MW00658409

CHARIOTS TO JORDAN

OTHER BOOKS AND AUDIO BOOKS

BY E. JAMES HARRISON:

The Tomb Builder

CHARIOTS TO JORDAN

A NOVEL

E. JAMES HARRISON

Covenant Communications, Inc.

Covenant

Cover image: *Water in Hands* © gaspr13, courtesy istockphoto.com

Cover design copyright © 2014 by Covenant Communications, Inc.

Published by Covenant Communications, Inc.
American Fork, Utah

Copyright © 2014 by E. James Harrison
All rights reserved. No part of this book may be reproduced in any format or in any medium without the written permission of the publisher, Covenant Communications, Inc., P.O. Box 416, American Fork, UT 84003. The views expressed within this work are the sole responsibility of the author and do not necessarily reflect the position of Covenant Communications, Inc., or any other entity.

This is a work of fiction. The characters, names, incidents, places, and dialogue are either products of the author's imagination, and are not to be construed as real, or are used fictitiously.

Printed in the United States of America
First Printing: August 2014

20 19 18 17 16 15 14 10 9 8 7 6 5 4 3 2 1

ISBN 978-1-62108-363-4

For my mom, a wonderful example of service and devotion. She is also one who has a skin condition that would have branded her as leprous had she lived during the time this novel takes place.

And to Hailey, Ryan, Chad, and Rhett, whose giggles and hugs make me happy.

Author's Note

In writing this novel, I have taken advantage (perhaps unfairly) of the confusion that exists among Biblical scholars about leprosy. The Hebrew word *Tsara'ath*, which has been rendered "leprosy" in the King James and other versions of the Bible, seems to be a sort of catchall phrase for a variety of skin diseases. Today when we think of leprosy, we generally think of the terribly disfiguring condition known as Hansen's disease. Although anciently, someone with Hansen's disease would most certainly have been considered leprous, so would someone with psoriasis, vitiligo, or any number of other more benign skin disorders.

Leprosy (again, not specifically Hansen's disease) is as old as mankind. Records from as early as 4300 BC have been found describing it, and it was not an uncommon ailment. In fact, many notable Biblical figures suffered from leprosy, including Moses, his sister Miriam, King Uzziah, and of course, one of the main characters in this book, the Syrian nobleman Naaman. Likewise, we can't forget those from the New Testament, especially those Christ healed, who were said to have leprosy. Did all these people suffer from Hansen's disease? While some may have, my personal belief is that not all of them did.

This is a novel, and because of that, Naaman's version of leprosy is unlike any other. At best it would have to be considered a combination of Hansen's disease and other skin disorders. There are details in the book that accurately depict how he might have contracted the disease as well as its progression and effect, but I have also taken some small literary licenses.

To any who suffer with Hansen's disease, I apologize for enhancing the myths. The reality is that although approximately 100 people in the United States and 250,000 worldwide are diagnosed with it every year, 95 percent of the world's population has a natural immunity. The disease is curable with a drug regimen, and those who are treated can lead normal, productive lives. Anciently, and even in more recent times, those with leprosy were shunned and ostracized. While some of that still occurs, there is no justification for doing so in today's world.

During the era in which this novel takes place, the world was a cruel, brutal, and harsh place. Wars and the complete annihilation of cities or towns—including women and children—were widespread and common. Historical records reveal instances of people committing suicide as attacking armies swept down on their village rather than face the atrocities they knew awaited them. While I have included some of that gritty reality in this novel, I have purposely chosen not to depict the extent of the horrific nature that historians tell us existed. As for the repulsive practice of slavery, it has been with us for millennia, and it is an ugly reality that continues today. Unfortunately, as I write this, in some African and Middle Eastern countries, humans can be bought and sold for as little as a few hundred dollars.

Finally, although some of the people and places in this novel actually existed, others were invented by me. Also, I've taken the liberty of making some changes—occasionally sweeping—in the earth's geography to make everything fit.

Enjoy!

E. James Harrison

Chapter One

Her screams shattered the night air and echoed off the mud and straw-block walls of the crude shelter. Although it had four walls and a roof of sorts, anyone giving it a quick glance would have thought it a shed for animals. It was a hut, nothing more, and crudely built at that. Bits of straw—the few stems which hadn't been nibbled off by goats—poked out from the shabbily made blocks at incongruous angles. The mortar, little as there was, had in many places simply cracked and fallen out, leaving gaps between the blocks. The roof was a series of wooden poles that had been lashed to the top tier of blocks with leather straps. On top of the poles had been interlaced a thatched roof of goat skins, dirt, and assorted bits of dried brush, all gingerly held in place with more strips of leather.

The wind rattled the makeshift wooden door against its frame, and if it hadn't been for the sturdy latch, the door likely would have blown off its leather hinges. Even with the door closed, the wind poured through the cracks, swirling gritty sand and coating everything with a fine layer of dust. As long as the wind held at a constant speed, the thatched roof and shaky walls could probably withstand the blowing, but a sudden gust would likely send the dilapidated mess crashing to the ground, and no one, especially the two women inside, wanted that to happen.

Another scream cut through the air, this one longer and more intense, causing the man and three small children huddled outside the hut to cringe. They sat clustered together with their backs to the wind like a small bunch of grapes, their bodies acting as a wind break for the small fire that struggled for life in front of them. Whenever the wind momentarily slowed, the orange flames licked at the faces of the pathetic group. The warmth took the raw edge off the chill of the desert night, but it did nothing to relieve the anxiety and fear that gripped their minds and hearts with each new scream that pierced the black night.

For more than two hours, the man had wrapped his arms around his sons and tried to console them. He did his best to explain why their mother was screaming in pain, but at two, four, and six years of age, even the simplest explanation was beyond comprehension and did nothing to relieve their concerns. The same question followed each scream, "Why is Momma screaming?" Followed by the same answer, "Because she's having a baby, and it is painful." Twice the man had attempted a more detailed answer, but he gave up when the six-year-old cut him short, "But the sheep don't scream when they have their babies; why is Momma screaming?"

With the last scream, the little two-year-old slipped from his father's arms and attempted to bolt for the door, crying, "Momma, Momma, Momma," as he went. He made it three steps before his father lunged out, grabbed the sleeve of the boy's hole-filled robe, and hauled him back. "I want Momma," he yelled, kicking and twisting to escape his father's grasp.

The man shook his head in a combination of disgust, anger, and remorse. It wasn't supposed to be like this. They were supposed to be living in a real house with solid walls, not this forsaken hovel, but nothing had gone as planned. For eight years he had labored countless hours building a life for himself and his family. They lived in a small but comfortable home on the edge of Jezreel, a growing and prosperous village of shopkeepers, shepherds, and farmers. Each year, he planted and harvested a little more wheat than the year before. While most farmers sold their surplus grain in the fall, immediately after the harvest, he stored his until springtime when demand was greater and prices were higher. His shrewdness had earned him a handsome profit year after year, and he had saved it all.

Over the same eight years, he'd slowly enlarged his flock of sheep. When Jehovah blessed an old ewe with twins or triplets rather than a single lamb, he would raise the extra lambs and keep them in his flock rather than sell them. He had also been shrewd when it came time to sell the excess wool. He never sold in the spring like others. He waited until winter when prices soared and demand was great.

For the last three of those eight years, he had kept his eye on a small farm outside the neighboring village of Shunen. Countless times the man who owned it told him he would sell—for the right price. The modest but sturdy house attracted his wife; the land mesmerized him. The ground was fertile and the hillside pastures thick with luscious grass in the late spring and early summer. As the weather turned hot and the grass in the lower valleys turned brown and dry, he could lead his sheep to the high mountain valleys of Mount Tabor with its cooler temperatures and abundant streams and grass.

For years they scrimped and saved every farthing to purchase the property, and at last it was so close it was almost his. But he had chosen to gamble with Mother Nature—and he lost.

Months earlier he had faced a difficult choice. He could continue as he had in the past, and in another two years he would have saved enough money to buy the house and land. Or, he could speculate. He could borrow money for more wheat seed and plant the fields his neighbor no longer used. By doing that, he would make a profit and have enough money to buy the property in only one year. He and his wife had carefully weighed the options and spent many nights discussing what would be best. She was more cautious and wanted to wait, but the lure of the land made him want to borrow the money and plant. It was a gamble. "But," he reasoned with her, "everything in life is a gamble." In the end, she reluctantly agreed.

All spring he worked night and day to get the seed in the additional ground. In the early stages of pregnancy, his wife had labored at his side as much as she was able, and even their small children helped clear rocks and chop weeds. The spring rains came, and the wheat sprouted, poking its head from under the soil into the bright yellow sunlight. The moisture-laden ground and warm sunshine caused the grain to grow rapidly, and before long the fields were green and lush. In not many weeks, the wheat was ten inches tall, and early summer breezes sent flowing ripples through it like gentle waves on a pond. It would be a perfect crop with greater yields than he had imagined, he told himself over and over. And then Mother Nature began toying with him.

The summer showers that usually bathed the land didn't come. Every afternoon, massive thunderstorms rose in the west like towering monsters and hurled lightning across the sky, but not a single drop of rain fell. As the days turned hotter, the tender shoots of wheat sent their roots deeper in the ground in a fruitless search for moisture. Finding none, the delicate plants changed from luscious green to yellow gold and, finally, dead brown. Eventually the hot winds snapped the dry stocks and blew them away, leaving nothing but barren fields of stubble.

At harvest time, the creditors arrived at his door demanding payment for the money he'd borrowed. He tried everything he could to stall their demands, but in the end, they would not be put off. "Pay what you owe, or in keeping with the law, we will sell your children into bondage to satisfy the debt." It took all the money they had saved as well as the sale of their little home and land to meet the creditors' demands, and now he sat huddled around a campfire while his wife gave birth inside a hovel that was better suited for birthing animals than humans.

The man wanted to take the children away from the screams, but there was no place to go. The night was too dark and the distance too great to take them to the home of even the nearest person, an old man whose pock-marked face and gaunt appearance would cause more terror in the children than the screams of their mother. In daylight he would have made the five-mile trek to his brother's home and left the children with him and his wife, but not at night; the terrain was too rough. Had a full moon lit the sky, he might have attempted it, but not on a black, moonless night like this. No, they would sit here on the ground, huddled against the stinging wind, and offer silent prayers to the Great Jehovah that their wife and mother would make the journey into the valley of death and safely return with a new life.

Another burst of noise shot from the hut. Not a scream, but an intense and labored groan followed by the muffled sobs of an exhausted woman. Less than a minute passed, and the same labored groan punctured the air, but this time it was followed by a loud sigh, a clear sigh of relief, the kind of sigh that conveyed it was finished.

* * *

"You did very well, Miriam," an aged female voice said calmly. "Jehovah has not blessed you with a son, but you have a healthy daughter."

The expended woman sank back off her elbows and lay on the make-shift bed of straw and animal skins. She knew the man outside would be disappointed with the news of a daughter, but she was thrilled. She finally had the daughter she had wanted for years. Every morning and night for nine months, she had begged and pleaded with Jehovah to send her a daughter, and her pleas had not gone unanswered.

"Let me hold her," the new mother pleaded anxiously. "Does she have all her fingers and toes?"

"Be patient, Miriam," the old woman said. "You would think this is your first child!"

"She may not be my first child, but she is my first daughter, and I want to hold her," she said as she expelled a long sigh and laid her head on the sweat-soaked piece of lamb's wool that was her makeshift pillow.

The ancient woman chuckled as she suspended the infant upside down by its feet and cleaned mucus from its nose and mouth. "Most Jewish women would be saddened with the birth of a daughter but not you."

Miriam started to speak, but her words were cut off by the soft cries of the newborn. It was a delicate cry, so different from the boisterous noise each of her sons made as they entered the world.

"I love my boys, but I have prayed Jehovah would bless me with a daughter. Please, Abish, can't you hurry? I want to hold her."

"Lie back and rest. You'll have her soon enough," the woman ordered as she expertly tied and cut the umbilical cord with a flint knife. Resting the infant on a shaky wooden table she had previously covered with a coarsely woven camel-hair cloth, she quickly washed the baby with a soft linen rag dipped in a clay pot of warm water. After the baby was bathed clean, the midwife blotted the infant dry and then rubbed salt over the tiny baby's skin as a cleanser and disinfectant.

"With the wind blowing as it is, this baby will be covered in more dust than salt," Abish said more to herself than to Miriam.

Miriam propped herself on her elbows and grimaced as a mild contraction coursed through her body. "Please tell me again, Abish, is she healthy?"

Abish smiled at the question as she poured oil from the earthen pot into her hand. Every mother is the same, she thought. "Of course, she's healthy. And more than that, she's beautiful. But considering the baby comes from you and Gideon, I would expect nothing less," she said as she coated the baby's arms, legs, head, and body with a fine film of lightly scented oil.

Miriam watched the old woman gently wrap the lightly whimpering baby in soft strips of swaddling clothes. "You'll be in your mother's arms soon enough," she cooed as her aged and well-practiced hands deftly wound the cloth around the tiny body.

With the baby wrapped securely, Abish shuffled to the bed and bent over, handing the small infant to her mother. "There's your baby girl," she said soothingly.

"Will you please tell Gideon that everything is well?" Miriam asked, accepting the baby and sliding back the cloth from around the newborn's face to gaze into her blue eyes.

"Not until I've taken care of you," Abish replied as she stepped to the far side of the shack and lifted a goat skin from the dirt floor. Holding it away from mother and baby, she brushed off what dirt she could and placed it behind Miriam's back to support her while she held the baby.

The women smiled at each other when they heard a voice from outside. "Tell me, Abish, do I have a son?"

"All men are the same," Abish said quietly as she moved the pot of water beside Miriam. "Sons, sons, sons, they all want sons, but without us women, no work would ever get done!" Then without pausing she called out over the noise of the wind, "You have three sons, don't you know?"

"No . . . I mean, yes, I know that, but do I have a new male child?"

Abish smiled as she tended to Miriam and called over her shoulder, "You have better than that; you have a daughter."

* * *

Upon hearing "daughter" the corners of Gideon's mouth pulled back into a smile and almost immediately gave way to a tooth-filled grin that seemed to cover his entire face. Down deep, he too had been hoping for a daughter, not so much for himself, but for his wife. Reaching out he scooped all three of his sons up in his arms and shouted, "You have a sister! You have a sister!"

"Oh no, not a sister!" exclaimed six-year-old Uzzi. "What good is a sister? She can't be a warrior."

Four-year-old Hanan clenched his fists and said, "I want a brother. Send her back; I want a brother."

It was all too much for two-year-old Caleb. His only reaction was, "Momma?"

"Abish," Gideon called out, "how is Miriam? Is she all right?"

The door of the small hut opened slightly, and the soft light of a single oil lamp flooded into the darkness. "She's fine. Come and see for yourself." Then pointing a crooked old finger at the three boys in their father's arms, she warned, "You boys must be very gentle to your mother and to your new little sister. Do you understand me?"

Each boy slowly nodded his head. They really didn't know who this strange old woman was—with her straggly gray hair and dressed in black robes, her sleeves rolled up to the elbows—but the sternness with which she spoke caused fear. Seeing each of them nod, Abish opened the door wider and stepped aside so the four of them could enter. "Hurry, hurry," she commanded, "before the wind blows any more dirt into this animal sty."

Stepping into the small shack, Gideon stooped over and set the three boys on the ground. As if they hadn't heard a word Abish said, all three instantly ran toward their mother, who was reclining on the makeshift bed with the tiny bundle wrapped in white rags in her arms. When they were still three feet away, a thunderous "Stop!" shattered the air. The word was hardly out of her mouth before Abish had inserted herself between the boys and their mother.

All three boys skidded to a stop then quickly backpedaled a step, their terror-filled eyes locked on the wrinkled woman.

"What did I tell you?" Abish said sternly as she pointed a menacing finger at them.

"They're just fine, Abish," Miriam said softly. "I'm sure they'll be gentle; won't you, boys?"

All three boys nodded in unison, still staring up at Abish. Only Uzzi spoke. "We promise to be gentle," he said with a quivering voice. With that, Abish moved from their path, and the boys cautiously eased to their mother's side without taking their eyes off the ancient woman.

A small cloud of dust stirred as the boys knelt on the ground beside their mother's straw bed. Without the slightest hesitation, little Caleb leaned over and hugged Miriam tightly around her neck, completely disregarding the infant in her arms. "Momma okay?" he said as he nuzzled his face against her neck.

"Momma's fine," Miriam said softly as she raised an arm to caress the boy's head. Running her fingers through his straggly hair, she lightly kissed him on the head and repeated, "Momma is just fine."

The two-year-old released his hug and sat back slightly. Then extending his hand, he patted Miriam lightly on the cheek and asked again, "Momma okay?"

Miriam reached up, took Caleb's hand in her own, and kissed each of his dirt-streaked fingers. "Yes, Caleb, Momma is okay."

It was only then that the worry drained from his eyes and his usual perpetual smile returned. Sitting back on his haunches, he folded his hands in his lap and looked at the small head with its layer of black hair that protruded from beneath the strips of white cloth.

"What are we going to call her?" Uzzi asked as he softly patted the back of the cloth-bound infant.

The question was not new. It had been debated countless times by the family as they spent Sabbath afternoons resting from their labor and eating a simple meal. In the end, they all agreed if the baby was a boy, he would be named Joshua. As hard as they tried, though, they simply couldn't agree on a girl's name. Uzzi was holding out for Ziklag, the name of his favorite dog. Hanan refused to even consider a girl's name because he refused to believe the baby would be anything other than a boy. Caleb was too young to care.

Gideon and Miriam each had their own favorites. His was Nirit, but Miriam grimaced at the name. "A plowed field?" she asked incredulously as she considered the interpretation. "You want to call our daughter a plowed field?"

"I like how it sounds not what it means," Gideon replied honestly.

Miriam said she preferred Renana because it meant singing or making a joyful sound. The longer they went without agreeing, the more convinced Gideon became that Miriam had another name, a secret name, she really wanted. Only two days before the baby was born, they reached a decision. If it was a boy, he would be named Joshua. If it was a girl, then Miriam could choose any name she wanted.

"So," Uzzi repeated, pointing at the bundle, "what are we going to call her?"

There was silence, and everyone, including Abish, looked expectantly at Miriam.

"I want to name her Gili," Miriam said as she hugged the child tenderly to her breast.

An understanding smile spread across Gideon's lips, and he nodded his head approvingly. "My joy, my happiness," he said softly as he considered the meaning. "Gili it is," he said proudly. "She will be our joy and our happiness."

Chapter Two

Naaman walked slowly through each room of the sprawling but empty house, peering in corners and running his fingers over the fine cedar woodwork that trimmed the windows and doors. He was a soldier not a craftsman, but even he could appreciate the high-quality materials and workmanship with which the house was constructed. The block walls were perfectly straight and had been covered with a smooth layer of mortar in delicate, swirling patterns. Each room had been painted different colors—some bold and some muted. Heavy drapes hung from each window and added a touch of warmth and elegance to the rooms. Massive beams crafted from cypress trees formed the basic structure for the roof and added to the impression that the house was built to survive nature's fiercest tempest or earthquake.

The stairway up which they had earlier climbed to the upper floor of the house was crafted out of some wood he'd never seen before, and carved into each step was a proverb or wise saying. The tile floors throughout the house were smooth and laid out in perfect symmetry. As Naaman walked he wondered how the craftsmen were able to keep each grout-filled seam exactly the same width.

"Do you like it?" Karinah asked as she clamped her hands together and held them at her chin, bobbing up and down on the balls of her feet. Her dark green eyes glistened with excitement and were a perfect match for her olive skin and nearly black hair. Her enthusiasm for the house was an extension of how she approached life, which contributed to keeping her remarkably trim and fit.

"Well, do you?" she asked with excitement that bordered on the giddiness of someone half her middle age.

"I don't know yet. I haven't seen it all," Naaman replied coyly in an awkward attempt to hide his own enthusiasm about the house.

Karinah rushed to his side and took him by the hand. "You love it, don't you?" she said as she clasped both of his hands in hers. Then almost skipping backwards, she pulled him down a long hallway. "Wait until you see the gardens out back." She pushed open a door that took them into yet another nicely crafted room. "Close your eyes," Karinah ordered when they were barely inside the room.

"No," Naaman responded. "You'll push me out a window, and I'll fall and break my neck. Then you'll marry someone else and live in this house," he teased.

Feigning offense she said, "If I promise not to push you, will you close your eyes?"

Naaman smiled and, closing his eyes, extended his arms so Karinah could lead him. As much as he loved and trusted his wife, the uncertainty of where she was leading him made him shuffle along, gingerly sliding one foot ahead of the other like an old man walking down an uneven path.

"Don't open your eyes yet, but we must stop for just a moment," Karinah said as she dropped his hands. Almost immediately he heard the sound of doors creaking as they were opened. With his eyes still closed, he could feel the coolness of a breeze on his cheeks and catch the faint scent of something sweet in the air. Flowery, he thought, perhaps citrus blossoms or maybe a rose. Whatever it was, the smell was pleasant.

"What's that smell?" Naaman asked.

"Which one?" Karinah replied. "There are dozens of smells just now."

"The sweet smell, the flowery smell."

Returning to Naaman's side, Karinah again took him by both hands. "Be patient, and you'll see. But first you must walk down two steps."

Naaman cautiously resisted the tugs on his arms. "The steps are still three feet ahead of you," Karinah said as she tugged more forcefully. "Stop being so cautious; just step forward."

"I stay alive by being cautious," Naaman said in response, slowly sliding his left foot forward until he detected the step. Easing down both steps, he said, "Karinah, may I open my eyes now?"

"Not yet, but almost!" she answered as she pulled him forward. Dropping his hands she stepped to his side and slightly rotated his body. "Okay, my love, open your eyes!"

Naaman slowly opened his eyes, and he was instantly awestruck by what he saw. Standing on a second-story veranda, he had a sweeping view of an expansive and perfectly manicured garden and courtyard. Rosebushes in full bloom ringed the perimeter, each spaced exactly twenty feet apart.

Placed evenly between the rosebushes were deep green cypress trees towering thirty feet in the air. The contrast of pink, red, white, and orange roses against the green of the cypress trees was startling and beautiful.

In almost the center of the garden was an ornate circular structure. It had no sides, and its domed roof was supported by four pure white marble columns, each about eight feet tall. Sheltered beneath the roof were marble benches, which had a slight pink cast. Perfectly straight flagstone paths extended in four directions from the marble structure and along both sides of each path were a variety of flowers.

Various greenery and bushes dotted the interior of the courtyard in symmetrical patterns and were interspersed with date palms and orange and lemon trees. In the far corner was a vegetable garden with neat rows of plants just beginning to crack the earth and begin their skyward reach. In the most distant part of the expansive yard, separated by a tall block fence, stood a small corral with an attached structure intended to shelter horses and a few other animals. But the most impressive part of the entire area was at the extreme rear of the property. There, beyond a short wall, flowed the beautiful clear water of the Albana River.

The river was slightly less than forty feet wide, and on the opposite bank was a beautiful block wall with trumpet vines cascading down to the water's edge. From his vantage point, Naaman could see that the water flowed smoothly with a slight but steady current.

"This is beautiful," he said as his eyes darted from one corner of the courtyard to another, struggling to take everything in.

"I knew it! I just knew it," Karinah said in delight. "I knew you'd love the garden more than anything about the house."

"Oh, the garden and courtyard are beautiful, but it's the river. It's so clear and peaceful it makes me want to jump in and swim," Naaman said without taking his eyes from the flowing water.

"Do you want to see the rest of the house? You've only been through a few of the rooms, and there's still much more to see," Karinah said anxiously. If he was hesitating at all about buying the house, she was confident the remaining rooms would be more than enough to nudge him toward a purchase.

Naaman smiled as he looked at his wife. "Do you want to live here?" he asked her quietly.

"Oh yes," she answered enthusiastically, "more than I can begin to tell you. What about you? Do you want to live here beside the Albana River?" The reference to the river was a deliberate attempt on her part to overcome the bit of hesitancy she could see in his eyes. The river was a soft spot, and she intended to exploit it.

Naaman hesitated slightly before he said, "It is a gorgeous house, and I truly admire the river . . ."

"But?" she prodded.

"I'm a little concerned that it's too nice," he replied with a suddenly serious tone. "You forget I'm only a soldier."

A look of surprise spread over Karinah's face, and she waved her hand in the air in a dismissive gesture. "Only a soldier?" she repeated. "You are now the captain over all of King Ben-Hadad's forces, his supreme commander. There isn't anyone he trusts more. He admires you for your bravery, your devotion, your cunning. Saying you are only a soldier is like saying the Albana River is a muddy trickle of water."

"I'm concerned about what others might think, us living in such a glorious place," he responded.

Karinah stepped closer to him and cupped his face between her hands. "Since when has my Naaman been worried about what others think?" she said with a tinge of sarcasm.

"Forever." Then looking into his wife's eyes, he said, "But if you want the house . . ."

"Thank you," Karinah interrupted with a squeal as she jumped up and wrapped her arms tightly around his neck. She gave him a quick kiss on his lips. "Thank you," she repeated. "You've made me very happy."

"And you've made me a very happy man," he replied as he encircled her in his arms and held her tightly, her feet suspended six inches off the floor.

It was as he gently lowered her to the ground that she focused on the red blotch on his cheek, just above his perfectly trimmed beard. "It's redder than usual. Does it hurt?" she asked softly as she lightly touched the spot with her index finger.

Naaman reached up and took Karinah's hand in his, moving it away from his cheek. "No, not really. It's a little tender to the touch, but it doesn't hurt."

Karinah extracted her hand from his and wrapped her arms around his waist. "I don't like how it looks," she said softly, unable to conceal the slight anxiety in her voice.

Naaman gave her a gentle squeeze and said reassuringly, "It's nothing. Go. Look around the rest of the house; I'm going to walk down to the river."

Chapter Three

The almost imperceptible sound of the slow-moving water lapping against the sandy riverbank was the only sound that found its way to Naaman's ears, and the quiet caused a contented smile to form on his lips.

Someone else must have liked this spot too, he thought, seeing a small wooden bench perched on the river's edge a few feet away. Walking in the soft sand, he sat down and impulsively removed the sandals from his feet. Placing his sandals beside him, he stretched his legs out so that his feet and ankles were covered by the refreshingly cool water and watched as specks of dirt and sand were swept from between his toes. Leaning back he folded his arms across his chest and sat motionless. This was a world away from the clang of swords and screams of dying men that were so much a part of his life, and he relished the peace and serenity.

Staring down at his feet, Naaman chuckled as half a dozen two-inch-long fish cautiously swam up and investigated his toes. Curious to see what the tiny fish would do, he sat perfectly still until a fly buzzed around his head and landed on his nose. He sat unfazed, concentrating on the fish, while the fly walked down the side of his nose. As the fly started across his cheek, the slight tickle of its feet was more than even his leathery skin could endure, and he slapped at the insect, instantly regretting it. The tips of his fingers slammed into the red spot on his cheek, causing an intense burning pain that made him bolt upright on the bench. Without thinking, he leaned down and scooped up a handful of water and splashed it on his cheek. The cool water eased the sting, and he scooped up another handful and doused his cheek again.

Slowly, the pain dulled to the slightest throb, and Naaman reached for his sandals.

"It hurts, doesn't it?" Karinah said softly.

The unexpected voice startled Naaman, and he turned around to see his wife standing a few feet behind him. "What?" he asked in feigned innocence.

"The red spot on your face," she said flatly as she walked down the gently sloping riverbank and sat down beside him. "How much does it hurt?"

"Not much," he lied.

Karinah leaned toward him and raised her hand to his cheek.

Naaman pulled his head away from her approaching hand and said, "Please, don't . . ."

"I wasn't going to touch it. I was going to . . ." but her voice trailed off to nothing. Shifting her body so she faced the river, she straightened her light blue robe and folded her hands in her lap. "What do you think it is?" she asked, still looking at the unhurried river, although she knew the answer before asking the question. They both did, but they didn't speak of it—at least not to each other. For her part, Karinah had discussed its existence with her closest friend several times, and after describing it in exacting detail, she and her friend had accurately diagnosed the disease.

Naaman was different. He spoke to no one of the small red spot because he knew what it was. More, he knew exactly how it came to be: an unwelcome gift from his fellow soldier and closest friend as the man lay dying in his arms exactly two years earlier.

It should have been an easy assignment. He and Joram, his second-in-command, were to lead a contingent of three hundred Syrian soldiers in protecting seven thousand pieces of gold and twenty thousand pieces of silver that were being paid as tribute to their king, Ben-Hadad. The precious coins were securely packed on the backs of two dozen camels, and for a week the convoy had traveled across the uninhabited reaches of northern Arabia without the slightest hint of trouble. But with only one day left until they reached the safety of Syria's borders, it happened.

Unknown to Naaman and his column of soldiers, two hundred mercenaries were waiting in ambush in the rock cliffs above a narrow pass through which he and his soldiers would go. Fifty mercenary archers were crouched near the upper reaches of the pass, hidden behind boulders and bits of scrub brush, the polished shafts of arrows notched in their powerful steel bows. Slightly below them, on more gently sloping ground leading to the bottom of the pass, were hidden another 150 men. They lay on top of their shields, spears, and swords to keep the sun from reflecting from the bright metal and revealing their hiding place. To mask their existence even more, they had thrown dirt, sticks, and brush on their backs to blend with the dreary landscape.

The mercenaries were loyal to Tiglath-Pileser III, the King of Assyria, but it was an uneasy loyalty, valid only for as long as the promise of plunder and money was within their grasp. They couldn't care less about lands and borders or who controlled whom. They fought for money, pure and simple, and were loyal to whichever king paid the most; for the moment that was Tiglath-Pileser. They were bloodthirsty, battle-hardened men who relished the fight but delighted in the plunder even more.

From their elevated perch, the mercenaries watched with eager anticipation as the long line of three hundred Syrian soldiers marched toward their ambush like unsuspecting ants. It wasn't the highly disciplined soldiers in the column who held their attention though. Virtually every set of eyes was focused on the two dozen camels in the middle of the column—the beasts with the precious coins. It was a small fortune but more than enough to warrant the ambush. Tiglath-Pileser would get most of the wealth, but within a couple hours, each surviving mercenary would get his share of the booty plus a bounty for the head of each Syrian soldier he hacked off after the fighting was finished. They would spare no one; the mercenary who collected the most heads would get the most money. In keeping with tradition, there would be a literal head count.

The Syrian soldiers approached the narrow pass with trepidation. Every one of them knew this pass held the potential for ambush. With only a narrow trail leading through its steep, high walls, they would be as vulnerable as a baby bird surrounded by hungry cats. Naaman had warned of its dangers before they broke camp earlier that morning, and he had reminded them again when they stopped for a brief rest. Every set of eyes, including those of the camel drivers, scanned the rocky cliffs and ridges looking for the slightest hint of anything unnatural: a flock of birds that suddenly took flight, the dark color of a cloak or tunic against the light tan of the dirt and rock, a glint of metal in the sunlight, a dislodged stone or rock tumbling down the side of the cliffs. Their survival depended upon their powers of observation, and they all searched rocks, crags, and brush.

They marched four abreast; the outermost columns were archers who walked with their bows at the ready. The inside columns were muscular men, each carrying a spear in one arm and a shield in the other. A three-foot-long sword made of Damascus steel—the hardest steel known to man—hung from a leather sheath at each man's side. The swords were formidable weapons. Unlike the swords of the mercenaries and Israelites made of inferior steel, the Syrians' swords were honed, razor-sharp, and could slice through flesh and bone time and time again without becoming blunted. Their enemies feared the swords in battle and eagerly claimed them as prized spoils of war.

While still hundreds of yards from the pass, Naaman raised up in the stirrups of his saddle, lifted his arm in the air, and shouted, "Halt." He was a big man, standing over six feet with broad shoulders and massive muscles in his arms and legs. His conical bronze helmet hid most of his dark hair, but the few gray streaks in his beard attested to his years of experience. His gray horse pranced uneasily as it fought the bit and reins that held it in check.

The command to stop was relayed down the length of the long column by a series of subordinates, and the ponderously long column came to a standstill. Not a soul broke rank until another order sounded allowing the men to drink water from the sheepskin bags they carried over their shoulders. The water was warm, but it would slake the men's thirst from walking in the heat of the sun and would wash down some of the dust of the desert that had drifted into their mouths and throats.

Perhaps it was their fascination with the chests of gold and silver on the camels below that prevented the hiding mercenaries from noticing the three men silently traversing the steep sides of the canyon. They were scouts sent out by Naaman with simple orders: they were to survey the area for potential danger and if they discovered anything out of the ordinary, no matter how seemingly insignificant, to shout a warning.

The three men were experienced at their task. Unlike their compatriots in the columns, these men wore no heavy metal body armor. They were dressed in linen tunics over which they wore thick leather jackets. They were not dressed for battle; they were dressed to travel quickly and blend with the landscape. They moved cautiously and noiselessly from one protected spot to the next so they could see without being seen. They moved forward one at a time, leapfrogging as they went. While one moved forward, the other two scanned the cliffs below and on the opposite side of the pass in search of any threat that might be looming.

It was the briefest reflection of sunlight that stopped the lead man in his tracks. He had only seen it out the corner of his eye, but he instantly froze. Crouching behind a boulder, he cautiously raised his head to scour the cliffs and ravines on the opposite side of the pass. From his vantage point he scoured the rock-strewn cliffs as carefully as a hawk searches for a mouse, and that's when he saw them: first two, then ten, and finally dozens of men lying on their stomachs in hiding.

Motioning for his two companions to remain where they were, he pointed at the hiding ambushers on the opposite side of the pass. In an instant, they too saw the hiding attackers. Noiselessly the lead man crept back to his companions, and the three of them began to retrace their path back to Naaman and the column of soldiers below. They would have made it undetected except for a single rock no larger than a watermelon. As they hurried along, the last of the three men slipped on the steep hillside and sent the rock tumbling noisily down. The noise echoed off the walls of the pass, and both the mercenaries and the Syrians instantly knew something was wrong.

Their cover broken, the three men stood and began scrambling over boulders and down the steep side of the pass as quickly as they could, shouting at the tops of their lungs that mercenaries lay in ambush.

Realizing they had lost the element of surprise, the leader of the outnumbered mercenaries rose to his feet and yelled a command for his forces to attack. Like dead men rising from graves, the ambushers clambered to their feet and hurtled down the steep hillside toward the Syrian soldiers, dust and dirt falling from their robes as they ran. And the killing began.

The mercenary archers were the first to enter the fight. From their high perch, they let fly a swift volley of arrows, but even with their steel bows, the distance was too great to be effective, and the arrows fell harmlessly to the earth, well short of the four columns of Syrian soldiers. For their part, the disciplined Syrian archers formed a solid line against the oncoming mercenaries but held their arrows until the last moment. Then on command, a hundred arrows flew through the air. A dozen missed their mark entirely, and two dozen more bounced harmlessly off the metal helmets and breastplates of the enemy. But the most skilled archers had aimed for the unprotected legs of their attackers, and the leading group of mercenaries stumbled to the ground, arrows protruding from their thighs and calves. The archers quickly sent another volley of arrows flying, and more mercenaries fell wounded. None of the wounds would have been fatal had the men been able to withdraw from the battle and treat their wounds, but injured as they were, they were no match for the Damascus steel swordsmen that would shortly descend upon them.

The Syrian bowmen hurriedly notched arrows and let a third volley fly. This time they took aim at unprotected faces as well as legs, but their attackers took a defensive posture. An instant before the arrows were unleashed, the mercenaries stopped running and crouched beneath their large metal-and-leather shields. Arrows rained from the sky but bounced harmlessly off the shields without injuring a man. Rising to their feet, the men raced forward to close the gap before the archers could shoot again.

Naaman spurred his horse and raced to the head of the column, where he gave the command for the archers to fall back and make way for the soldiers with spears and swords. It would now be hand-to-hand combat—a fight to the death, for neither side would take prisoners.

For two hours, the battle raged as death and carnage spread their ugly faces over the desolate landscape. Although outnumbered, the ragtag mercenaries fought with the intensity that had earned them their reputation as a bloodthirsty army. In the end, though, their ferocity was no match for the discipline of the Syrians and the keen edge of the Damascus steel blades. Before the battle was over, every mercenary had been speared or hacked to death, but not before they had killed or wounded almost the entire columns of soldiers.

His horse cut out from under him, Naaman led the battle on foot. He charged into the fray and, for nearly two hours, alternately slashed at the mercenaries and cheered on his own men. Against all odds he managed to stay standing until almost the end, but the wounds to his arms and legs had taken their toll. When a huge mercenary charged him, sword slashing, Naaman struggled to fend off the relentless blows. He might have succeeded had he not tripped over the severed arm of a downed soldier. Off balance he couldn't parry the mercenary's thrust, and the sword pierced Naaman's side just below his ribs, sending him to the ground in pain.

It was only a well-placed arrow from one of Naaman's bowmen that saved him. As the mercenary raised his long sword high above his head to deliver the killing blow, the bowman sent an arrow deep into the man's chest. The last thing Naaman saw before losing consciousness was the bowman who had saved him from being felled by a mercenary's sword.

The gritty sand digging into Naaman's cheek was the first sensation he felt as his brain slogged from the world of unconsciousness. With the exception of his eyelids, he moved nothing as he lay on the ground, waiting for his fogged brain to sort reality from hallucination.

Quiet. Everything was quiet. Gone were the screams of dying men, the clash of steel on steel, and the incessant yelling of battle. Slowly rolling onto his side, he pushed himself almost to his elbows and knees before searing pain from his left side made him crumple to the ground. He blinked only a single time against the brightness of the sun before his world went dark, and he drifted into blissful unconsciousness once more.

It seemed as if the sun had barely moved when Naaman again opened his eyes and blankly stared heavenward. With the little strength he could muster, he wrapped his hand around the hilt of his sword and struggled to his knees, shoving the point of the sword into the blood-soaked ground before him. Clenching his teeth against the pain, Naaman used the sword to steady himself as he slowly rose to his feet. His world swirled in uncontrollable chaos as he fought off the dizziness that made him sway as if he had drunk too much wine, and for a moment he thought he might pass out again. He quickly placed both hands on the hilt of the sword and leaned against it for support, hoping the world wouldn't go dark.

Blood ran freely down both arms from gashes in his biceps and made the grip of his sword slippery. The left side of his tunic was saturated with blood, and searing pain burned from the gaping wound just below his ribcage. He hung his head and closed his eyes in the hope it would give him a better sense of balance. It didn't, and only a quick shift of his legs stopped him from tumbling to the ground.

The rapid movement caused his world to swim. He yanked the helmet from his head and took several deep breaths in an effort to calm the wave of nausea that poured over him like a waterfall. His effort was too late, and he spewed a stream of green bile onto the back of a disemboweled man on the ground beside him. He looked at the vomit with a small sense of relief. At least there was no blood, he told himself as he wiped his mouth on his shoulder, vowing not to vomit again. The retching caused a surge of blood to flow from his side, and he clamped his hand over the wound to staunch the flow. Strangely, after vomiting he felt better. Even the swirling in his head slowed as he scanned the ugliness that surrounded him.

As the fog in his brain lifted, his senses slowly began absorbing the sights and sounds of the aftermath. First came the moans and cries of the wounded and dying, followed by the grizzly sight of an ended battle. In the yellow glow of the late-afternoon sun, Naaman could see the horror of the carnage. The killing field was strewn with bodies, some with arrows and spears sticking from them, others with arms and heads missing. He had already been hardened to the gore of battle, but he could never accustom himself to the sickening stench of death that filled the air after the killing had stopped.

His world no longer rocking, Naaman straightened up and pulled his sword from the earth. Weak as he was, he had no intention of returning it to its scabbard; too many times in the past, he had watched a mercenary feign death, waiting until an unsuspecting enemy got too close, and then rise up to fight again. Now, though, he wasn't looking for wounded mercenaries to kill; he was searching for his second-in-command—his friend.

"Joram," he coughed out as loudly as he could while looking over the bodies littering the ground. "Joram!" he repeated. It was meant as a yell, but what came out was only slightly louder than a hoarse whisper.

"Where are you?" Naaman mumbled to himself. The two of them had been fighting almost side by side for the entire battle. It was only in the final few minutes they had become separated, but even then Naaman was close enough to watch his friend drop under the crushing blow of a mercenary's sword.

It was the soft moan from thirty feet behind him that made Naaman turn around. Lying in a heap, beneath the crimson cloak of a Syrian army officer, was Joram. Stepping over a crumpled body and walking around another with the shaft of a spear protruding from its throat, the captain knelt beside the groaning man. Gently rolling him onto his back, Naaman scooped his friend up and cradled his head and shoulders.

Joram gasped in pain but looked up into the eyes of the man who held him. "Naaman, I think I'm wounded," he croaked out. "What do you think?"

Naaman managed a smile at the remark. The characteristic humor of his good friend came through even while the man pounded on death's door. "Only slightly, my friend," Naaman lied. The frothy blood dripping from the corner of Joram's mouth, along with the deep red blood pumping from the stomach wound told Naaman that death's dark horseman was galloping near to claim another victim.

"You've never been able to lie," Joram said with a cough, spraying a mist of blood on Naaman's cheek. "We've been through a lot, you and me. But now it ends."

"Nonsense," Naaman snorted. "You're going to return home to that beautiful wife of yours."

Joram slowly shook his head back and forth a single time and grimaced as pain shot through him. "Stop lying. We've both seen too much death and dying. We're warriors, you and I. We know. You will recover; I will die."

Naaman held the dying Joram in his arms and unconsciously rocked, as a mother would rock her injured child. The blood from their wounds mingled and flowed freely down onto the pebble-strewn sand. "Don't exert yourself by talking," Naaman said softly as he removed the man's helmet and brushed sweat-soaked hair from his forehead.

Joram stiffened slightly as another jolt of pain coursed through his body. He coughed again, spraying blood all over Naaman's face and into his eyes. His body went slack, and had Naaman not been able to see the blood still pumping from the wound in Joram's stomach, he would have thought his friend's heart had stopped and the man dead.

After a moment Joram said in a strained voice, "I've never thanked you."

"For what?"

"For many things," Joram said breathlessly, "but especially for never revealing my . . . sickness to our superiors."

Confusion spread across Naaman's face. Of all the things his friend could have said, this was the last thing Naaman expected. "It was a very small thing," he replied in a hushed voice.

Joram moved his head from side to side. "Leprosy? A small thing?" he said in a weakening voice. "Knowledge of it would have ruined me, and being a soldier was all I ever wanted."

Naaman gazed down at his friend through moistening eyes. He was right. Had knowledge of his leprosy become known to those higher in command, Joram would have been cast out of the army and shunned. To Naaman's knowledge, only three people knew of the leprosy: Joram; Naaman; and Joram's wife, Lilith. Over the past several months, she had done a marvelous job of disguising the small gray and white patches of dead and dying skin on his hands, ears, toes, and face when her husband went out in public.

Joram's breathing became more labored, and a gurgle came from deep in his throat. "I have one last favor to ask of you," he said after a long pause.

"Anything," Naaman said softly as he held his friend more tightly.

"Please tell Lilith and my sons that I love them and that they were my last thoughts as I died."

Naaman drew a breath to respond but slowly let it escape through his parched lips as the last bit of life ebbed from Joram's body. No more raspy breathing escaped his mouth, and the blood coming from the wound in his stomach slowed to a trickle and then stopped. Naaman clutched the man tightly in his arms and continued rocking back and forth as tears streamed from his eyes and washed down his cheeks.

It was only the pain in his own side—and the sound of someone calling his name—that made him tenderly lay his friend's lifeless body on the ground.

"Captain Naaman! Praise the gods that you are yet alive," the man said as he leaped over bodies and rushed to Naaman's side. Upon seeing the still body of Joram, the man added, "And may the gods be merciful to Joram."

Naaman looked up at the man standing above him but said nothing. As much as he wanted to continue kneeling beside his dead friend and let memories of better days play through his mind, he knew he couldn't. "Please, help me to my feet," he finally said.

The soldier grasped Naaman under his arms and slowly lifted. The captain struggled to his feet and asked, "What is our situation? Do you know any details?"

"Including you," the soldier began, "I have counted thirty-two soldiers who are alive, all with injuries. Four, maybe five, are seriously wounded, and I don't expect them to live until sunset." Looking at Naaman's bloody tunic, he continued, "Ten or twelve more have injuries that are serious, like you, but with proper attention and rest, they should recover. The rest of us have only flesh wounds, which we can easily bandage."

"What of the mercenaries? How many of them survived?"

"I'm not certain. We pursued three or four who fled, but they outran us and disappeared into the hills." Sweeping his arm out over the battle scene, he added, "There are probably a few others who are wounded, but we haven't looked carefully."

Naaman nodded in acknowledgement and asked, "And what of the camel drivers and the camels? Where are they?"

The soldier took a deep breath. "The drivers fled to the hills at the first sign of attack. All but two of them have now crawled out of their hiding places." Pointing to a small hill a quarter mile away, he said, "We've placed the seriously injured men on top of that hill. The camel drivers are huddled over by them. The camels are gone. They bolted early in the attack."

Naaman considered all this as well as the challenges that lay before him. After a moment he issued a string of commands. "Tell the camel drivers to immediately begin searching for the camels." He pointed into the distance. "They've probably taken refuge up one of the side canyons. Continue your search for survivors. Kill any mercenaries who are still alive. Assemble everyone else at the hill. If we can find the camels before sunset, we'll push on. If not, we'll camp there for the night."

Looking down at the trickle of blood oozing from between Naaman's fingers clutching his side, the soldier asked, "What of you, Captain? Do you want me to help you?"

"No," Naaman replied. "See to the others first."

The soldier looked down at the expanding blotch on Naaman's blood-soaked tunic. "But, Captain, you're—" he stopped in midsentence. Seeing the determination in his leader's eyes, he said, "What of the dead? How shall we take care of them?"

Naaman scanned the hundreds of dead soldiers that littered the ground and then slowly lowered his eyes to Joram's lifeless body. Reaching up with both hands, Naaman gently rubbed his eyes with the tips of his fingers and then wiped his face clean of the blood Joram had coughed on him. Sighing heavily he answered, "Leave them where they lay. There's no time to attend to them. We must leave here before other mercenaries discover us and attack."

It took the rest of that day and most of the next morning to find all the frightened camels and their precious cargo. After two more days of painfully slow travel, the badly decimated column finally trekked into Damascus. King Ben-Hadad praised Naaman for his courage during the battle. But mostly the king praised him for safely delivering every one of the gold and silver coins. To show his gratitude, King Ben-Hadad even rewarded the captain with two hundred gold coins and five hundred silver ones, all of which Naaman gave to Joram's wife.

Now, two years later, as Naaman sat on the bench contemplating his wife's question, he reflected on the battle scene. But more, he reflected on the blood Joram had coughed into his face and eyes, and the wounds where their blood had so freely mingled. He knew what the small red spot was, and he was certain she knew as well. What he didn't know was how she would react when they both finally acknowledged the truth. Now, as they sat on the banks of the river, he decided it was time to face the demon.

Letting out an almost imperceptible sigh, Naaman looked at his wife, who was still gazing at the clear water. “Karinah,” he said as he raised his hand to the red spot on his cheek. “I think this is—”

“Leprosy,” she blurted as she turned to face him. “It’s leprosy.”

Chapter Four

He was dressed neatly but not nearly as well as people would expect for someone of his position and stature. His loose, flowing robe hung from his shoulders to slightly below his ankles. It was tan, slightly darker than the endless hills of desert sand and rock over which he passed. The sleeves were long, reaching to his wrists, and about his waist was tied a sash of emerald green. Shielding his head from the intense rays of the sun was a soft scarf, almost as white as snow. But the most striking article of clothing he wore was his mantle. It was deep red with strands of gold thread woven into its long fringed edges and tassels. It was thrown over his left shoulder then draped well under his right arm and then up across his chest to where it once again went over his left shoulder. The quality was beyond comparison, and that article of clothing alone distinguished him from every other man on earth.

"Gehazi, we must hurry or night will overtake us before we reach Ramoth-gilead," the man said in a calm, dignified voice.

"Yes, master," the thin-framed wiry man responded without much enthusiasm. He had been pulling, pushing, slapping, and coaxing the recalcitrant donkey on which his master was riding for most of the last two hours, and the animal's stubbornness had delayed them considerably.

"Stop. Let me get down," the man commanded. "Perhaps we'll make better time if I walk and we lead him behind us."

"As you wish, master," Gehazi said. He yanked sharply on the lead rope to stop the donkey. It was an unnecessary gesture, but he was frustrated and mad at the beast and wanted to inflict a little unpleasantness in its life.

"Even walking, master, I fear we won't make it much beyond Edrei until long after dark. Perhaps we should seek shelter somewhere along the way," the servant suggested hopefully.

"Perhaps," the man said. "But let us do the best we can for as long as we can."

The two men walked side by side in silence, Gehazi leading the donkey and looking mostly at the ground ahead of him. Although the other man was old and had witnessed much of life, he walked with his shoulders back and head erect, his eyes scanning the grass-covered rolling hills in the distance and the rugged mountains beyond. He wasn't searching for anything in particular. He was simply soaking in the details around him: the small sparrows darting through the late afternoon sky, the lizards scurrying over rocks and sand, the grass gently swaying in the breeze. He marveled at it all. He had walked this road many times in the past, but he never tired of the contrast between the serene welcome of the fertile plain and the steep harshness of the mountains.

After an hour of walking, the sun was sinking quickly in the sky, and it was obvious they would never make it to their destination before dark. "Gehazi, we will seek shelter for the night in Edrei at the home of Ziba, the widowed man."

Although Gehazi had never met the widower, he knew exactly about whom his master was speaking and where the home was located. "Excellent, master," he replied with enthusiasm. He was tired after a day of walking and wrestling with the donkey, and he was ready for food and a bed—as poor and uncomfortable as the food and bed would be.

Fifteen minutes later, just as the sun was casting its last bit of light over the western hills, the two men approached the door of the home. It was perfectly situated on a slightly sloping hillside: far enough from Edrei to afford privacy but close enough to have the conveniences of civilization. The home wasn't large, but it was well built and had once even been attractive, but now it showed signs of neglect. The walls were made of thick square blocks stacked straight. The once-white paint was faded and flaking off in many places. The house was one level, with a roof that sloped gently from front to back. A fence made of cedar post and rails encircled the home, and inside the fence, a short distance from the front door, was a short wall of rocks that formed a circle around a deep well of cool, crystal-clear water. On the far side of the yard, a narrow path descended down the steep hill to an enclosure for cattle and sheep.

Gehazi tied the donkey's lead rope to a rail of the fence, and the two men walked to the door, where Gehazi rapped sharply with his knuckles.

When there was no response, he rapped again, this time more vigorously with the heel of his hand.

"I'm coming. I'm coming," came a raspy voice. And then, with a distinct tone of irritation and annoyance, came the words, "Be patient."

With a quick yank from inside, the door flew open to reveal a stooped old man with a single crutch tucked firmly under his left armpit. He had shed his robe after a day's hard labor and stood clothed in what had originally been a white linen tunic. It was now brown with dirt, filled with holes and poorly mended patches, and stained with sweat; the man smelled as though he hadn't washed in several days. His face was streaked with dirt—at least the part of his face not hidden by a matted gray beard and long, stringy hair. His hands were stained with pomegranate juice, and his broken and chipped fingernails had grime caked beneath them.

Upon seeing the men at his door, he did what any believing Israelite would have done: he bowed very deeply. Still looking at the ground, he uttered the familiar Israelite greeting with reverence, "Jehovah with you."

"And Jehovah bless thee," the man in the red mantle replied in a gentle voice.

Rising slowly, the grimy and smelly old man said, "The prophet of Jehovah does me a great honor by stopping at my house. I am unworthy, but please enter." Clinging to his crutch, Ziba awkwardly stepped to the side to allow his visitors to enter.

The inside of the home resembled the man who lived there—cluttered and dirty. The old man closed the door and hobbled to the nearest chair, where he removed clay pots, broken trinkets, and rags and placed them on an already overcrowded table. "Please, sit, kind sir," he said, motioning to the empty but still dust-covered chair.

The prophet Elisha offered a warm smile, seeming not to see the dust on the chair or the clutter that littered the room. "Thank you," he said with genuine gratitude as he lowered himself into the chair.

The man looked at the prophet as if in a trance, overwhelmed by his presence. He appeared to have forgotten that Gehazi was also in the room.

Pointing to Gehazi, the prophet said, "This is my servant, Gehazi."

Realizing he had forgotten to offer the servant a place to sit, the man quickly removed clutter from a chair in the corner and motioned for Gehazi to sit. Gehazi said nothing as he plopped down and let out a deep sigh.

"We have come from Samaria," Elisha explained, "and are on our way to Aphek. We began our journey later than intended, and it has taken longer than expected. We are in need of a place to spend the night."

Ziba's eyes widened. "And you've chosen to spend the night in my humble dwelling?" he asked incredulously.

Elisha smiled and nodded his head but said nothing.

"Jehovah be praised," Ziba said, seeing the smile. "I have very little to offer, but such as I have I freely give. Come. First you must wash and refresh yourself, and while you're washing, I shall fix a meal for you."

Looking at the dirt on the man's hands and clothes, Gehazi wasn't sure he wanted to eat food prepared by Ziba. He quickly offered, "Kind Ziba, you must be tired from your day's labor. If you will but show me where your food is, I will be happy to prepare the meal while you and the master rest and talk."

With obvious excitement, Ziba said, "You are gracious to offer, and I will agree. First, we will all wash, and then I will happily allow you to prepare a meal."

Ziba provided warm water for Elisha and Gehazi to wash their faces, hands, and feet as well as oil and salve for their feet. He showed Gehazi where he kept the mutton, goat cheese, and unleavened bread; then he disappeared into another room.

It was nearly an hour later when the three men again assembled in the same room. When Ziba entered with his crutch, neither Elisha nor Gehazi was certain they were looking at the same man. He was clean. The dirt and grime from his hands and face were gone. His hair and beard were clean and had been brushed. The dirty tunic had been replaced with a clean one. But most noticeable was the smell. The foul odor that had previously emanated from him was replaced with the sweet scent of spiced oil. He was a changed man.

Gehazi had cleared the clutter from the table and set it with three small plates he'd found in a cupboard. He had prepared some salted, dried mutton and thick slabs of fresh goat cheese and placed it all on the table. Brass cups were filled with cool water he had drawn from the well, and the three men sat down at the table.

"Shall we give thanks to Jehovah?" Elisha asked.

"I would be honored if you would do so," Ziba responded, bowing his head.

Elisha and Gehazi both bowed their heads, and Elisha offered a simple but heartfelt thanks for the food they were about to eat and for Ziba's generosity.

Once Ziba got over his anxiety of having the prophet of God in his home, the conversation came easily. It drifted pleasantly over several topics before it settled on Ziba's situation. "She's been gone two years," he said when Elisha asked how long he had been living alone.

"And what of your children?" Elisha asked.

"Jehovah blessed me with a wonderful wife, but we did not have any children," Ziba replied sadly. "And now I am a lonely old man without family."

"What are your plans for the future?" Elisha asked, taking a small bite of the soft goat cheese.

"Only to sell this place and move. Since my wife died, I have lost interest in it, and as you can see, I no longer take care of things as I should. A few weeks after my wife died, I tripped while herding a cow, and she stepped on my leg. She is a huge animal, and the bone snapped like a twig. Since then," he chuckled, holding up his crutch, "this piece of wood and cloth has become my best friend." More seriously, he added, "Since then I have had difficult times, and my money is gone. I have a brother whom I visit in Tirzah. Perhaps I will move nearer to him."

Elisha nodded his head as if he understood and approved of the man's plans, but then he abruptly stopped. A slight wrinkle creased his forehead, and he placed the small crust of bread he was holding onto his plate, resting both forearms on the edge of the table. He looked deeply into Ziba's eyes for a full minute, long enough for Ziba to shift uncomfortably under his gaze, and then Elisha peered out the small window into the dark night.

Ziba watched in silence as Elisha's countenance changed. The wrinkle in his forehead disappeared, and a quiet peace visibly spread over him. After another full minute, he said to Ziba, "In less than six months' time, two men will come to you seeking to purchase your house and property. The first will offer you very little money. The second will offer you far more than the land is worth. If you sell to the first, you shall be blessed with a great posterity. If you sell to the second, you shall have the riches of this world and live in comfort all your days."

Ziba's hands dropped to his side, and he looked at Elisha in confused awe, unable to respond. *Great posterity? Riches?* he thought. The promises the prophet of Jehovah had just given him were overwhelming, and he sat quietly, completely lost in his thoughts. It was Elisha's voice that jarred him back to reality.

"Ziba, we are tired from our day's travels. Will you show us where we may rest our weary bodies in sleep?"

"Huh? Oh yes, yes, of course," Ziba said as he jumped from his chair. Lighting an oil lamp, he said, "Follow me, and I shall lead you to your room."

* * *

Sleep came late to Ziba. After sitting in a chair in his room and pondering for hours about how an old widower could have a great posterity—especially when he didn't have any prospects for a wife—or how he could be rich when all he had was this farm, he lay down on his bed only an hour before the first golden rays of the sun burst over the mountains to the east. He was so weary that he didn't hear Elisha and Gehazi walk from the house, retrieve their donkey, and continue their journey.

Chapter Five

Uzzi raced around the corner of the hut, his short legs whirling at top speed, and forcefully collided with his younger brother, Hanan. Both boys hit the ground with a thud and sent a cloud of dust into the morning air. Hanan was the first to struggle to his feet and rubbed his forehead with the palm of a very dirty hand. "You hurt me," he said to Uzzi, who was still lying on his back in the sand.

"Why weren't you watching where you were going?" Uzzi asked as he jumped to his feet, uninjured in the collision.

"I was watching where I was going. You ran into me. I didn't run into you," Hanan replied.

"I did not. You ran into me," Uzzi said, his voice growing louder with each word.

"Boys!" Miriam shouted over the noise of the escalating argument, "Gili is sleeping, and if you wake her, I'm going to make you play with her while I finish milking the goats."

Uzzi and Hanan looked at each other with wide eyes and instantly began to whisper. "Let's go to the sheep pens and play war. I'll be an Israelite general, and you can be a Moabite general," Uzzi said.

"That's not fair," replied Hanan in a voice only slightly quieter than he had used before Miriam threaten them. "You always get to be the Israelite." Turning away, he walked to where his mother stood. "Momma, I never get to be the Israelite," he whined. "Tell Uzzi he must be the Moabite this time."

Miriam drew a deep breath and began the same lecture about taking turns that she had given a hundred times before when she was interrupted by the soft cries of a baby. All three of them froze as still as statues, barely breathing, each hoping that the cries would cease. After thirty seconds of on-again off-again whimpers, the little voice from inside the hut erupted into full-scale crying. There would be no playing war and probably very little goat milking for the next hour.

Uzzi was the farthest from Miriam and began slinking backwards into the shadow of the hut to avoid playing with his little sister. He probably would have made it had he not tripped over the dog that had crept up and was lying on the ground behind him. The dog let out a yelp and jumped to its feet, drawing Miriam's complete attention.

"Uzzi, where do you think you're going?" Miriam barked as she looked sternly down her nose to where the boy stood. "I told you if you woke Gili, you would be playing with her. You march straight to the door. And you, Hanan," she said, looking at her other son, "will join him."

"Ah, Mother, do we really have to watch her?" they both asked simultaneously. "Can't she play by herself?"

"No, she can't play by herself, and yes, you really do have to watch her!"

Both boys lowered their heads and began walking to the door of the hut, kicking at dirt and small pebbles with each step.

"When will Father be home?" Hanan asked as he shuffled along.

"Tomorrow for sure, but perhaps later tonight," Miriam replied as she walked quickly toward the crying baby.

"Tell me one more time. Where did he go?"

"Shunem," Miriam replied, lifting the latch and going through the door.

Miriam walked up to the small wooden box in which Gili lay. "My, how you've grown these past six months," she said as she picked the baby up, holding her and gently stroking her fine strands of dark brown hair. Upon hearing her mother's soft voice, the baby changed her cries to contented gurgling sounds. Miriam was continually amazed at how quickly the child calmed. In the six months since her birth, Gili had cried longer than a minute only three, maybe four times. She was simply the happiest, easiest baby Miriam had ever had. On those days when she trekked into Jezreel to the produce market and stopped to visit with the gathered mothers, invariably Miriam was the envy of them all when she told of Gili's sweet personality.

Miriam picked up a goat skin from a bench in a corner of the small dwelling and gave it a quick shake to dislodge some of the dust that seemed to cling to everything. Placing it on the hard-packed dirt floor, she retrieved a soft woven blanket and spread it out on top of the goat skin. Placing Gili in the center of blanket, Miriam called to Uzzi and Hanan. "Come, boys. You need to keep Gili occupied for a few minutes while I milk the goats." Turning to her third son, two-year-old Caleb, who had been standing at her side the entire time, she clasped his hand and said, "You come with me to the goats."

Milking three goats took little time. Anxious to eat the few handfuls of wheat and barley Miriam dumped in the tray, each goat readily jumped up on the wooden stand when it was her turn. As the goats attacked the grain, Miriam expertly milked them. With the milk in a small bucket, she and Caleb left the small pen and began walking toward the hut.

They had only taken three steps when Caleb yanked on her robe and with his arms extended said, "Carry me."

With barely a pause in her stride, Miriam stooped down, wrapped her right arm around the boy's waist, and hefted him onto her hip. Caleb wrapped his arms around her neck and held on tightly as she navigated her way over the rock-strewn path, the fresh goat milk sloshing in the bucket in her left hand.

Every morning for the past three days as she walked from the goat pens to the hut, she scanned the barren land in hopes of seeing her husband's lone figure approaching the hut. He was two days overdue, and her anxiety was building. This day anxiety turned to excitement as she scanned the flat, treeless plain that stretched beyond the hut.

Setting the bucket of milk on the ground, she extended her arm and pointed in the distance. "There's Daddy," she exclaimed. The young boy instantly wriggled around in her arms so he could see where she was pointing. He was still too far away to make out his features, but Miriam could tell from his loping gait that it was her husband.

It took Gideon only fifteen minutes to cover the distance to the ramshackle hut and the waiting arms of his wife and children. After the hugs, bursts of laughter, and excitement had died down and the children had scampered off to play, Miriam took out a loaf of unleavened bread and began cutting Gideon a thick slice. "Well, how did it go?"

Gideon forced a smile and said, "The bread smells delicious, and I'm starving."

"But how did it go?" Miriam asked, unable to conceal the anticipation in her voice as the blade of the knife sliced through the bread and lightly gouged the wooden table.

Gideon watched Miriam's rapid sawing and chuckled. "If you continue sawing away like that, I'll have to build a new table."

Miriam dropped the knife and set the slice of bread and a cup of the fresh goat milk in front of Gideon then plopped down in a chair. "Gideon," she said eagerly, "what did he say?"

Gideon looked at the excitement in his wife's eyes and dreaded what he was about to say, but there was no way to ease into it. He let a small sigh escape from his lungs. "Not well, not like I expected."

The smile faded from Miriam's face, and her body visibly slumped. "What do you mean, not like you expected?"

Gideon looked down at the few crumbs that littered the table and pursed his lips. He knew his hopes of moving from this crude hut paled in comparison to his wife's. She had been hoping and praying the old man and woman in Shunem would consent to sell their house and property to Gideon. More than anything else, she wanted to leave this despicable hut, with its parched land and rocky fields. Anywhere would be better than this, she had told herself countless times.

"He said no?" she asked anxiously.

Gideon licked his lips and nodded his head slowly. "He wouldn't even consider it. He told me I was trying to take advantage of him."

Miriam's shoulders sank in despair, and she sat motionless, staring at Gideon, her hopes shattered. Their only chance of escaping this forsaken place was gone. The dreams that had filled her nights—abundant water from a stream, tall trees, and especially a house—were gone, replaced with the gritty reality of more days in this dreary place.

Gideon leaned across the table, tenderly clasped her hands in his, and gave them a gentle squeeze. With the slightest smile on his face, he continued, "But a strange thing happened as I was traveling back."

Miriam's thoughts were far, far away. She looked at him blankly and said without interest, "What was that?"

"As I was walking from Shunem, I came upon a man traveling the road. He was an old man with a crutch, who had a difficult time walking. Since we were both going the same direction, he asked if we could travel together. I agreed and offered to carry the pack he had slung on his back. At first we spoke of small things: the weather, the birds, and such. Eventually he told me he had been to visit his brother in Tirzah and was returning to his home in Edrei."

Miriam managed to shove enough of the disappointment she was feeling from her mind to ask, "Where is Edrei?"

"It's a village north of Ramoth-gilead. It sits in a valley on the edge of the volcanic fields, near the border of Syria."

"Hmm," Miriam acknowledged, not really certain where he was talking about and struggling to concentrate on what he was saying. "And then what?"

"He asked where I had been and the purpose of my trip," Gideon said. "When I told him I had been to Shunem, trying to buy a house and farm with little more than a few pieces of gold and a promise to pay more, he asked if I had ever been to Edrei."

"Have you?" Miriam asked quizzically.

"No, never," Gideon replied. And then with a coy smile, he added, "That is, until yesterday."

Miriam tilted her head and looked at Gideon, confusion all over her face. "You went to Edrei?"

Gideon caressed Miriam's face and said facetiously, "I know you love this place and would hate to leave it, but would you consider moving to Edrei?"

"Edrei?" Miriam replied cautiously.

"The house needs a little repair, but it's nestled against a hill with tall cedar trees out back and a well out the front door. It even comes with three cows!" Gideon said with a smirk.

Chapter Six

Thankfully, the streets of Edrei were nearly empty as Gideon and Miriam led their ragtag caravan of three donkeys, five goats, a dozen sheep, and a dog to the edge of town in the late afternoon. Miriam held a sleeping Caleb in her aching arms and had a sleeping Gili secured in a neat little bundle on her back. Fresh blood dripped from her dirty toes, evidence of battles she'd lost with rocks and brush that cluttered the trail. Uzzi, ever the adventurer, scampered energetically between the front of the column and the rear with a stick in one hand and pebbles in the other, motivating straggling sheep and goats with a swat of the stick or the sting of a thrown rock.

Hanan sat perched on Gideon's shoulders, with his hands cupped tightly beneath his father's chin. His deep brown eyes were more closed than open, and his little head bobbled with each step. In one hand Gideon held a rope leading a donkey that was nearly buried under a pile of goat skins, sheep skins, and assorted cloth. Tied to the tail of the first donkey was a leather strap leading to the halter of the second. Its burden was a cage filled with squawking chickens, plus an assortment of clay pots, an iron pan, and two chairs. The third donkey was by far the largest but struggled under a load of wheat and barley in large bags. Gideon shook his head, amazed that all their worldly possession could be carried on those three animals, two of which he had borrowed from his brother.

"This village is larger and nicer than I thought it would be," Miriam observed, stepping up beside Gideon. "I like it already!" she added with a weary but content smile.

Gideon gazed at his wife with genuine relief. He had done his best to describe the village as accurately as he could. If anything, he was guilty of understating not only the village but their new house. "I'm glad you like it. Only two more miles, and you'll be to your new home," he said with far more energy than he felt.

Uzzi came running up beside Gideon and pointed beyond the last row of houses. Atop gently rising terrain that extended the entire length of the village was a high cliff of volcanic rock. Scattered throughout were a series of cave-like openings. "What are those?" he asked.

"Entrances to another village," Gideon said with a twinkle in his eye.

"Really?" Uzzi replied, his eyes bulging in amazement. "An underground village?"

"An underground village," Gideon replied with a nod.

An involuntary shiver coursed through Miriam. "You never said anything about that. Why an underground village?"

Sensing her slight anxiety, Gideon said lightly, "I don't really know, but Ziba, the old man who sold us his house, says an entire village exists in the caves. It was tunneled out hundreds of years ago as a place of refuge from marauders. It hasn't been used in decades, but there's even an underground stream that flows through there."

"Can we go explore it?" Uzzi said, hardly able to contain his excitement.

"Yes, but not today."

"When?"

"After we're a little more settled," Gideon promised.

Edrei's main street was narrow, hemmed on either side by a mishmash of two-story structures. Some were made of brick, but most were built from chunks of black volcanic rock held together with white mortar. Leather awnings extended from the fronts of each building, providing patches of shade where shopkeepers and customers could haggle over merchandise without the sun beating down on them.

Jutting off at right angles were even narrower side streets, where shirtless, barefooted children played, oblivious to the sharp cinders that littered otherwise light brown dirt. The deep green leaves of a few pomegranate and fig trees mingled with colorful laundry that had been draped over lines to dry in the sun and created a lived-in, homey atmosphere.

Miriam surveyed the village and smiled as a sense of contentment replaced the uneasiness she felt when looking at the caves. This was a pleasant village, a place she would feel comfortable raising her children. Leading the way down the main street, Gideon and Miriam exchanged warm greetings with an occasional shopkeeper who had yet to close his business for the day.

The far side of the town was a different world. The gently rising terrain was dotted with cedar trees, and in the distance a stream ran down a narrow channel lined with thickets of bushes and trees. This side of the town was far more inviting than around the caves.

The last two miles seemed to take the longest, but while they were still several hundred yards from the house, Hanan came to life and begged to be taken off his father's shoulders so he could run. "Gladly," Gideon said, relieved to be free of the added weight. Then turning to Miriam, he said, "Let me take Caleb."

"Gladly," she replied with a smile.

The new house was more than Miriam could have hoped. It sat on a slight hill with its back tucked against an even higher hill which was covered in a thick stand of cedar trees. In front of the house was a three-foot-high rock wall that surrounded a deep well. A rocky path sloped down the hill, turned a corner, and disappeared from sight. This, Miriam supposed, was the path that led to the cattle enclosure, and she was sure if she followed it, she would find three large cows chewing their cud.

"I'll include the cows as part of the deal," Ziba had told Gideon weeks before when they'd negotiated the agreement. "They will be of no use to me in Tirzah, and they'll be of great benefit to you. But be cautious with the largest one, especially when she has a newborn calf; she's very mean and protective," he warned.

Unpacking their few belongings took far less time than packing had, and as Miriam arranged them inside the house, Gideon saw to the animals.

As the sun began sinking in the sky, Gideon trudged up the path from the animal enclosures to the well. Lowering a bucket, he drew it up filled with cool water. Lifting it to his lips, he tipped his head back and took several deep swallows then dumped the rest over his head. Rivulets of water ran off his black hair and beard and soaked into the shoulders of his leather vest and linen tunic.

Miriam silently glided up beside him and slipped her hand in his. "Beautiful!"

"You certainly are," Gideon said in return as he lowered the bucket to the ground.

"Not me," she said, obviously pleased by the compliment. "This place." She waved her arm all around her.

"It will do, then?"

"I love it already. I never want to leave."

Gideon smiled at her. "It is remote and far from family."

"My family is here," she said as she clasped both of her hands around Gideon's hand. "You and the children are all I need."

In spite of the enthusiasm, Gideon had sensed a twinge of uneasiness in his wife ever since she learned where Edrei was located. "It bothers you that we're so close to the border of Syria, doesn't it?"

Miriam gazed up at her husband. "A little," she answered. Then pausing, she added, "Perhaps a little more than a little. What about you? You were once a military commander. Does it concern you?"

Gideon thought about glibly telling her that it didn't bother him in the least, but he was certain Miriam would see through his false bravado. "Would I prefer the security of Shunen, surrounded by a hundred miles of Israelite territory and no fear of invasion? Yes," he answered truthfully. "But as close as we are to Syria, Edrei has one very important factor in its favor."

Miriam inclined her head slightly, arched her eyebrows, and asked, "And that is?"

"The Shahba."

"The what?" Miriam asked in confusion.

"Syria only has two directions from which it can attack. If they come from our front, they must pass through Israelite territory—something they couldn't do without being discovered. We would have plenty of time to flee." Pointing to the hills and cedar trees behind the house, he smiled reassuringly and continued, "Our backs are protected by a thousand square miles of the most forsaken, desolate, inhospitable, and inaccessible lava fields in the world—the Shahba. It is impossible for an army to cross such unforgiving terrain. Attempting to do so would be suicidal." Squeezing his wife's hand gently, he said, "We are quite safe."

Chapter Seven

Five years later

Naaman looked around him with pure contentment as he walked through the garden behind his home. In the many years since he and Karinah had moved in, they had made countless improvements and changes. He loved everything about it, but mostly he loved the water.

Naaman draped the luxuriously thick towel over the block wall and eased down the gently sloping bank of the Albana River. The thick, black mud on the river's bank was warm from the August afternoon sunshine, and it oozed between his toes. He welcomed the coolness of the clear, clean water as he waded in, stopping only when the water lapped at his waist. Cupping the small brush made of pig bristles in his right hand, he softly scrubbed the snowy-white skin on the fingers of his left hand and watched the tiny particles of dead skin drop to the water and float away. Switching the brush to his left hand, he scrubbed with slightly more intensity at the thumb and forefinger on his right hand. He frowned as little specks of blood appeared where, only a moment before, scaly bits of flesh had been. It was getting worse.

Moving back to the bank, he sat down and swished his right foot in the water to remove the mud. Then he rested that foot on his left knee to examine his toes. Over the past three months, two of his toenails had fallen off as the skin around them had flaked and fallen away. He gently brushed at the white of his toes but stopped after only two strokes—it was too painful. Letting out a sigh, he plopped his right foot back in the water and lifted his left foot to examine. Good, he thought as he carefully looked at each toe, no red or white spots . . . yet.

Leaning to his side, he looked at his face reflected in the calm water. Bending closer to the surface, he moved the hairs of his beard aside so he could examine his cheek. Over the years, the small, red blotch had become two and then three and then turned gray and eventually stark white. But Naaman had managed to hide it with his beard. It had progressed slowly, and at times it seemed to shrink. For a while he'd held out hope that the leprosy would disappear. It didn't. Fortunately, rather than spreading up his cheek and to his nose, like so many others' did, the creeping disease had chosen a different route. It had worked its way across his cheek and was slowly spreading to his ear. As the skin began dying and decaying, his beard had become thinner but had never fallen completely out. With careful brushing, he could rearrange the hair to make it appear as if nothing was wrong. As he sat and studied his reflection, he wondered how long it would be before he could no longer hide the disease.

Rising to his feet, Naaman waded back into the river as he pulled a small cloth from the waistband of the white linen pants he wore and gently rubbed his right earlobe. Although not as obviously affected as his hands, his ear was more painful to touch, and he lightly dabbed at it with the water-soaked cloth. His right ear done, he shifted the cloth to his other hand and worked on his left. There were no signs of the disease on that ear, but he was confident it was only a matter of time. His ears clean, Naaman wrung water from the cloth, formed it into a ball, tossed it to the bank, and then slowly lowered himself below the water's surface, vigorously rubbing his face and hair as he blew a stream of bubbles from his mostly closed lips.

Rising above the surface, he shook his head from side to side and sent a shower of water drops through the air and waded back to the bank. He picked up a thick bar of lye soap, lathered his head and body, then dove headfirst in the water and swam several strokes upstream, leaving a wake of white soapy bubbles.

His bath complete, Naaman sighed as he walked up the slope and dried himself with the towel. He loved the cool, sparkling water of the river and hated to leave it. Clean and rejuvenated, he walked slowly to the house and dressed in a fresh robe for his meeting with the king.

Ordinarily he would have summoned his chariot for the mile trip to the opulent palace, but today he chose to walk. He wanted time to mull over the things he would say and hear.

At the palace, Naaman waited patiently in the huge room and scanned the mural on the wall. Ordinarily he found the thousands of pieces of colorful tiles arranged in a battle scene to be intriguing, and he would search it for details he'd overlooked on previous viewings. Today, however, weightier matters pressed on his mind, matters of battle.

The door burst open, and a boisterous voice boomed through the room. It neither shocked nor startled Naaman—it was expected.

"Ah, my very favorite commander," said an exuberant Ben-Hadad II, king of Syria. He strode with a retinue of servants following behind like puppies trotting behind their mother. "It is so good to see you!" he said with genuine affection.

Naaman smiled. It was impossible not to like this man. He could be vengeful and frightening to his enemies, but he would give the world to those he admired and respected.

Naaman grasped the edges of his flowing cape and bowed deeply. "I'm equally pleased to see you."

"Come, come. Join me at the table," Ben-Hadad said, motioning to a table large enough to seat fifty people.

Two servants raced ahead of the king. One slid back the ornate chair at the head of the table and waited for the king while the other did the same for Naaman. Everyone else took up standing positions at various places around the room, each waiting patiently should they be summoned.

"How have you been?" Ben-Hadad said as he pulled his deep red cloak around him and sank into the soft cushions on the chair. The servant behind the chair tried pushing it toward the table, but his hundred-and-twenty-pound frame was no match for Ben-Hadad's ample three-hundred-pound body. Ben-Hadad smiled at the servant and dismissed him with the wave of a hand; then he pulled the chair nearer the table himself.

"I've been fine, thank you," Naaman said as he sat down and slid his chair up to the table. "And you?" he asked.

"Glorious! I'm just wonderful!" Ben-Hadad said with a smile. He unfastened the buckle on his leather belt, removing it and the sword attached to it. Laying them on the table, he continued in a lower and more serious voice, "But tell me, now that you've had a chance to consider my plan, what are our chances of success?"

Naaman looked into the man's dark green eyes and inhaled a deep breath. It was the question Naaman had been wrestling with for the better part of a week and had caused him several nights of fitful sleep. Naaman expelled the breath and said guardedly but truthfully, "Fair."

Ben-Hadad raised his eyebrows in surprise and leaned backward in surprise. "Only fair?"

Naaman nodded his head.

Clearly stunned at the response, Ben-Hadad prodded, "Come, Naaman. Don't make me drag it out of you. What don't you like about it?"

Naaman leaned forward and carefully considered his response. Ben-Hadad was a strong leader, well respected by his people, but not a military genius, though he often thought of himself that way. And as pleasant as he generally appeared, he did not like being told his ideas were flawed in any way. Naaman had churned these issues over his mind as he walked to the palace and, in the end, decided he would be tactful but honest. "There are many unknowns, and the risk of failure is significant."

Naaman watched as the smile melted from Ben-Hadad's lips and his brow furrowed. There was no anger, but there was defensiveness in his voice when he said, "Of course there's risk; there always is in a military campaign. And what's unknown?"

"I agree there's always risk, but we should do everything possible to reduce the risk and—"

Ben-Hadad cut him off in midsentence. "Are you afraid of this raid? Are you afraid of the Israelite forces?"

"I'm fearful every time I go into battle," Naaman said carefully. "But it isn't the battle; it's getting to the battle that causes me anxiety."

Ben-Hadad's eyes opened wide in surprise. "Getting to the battle? You mean trekking down through the Shahba?"

"Yes."

"But I've dealt with that," Ben-Hadad exclaimed in mild irritation, waving his hand in the air. "You'll have an expert guide."

"I don't relish putting my life and the lives of my men in the hands of someone I've never met and know nothing about," he said candidly, and then added with emphasis, "especially when it comes to someplace as treacherous as the Shahba."

Ben-Hadad dismissed the comment as if he was shooing away a fly. "He can be trusted, I assure you."

The expression on Naaman's face made it clear he wasn't willing to accept Ben-Hadad's assurances on face value.

Ben-Hadad leaned forward against the table until his hefty stomach would let him go no farther. With breath reeking of garlic and spices, he said forcefully, "Naaman, this raid is important. The Israelites must understand we will not allow them to expand any farther into our territory. We need to create fear, to make them uneasy and uncertain. This raid will do that. When you're finished, they will understand that even the volcano fields of the Shahba do not deter us. You must do this! You simply must! I would trust this to no one but you. And besides, you will be rewarded handsomely."

Naaman listened to what was said, but he was also paying close attention to what wasn't being said. Ben-Hadad was seeking his input only as a formality—Naaman wasn't being given a choice. Resigned that nothing he said would sway Ben-Hadad from the ill-conceived plan, Naaman drew in a deep breath and, looking the king in the eye, said simply, "I'll do my best."

"That's what I wanted to hear," roared Ben-Hadad as he slapped the table with the palms of both hands. Then standing up, he added, "I knew I could count on you." Grasping Naaman's arm, he offered a big smile. "And now I must be off. Send me reports when you can. Best of luck to you!" He began walking from the room. Pointing to a servant trailing behind him, he ordered, "Get my sword from the table," and then he disappeared out the same door he'd entered, his gaggle of aides and servants following.

Naaman slowly rose from his chair and ran his fingers through his hair as he shook his head from side to side. Expelling another deep sigh, he slowly walked from the room, down the corridors of the palace, and out into the bustling streets of Damascus. The sun beat down on him, and sweat instantly began trickling from his armpits in little rivulets. Fighting his way past a camel caravan loaded with spices, food, and a hundred other items to trade and barter, Naaman made his way to the merchant quarter of the city. Noisy shopkeepers hawking clothing, jewelry, and intricate figurines of precious metals lined the streets and held out their wares, enticing him to enter and buy, but he pushed on, lost in his thoughts.

Leaving the main road, he turned up a side alley and walked to an inordinately large dwelling that looked neglected and deserted. What should have been smoothly plastered walls were pockmarked, and small chunks of plaster littered the ground. Boards and bits of wood were strewn about and looked as if they hadn't been moved in years. A few healthy weeds peeked out from cracks in the stone walkway leading to the door.

Naaman smiled as he approached the dwelling; it looked exactly as it had twenty years earlier when he saw it for the first time. Bending over, he picked up a small rock and used it to give three loud raps on the solid door. He waited patiently for a moment, and when no one answered, he rapped four more times, only louder.

"I'm coming. I'm coming! Be patient."

Naaman listened as two heavy latches were unbolted and the door slowly squeaked open on its hinges. An ancient man dressed in an immaculate black satin robe with a deep red sash stood in the doorway.

"Hello, Grandfather," Naaman said cheerfully, even though the man wasn't. In fact, he was no relation at all, only a man Naaman had met many years before and had become close to.

An instant smile spread across the old man's toothless mouth as he exclaimed loudly, "Naaman, my friend, you are a wonderful sight for these tired old eyes. Come in. Come in."

The inside of the house was the exact opposite of the outside. Beautifully woven rugs adorned the floor, and luxurious chairs and couches were placed uniformly around the room. Ornately carved tables inlaid with various types of wood and ivory stood in the corners, with decorative silver lamps glowing on them. The walls were adorned with what Naaman assumed were pieces of art from distant lands.

"Come and sit." The old man shuffled across the floor and pointed to one of the couches piled high with pillows. "What refreshment can I get for you? Something cool to drink? A meal? How about some figs or dates?"

"I'm not hungry, but water would be nice."

"Water it is," he said, then he called loudly, "Sophia, please bring some cool water."

Only a fraction of a second later, a servant girl entered the room carrying a wooden tray on which rested a silver goblet of water.

"Thank you," Naaman said as he removed the goblet from the tray.

"Tell me, how have you been?" the man asked as he watched Naaman take several deep swallows from the goblet.

"I'm fine."

"And what of that lovely wife of yours? How is she?"

"As beautiful as ever," Naaman said proudly. "But what of you? Are you well and still trading as much as you always were?"

"More!" the man said with a twinkle in his eye. "I can't stop trading or I'll die."

Naaman smiled at this. He had no idea how old the man was, but he'd estimate close to ninety years old.

Naaman set the goblet on the table beside him and let out a faint sigh. "Bisha, I've come seeking advice."

The old man leaned forward in his chair and said almost conspiratorially, "I think you should divorce your wife so I can marry her. That's my advice to you." Then he burst into laughter.

Naaman chuckled and shook his head. "I don't think I'll take your advice."

"Hmm, too bad for me," the grandfatherly man said with feigned sadness. Then more brightly he said, "What is it I can help you with?"

"I know of no one who has traveled the deserts of Syria more than you," Naaman began.

"That's because there isn't anyone," Bisha said as he leaned back in his chair and puffed out his chest.

"I've come asking your advice about crossing the volcanic fields of the Shahba."

"Oh, that's easy." Bisha leaned forward in his chair and said emphatically, "Don't do it!"

The corners of Naaman's mouth pulled back in a halfhearted smile. "What if I tell you I must?"

The smile drained from Bisha's face as he considered Naaman's statement. He leaned back and propped his elbows on the arms of his chair, interlocking his fingers and peering at Naaman in silence. After a moment he said very seriously, "Naaman, tell the king that a surprise attack on Ramoth-gilead is not worth the cost you'll pay for crossing the Shahba."

The response startled Naaman, and he shifted in his chair uncomfortably. "I've said nothing about an attack on Ramoth-gilead," he protested in a weak denial of his mission.

"You don't have to," Bisha said as he raised his joined hands to his chin. "There's only one reason a military man like you would want information about the Shahba, and that's for a surprise attack on Ramoth-gilead or perhaps Edrei."

The corners of Naaman's mouth dropped into a frown as he looked intently at the old man. Denying his supposition would only confirm what the astute man had already figured out. "Ramoth-gilead," he confirmed softly.

Bisha slowly lowered his hands and let out a long, weary sigh. "It's an unforgiving place even the gods of Syria refuse to go. It is hundreds of square miles filled with twisting canyons whose sheer walls are so steep you can't climb them. Once you enter, you're trapped in a maze from which there is only one way out, and if you don't know how to find it, you die. There's no water, the wind blows so hard it obliterates your tracks in a matter of minutes or at most a few hours, and there's no vegetation. Scorpions are the only living creatures within its confines. Even the birds refuse to fly over its desolate nothingness. The sun beats down on the black sand, making it so hot it burns your feet. And at night it gets so cold you think you'll freeze."

Naaman looked intently at Bisha through ever-widening eyes while he considered everything he'd been told. "Have you crossed it?"

"Many times, but those were days long, long ago. I would never attempt it now."

"How long does it take?"

"That depends on many things. Will you be on camel, horseback, or foot? Will you go in the spring or fall? You should never go this time of year—it is too hot!"

"If we go on foot, with camels, how long will it take?"

"If everything goes perfectly, no wrong turns, you can cross it in three and a half days. But you should plan on five."

Naaman let out a long sigh and sank back into the plush couch. "Can you give me any words of wisdom?"

"I've already told you: don't do it!" the man said earnestly. After a long pause and knowing Naaman couldn't heed his advice, he said, "Never turn back, and always go right!"

Naaman looked at Bisha quizzically and repeated, "Never turn back, and always go right?"

"When you get lost—and you certainly will—never backtrack unless you are absolutely positive where you made your mistake. It wastes precious time. And whenever you come to a fork in a canyon, always take the trail that goes to the right," Bisha said. "It doesn't always work, but it's the safest bet. The only exception is if the left fork descends more rapidly. In that case, go left."

Naaman sat deep in his chair, more than a little perplexed at the information he'd just been given. Always go right, except sometimes left, and never backtrack, he thought. It was hardly the kind of information he had hoped to get. Pushing himself up from the chair, he walked to where the old man was sitting and extended his hand. "Thank you, Bisha. You have helped me." He wanted to say the man had been a big help, but he wasn't sure that was true.

Bisha smiled and said, "I hope to see you again soon. And may it not be after we are dead."

Chapter Eight

Travel from Damascus to Lajat was easy. The contingent of one hundred foot soldiers, six men on horseback, and string of ten camels drew stares and curious glances from isolated settlers and nomads herding goats in the almost-barren hills, but civilization soon disappeared in their dust. Except for a horse stepping in a gopher hole and breaking her leg, the three-day trip to Lajat had been uneventful.

Lajat wasn't the ideal place to wait for their guide, but they could make do. At one time, civilization had taken a sip of the isolated settlement, swirled it around in its mouth, then quickly spat it out as being too bitter. Remote and desolate, the only evidence that humans had even tried gaining a foothold was a shallow well with surprisingly good water. Besides the well, Naaman was also satisfied with Ben-Hadad's rendezvous spot for another reason. Enough grass, dry and tough as it was, managed to push up through the parched ground to provide a limited supply of feed for the horses and camels. The water was plentiful enough it would slake the thirst of man and beast for days, and as long as the guide arrived as planned, the grass would keep the animals content.

Anticipating their guide might be late, Naaman had timed the group's arrival for the exact day their guide was supposed to meet them. If necessary, the horses and camels could grub out an existence for two or three days but no more.

On the evening of the fourth day, when their guide still hadn't arrived, Naaman turned to his second-in-command and asked, "Malik, what is your recommendation?"

The man didn't hesitate. "We turn back."

"Do you mean back to Damascus or jut backtrack a few miles for more grass?" Naaman asked.

"To Damascus," Malik replied firmly. "Backtracking gains us little, possibly nothing. We must still bring the horses here for water at least once a day, perhaps twice, and each day we'll have to backtrack even farther to find more grass for the animals." And then in an afterthought and with a smile, he added, "In a week we'll have worked our way back to Damascus anyway, so we might as well go there now."

Naaman had already considered this. "Returning will not put us in Ben-Hadad's good graces."

Malik shrugged his shoulders. "Better to retreat and live to fight another day than to perish in this forsaken place. Besides, how long do we wait for this mysterious guide to appear?"

Naaman smiled at Malik. He had reached the same conclusion much earlier in the day but wanted to know if Malik agreed. "We'll leave tomorrow at sunrise," Naaman said. "Please make sure the men are ready."

"Yes, Captain," Malik said with a smile and left the tent.

Naaman sat cross-legged on a small rug studying the map before him. Admitting defeat did not come easily, but regardless of how long he stared at the map, he could see no possible way to avoid the desolation of the Shahba and still attack the small village of Ramoth-gilead without using the main trade routes, something Ben-Hadad was loath to allow.

"Captain," Malik's voice called from outside the tent.

"Enter," Naaman replied without looking up.

Malik walked into the tent followed by a young soldier. "Captain, this is Zeri, a bowman. He says he might be able to help us."

Naaman eyed the young soldier. Every year they seemed to get younger and younger, he thought. "What is it?"

"Captain, as a young child I grew up herding sheep near here," he said with an air of authority. "On a few occasions, my father led us across the volcanic fields to Ramoth-gilead and Edrei to trade with merchants." Seeing a look of interest on Naaman's face, he puffed out his chest and added proudly, "I can lead us across the fields."

Naaman shot Malik a questioning look. The second-in-command offered a slight shrug of the shoulders.

"How long ago?" Naaman asked.

"Sir?" the overly confident soldier replied.

"How long has it been since you traversed the volcanic fields?"

"Not long; five, maybe six years?"

Malik let out a snort. "Five or six years? How old where you then, maybe ten?"

"Younger," Zeri responded. "Probably only eight or nine."

Malik rolled his eyes and scoffed at the remark. "What makes you believe you can remember how to get through the fields? You were only a child, and it was years ago." Malik clasped his hand around the soldier's arm in disgust and began pulling him from the tent.

"It's not as difficult as it seems," Zeri said quickly. "That is, if you know the signs or monuments to follow!"

Naaman raised his hand to Malik, signaling him to release his grip on the soldier. "What signs or monuments?"

Zeri tugged his arm free from Malik's grasp and straightened his tunic, shooting him a look of superiority. "If you know where and what to look for, the way is clearly marked. If you don't, it's a maze from which you never return."

"And you know these signs?" Malik said skeptically.

"Yes," Zeri said proudly. "I do."

"Can you describe them to me?" Naaman asked cautiously, surprised that his grandfatherly friend Bisha had said nothing about monuments.

Zeri hesitated. "Well . . . it's complicated."

Naaman and Malik exchanged nervous glances, their skepticism growing with each statement the young soldier made. But before either man could respond, Zeri continued, "There are some places where the monuments show the way to proceed. At other places, they show the way not to travel. By knowing the monuments, you can safely travel through the canyons and come out on the other side."

Naaman looked at Zeri and mentally shook his head; the men really were getting younger. This young soldier was nothing more than a man-child. His matted jet-black hair was thick and wavy, and it clung to his head from being trapped in a helmet all day. His face was smooth—he lacked the maturity to even grow a beard. Deep gray eyes were almost hidden behind bushy black eyebrows, but what Naaman could see of them bespoke innocence not the detached hardness of more experienced men. There wasn't any fat on the young man, and his arms were so skinny Naaman wondered how he even had the strength to draw a bow. His face was thin and his eyes were close together, giving him an awkward appearance.

Naaman had spent years in command of troops and knew most of the men in this party very well, but this boy was a last-minute substitution for a battle-tested soldier who had become violently ill. Naaman knew nothing about Zeri.

"You're confident you can recognize these monuments? You're certain you can determine the difference between where to go and where not to go?"

Zeri shifted the weight on his feet and said, "Oh, I'm positive I can do it, Captain. I remember them as if it were yesterday."

Naaman ran his fingers through his hair then absentmindedly scratched at the stark white blotches on the lobe of his right ear. The heat and dirt aggravated the blotches, and he wished he could soak in the cool waters of the river behind his house.

Looking first at Malik and then Zeri, Naaman gave a weak smile. "Thank you for your information. Malik and I will discuss it. In the meantime, tell the cooks that you are to receive an extra portion of wine tonight."

"Thank you, Captain," Zeri said excitedly. Turning, he looked at Malik with the slightest sneer on his lips and walked from the tent.

"Well, what do you think?" Naaman asked Malik as they watched Zeri trot toward the cooks.

"I question if he could find his way from one side of Damascus to the other if there was only a single road and he had a map."

Naaman chuckled. "Returning to Damascus empty-handed would not make our king very happy, Malik."

"Not returning from the volcanic fields of the Shahba would not make me very happy," Malik retorted with only the slightest smile.

"You think it unwise to trust him?" Naaman asked.

"I think the odds are against him—and us."

Chapter Nine

Naaman reined his horse to a stop on the slight incline, rose slightly in the stirrups, and gazed over the desolate, narrow valley that stretched before him. He shook his head in disgust. For as far as he could see, it was the same: high black cliffs on both sides of a barren black-sanded nothingness. The intense rays of afternoon sun heated the desert floor and made the rock outcroppings in the distance shimmer and wave. At the very farthest point in the valley, there appeared to be a pond of water, but Naaman knew the sun and heat had joined an unwitting alliance to play tricks on his eyes. There was no water, not a drop. It was an illusion.

Every part of him rebelled at the heat. The dry air sucked moisture from everything, even his eyeballs, and he blinked several times to clear the dust that had been blown into them by the ceaseless wind. He tightened the once-white cloth, now a dingy gray, wrapped around his head to cover his nose and mouth. It was a futile attempt to keep the black sand from lodging in his nose or getting sucked into his lungs. He licked his parched and cracked lips, but the moisture from his tongue mingled with the dust to create a gritty paste. Lifting a corner of the cloth, he spit on the ground and instantly regretted it. Dusty spit was better than none. His mouth was as dry as the volcanic sand that surrounded them, and he'd had no water for an entire day.

"Order the men to halt," he said to Malik as he contemplated the oddity that lay in their path.

Malik shouted the order with greater intensity, and it echoed along the snake-like column of soldiers behind them until everyone came to a stop. Those who had spears shoved the ends into the hot black sand and leaned on them for respite. Others dropped their shields in the sand and let their arms hang limply at their sides.

Turning to his right, Naaman said, "We'll rest here for a few minutes. Malik, check on Zeri."

They were lost again—or still, depending upon how the captain looked at it. He knew it, and all the men behind him knew it, but there was no grumbling. They were just thankful he'd kept them alive this long.

Dismounting and dropping the reins of his beleaguered horse, Naaman walked forward and studied the stone monument at his feet. It stood slightly less than two feet tall and was about the same distance in diameter. It was really nothing more than a pile of volcanic rock, yet he knew it was of critical importance. He just didn't know why. "What are you trying to tell me?" he asked the stones softly.

Malik walked up beside Naaman and looked down at the monument; then he looked up in the barren nothingness before them, saying nothing.

"How is our young guide?" Naaman asked without turning to look at Malik.

"He is unconsciousness. Death will come soon."

It had happened two nights earlier, the second night after they'd left Lajat. It was a mistake a more experienced soldier or desert traveler would never have made, one a grizzled old soldier had warned the young man about only minutes before.

"You should never walk without your sandals," Dekar had said, ramming the end of his spear into the sand. He'd unrolled a thick blanket that would become his bed for the night and shook it vigorously, sending a cloud of dust and sand into the air.

"But my feet are tired, and if I burrow them deep enough, the sand is cool and feels good," Zeri replied as he wiggled his toes up and down and twisted his feet from side to side, burrowing them in the black sand. It wasn't that the sand was that cool; it was just that it wasn't as hot as the surface.

"Still, it is unwise. The deathstalker is never far away," Dekar warned ominously.

Zeri laughed at the reference to the illusive scorpion. "Scorpions don't kill people, except maybe children or weak old women. Not strong men like us."

"The deathstalker does," Dekar replied matter-of-factly as he smoothed a wrinkle in his blanket.

"How do you know?" Zeri asked skeptically as he spread his own thick blanket on the ground. He'd heard talk of the extremely deadly scorpion since he was a child, but no one he knew had ever even seen one, and he believed they were figments of people's imagination.

"I've seen it," the deeply tanned veteran said as he unfastened his sword and pulled it from its scabbard. Laying the scabbard to the left of his blanket, Dekar carefully placed the sword beside him on the right. He always slept on his back, his head resting on his shield and his sword within easy reach.

"You've see the scorpion or you've seen it kill someone?" Zeri asked, not convinced.

"Both."

Zeri snickered as he straightened a corner of his blanket. "You and your deathstalker."

"You can laugh, but if you value your life, there are two things you should never do in the desert."

"What?" Zeri asked condescendingly.

"Put your hand where your eye cannot see," Dekar said ominously. Then pointing to the boy's bare feet, he added, "And walk without sandals."

Zeri scoffed. "You worry too much."

Dekar raised his eyebrows at the boy's remark. "Perhaps, but I'm still alive," he said as he stretched out on the blanket and looked in the distance. The rays of the twilight sun streamed through the fine dust particles in the air and turned the western horizon a brilliant gold. In not many minutes, the sun would sink below the mountains, and the air would turn cool, making sleep possible.

Zeri finished smoothing out his blanket and walked the short distance to where his bow and quiver were propped against a rock. He undid the bowstring to relieve the tension then picked up the quiver. Turning, he stepped toward his blanket. As his right foot sank into the sand, an unexpected pain shot through the soft skin of his instep, bringing instant pain.

Dropping his bow and quiver in the sand, Zeri hopped to his blanket and crashed down onto it. Given the pain, he expected to find a large thorn sticking from the bottom of his foot, but there was nothing more than a small dot and intense stinging.

In a single, lightning-fast motion, Dekar sat upright on his blanket, sword in hand, and with a mighty swing, slammed the flat of his blade onto a small creature scurrying across the earth. The force of the impact buried the bright steel blade under a thin layer of sand. Relaxing his grip on the sword, he left it lying in the sand, the blade mostly covered. Rising to his feet, he picked up his scabbard and moved to where he thought the small creature should be. Using the tip of the scabbard, he carefully pushed sand from around the blade until he could see the flattened body of a scorpion. He picked up his sword and, with the sharp tip, gingerly nudged the scorpion to make certain all life had been crushed from it. Satisfied the creature was dead, he reached down and gingerly lifted it by its curving, segmented tail, letting it dangle in the evening light.

Unlike the millions of tan and brown scorpions that crawl and burrow in the deserts of Syria, the colorful hues of this one marked it as belonging to a rare group of deadly killers. Larger than most scorpions, it measured slightly less than four inches long from the black tips of its small pincers to its unusually thin tail, which came to a point so delicate and threadlike it was difficult to see in the waning light.

Clenching his teeth so his chiseled jaw muscles protruded, Dekar stepped to where Zeri sat on his blanket holding his foot and writhing in pain. Letting the scorpion drop from between his thumb and forefinger, he said calmly, "Take a close look at the deathstalker that killed you."

Zeri watched the scorpion fall through the air and land in his lap. He stared in disbelief through panic-stricken eyes and looked up at Dekar. "Do something! You must do something!" He frantically brushed the dead scorpion from his lap and onto the sand beside him.

Dekar slowly shook his head as he looked at the terrified boy-soldier. There was nothing to do except perhaps kill the boy now to save him the excruciating agony and pain that would last several hours if he was lucky, a few days if he wasn't. First would come the pain, beginning in Zeri's foot and quickly working its way up his leg until it eventually spread throughout his body, getting more intense by the minute until it became excruciating. If the boy was lucky, he would pass out; if not, he would pray for death. Then the burning fever would begin, causing body fluid to ooze out the pores of his skin and soak his clothes. Soon, very soon after that, the convulsions would begin, mercilessly wracking every muscle in the boy's body with repeated, violent contractions. Eventually paralysis would come and, finally, the blissful relief of death, but not before each internal organ slowly, agonizingly shut down. There was nothing anyone could do but let the insidious venom run its course.

Ending his misery now would be humane, but Dekar's thoughts had already turned from the boy's death sentence to a far more important matter: his life—and the life of every man in the contingent who had depended on their guide.

He looked at the boy, who sat shaking his foot and gritting his teeth as the pain crept from the bottom of his foot toward his ankle. "You must be calm," Dekar said sternly. "The more excited you become the more rapidly the venom spreads."

"The pain," Zeri moaned as he took a deep breath and tried to calm the terror in his mind. "The pain is getting worse and climbing up to my ankle."

Dekar nodded his head in sympathy. He had felt the sting of the deathstalker's less deadly relatives and knew what Zeri was feeling. Reaching for his sword, he sliced a long, thin strip of cloth from the edge of Zeri's blanket. "Lay back; I'm going to tie this around your leg to slow the venom." Tying the tourniquet snuggly just below Zeri's knee, Dekar rose to his feet and said, "Stay here. Don't get up. I'll go find others." Then he turned and rapidly sprinted away.

Dekar hadn't taken more than three steps before any thoughts of Zeri had vanished from his mind. The boy was as good as dead. What flooded Dekar's mind was the death sentence the pathetically small but deadly creature had issued for every man in the contingent. Without their guide, as careless and stupid as he had been, they stood no chance of finding their way out of the forsaken volcanic fields of the Shahba. Zeri's would be a slow and agonizing death by venom. Theirs would be death by dehydration and starvation. Either way, they were all now sentenced to die.

Zeri was groaning in pain as Dekar led Naaman and Malik to where the young man lay. "Out of the way," Dekar barked at the small group of soldiers who had congregated around Zeri. "The captain is here."

Naaman and Malik pushed their way between the men and stood on either side Zeri. Looking at the contorted grimace and the fear in the young man's eyes, Malik shook his head and demanded, "You must tell us everything you know about getting out of this forsaken place—now!"

Naaman shot Malik an angry glance to silence him; then the captain dropped to his knee beside the boy. "Zeri," he began calmly, but the young soldier cut him off.

"Captain," he said in a quivering voice, "I'm sorry I have already failed you."

Naaman looked quizzically at Zeri. "Failed? What do you mean? How have you failed?"

The boy grimaced and grabbed at his thigh as a jolt of pain spread farther up his leg, but his voice was remarkably calm. "Dekar tells me I will die. Nothing can be done to save me."

Naaman rested a hand on the boy's shoulder but said nothing, a tacit acknowledgment of the truth: nothing could be done for him.

Zeri gave a weak smile and began grinding his clenched teeth together. Sucking in a deep breath, he looked Naaman squarely in the eyes and blurted, "We're lost!" Then without any hesitation, he continued, "Since yesterday at noon. As we've come upon each monument, I haven't been certain of the direction we were to travel."

Naaman's eyes widened, and he shook his head in confusion. "What?"

"I've been guessing."

Standing above, Malik and Dekar looked at each other in disbelief. Had Naaman not been in their way, either one of them would have likely strangled the boy out of anger.

Naaman pulled his hand back from the boy's shoulder. "You have no idea where we are or which way we should go?"

Zeri clenched his teeth and slowly shook his head. "When I saw the first few monuments, everything from my childhood came back, and I was confident I could guide us through. For the first day, everything was exactly as I remembered. But yesterday morning the very first monument we came to didn't make sense. I was uncertain, so I guessed. An hour later when we came upon the next monument, I was relieved. Everything was fine again until just before noon. When we came upon the next monument, nothing about it was right, and so I guessed once again. Since then I haven't recognized anything."

Malik dropped to his knees beside the boy and angrily shouted, "Why didn't you say something, you fool? Don't you realize—"

Naaman held up his hand to cut off Malik's outburst. "Be quiet, Malik," he commanded. A thousand questions needed to be asked, and Zeri needed to be calm and helpful, not frightened into silence. Looking at Zeri, Naaman said, "I know you're in pain, Zeri, but I must ask you some questions."

The boy rolled to his other side, facing away from Naaman, and began moaning as pain gripped his stomach. "I'll do my best," he said in a voice not much louder than a whisper.

Naaman stood up, stepped over the boy, and knelt in the sand so he was facing him once more. "What made you decide to lead us the direction you did? Was anything familiar to you? Did you recognize anything?"

Zeri shook his head only slightly. "No."

Naaman shook his head. There had been thousands of footsteps, hundreds of turns, and dozens of forks in the trail since yesterday. It was impossible to sort them out.

Zeri screamed out as the deadly toxins intensified their attack, spreading to his chest and shoulders. Despite the coolness of the evening, large drops of sweat popped out from beneath his matted hair and ran down his face in an almost steady stream, saturating his blanket. "Please, Captain, do something!" he begged. "I can't stand the pain."

Naaman put his hand on the young man's sopping wet head and, in the most soothing voice he could muster, said, "The pain will subside." It was a lie. The pain would only get worse until his body was so wracked and tormented that he could no longer withstand it and passed out; then, and only then, would relief come. Standing up, Naaman shouted, "Bring the physician."

In the fading light, Naaman couldn't see the diminutive man rushing toward him with a goatskin bag tucked under one arm. "I'm here, Captain," the man said as he slid to a stop. "I was getting water and rags."

Pointing down at Zeri squirming on the blanket, Naaman said, "Scorpion bite, deathstalker; see what you can do for him."

The man's shoulders visibly slumped at the words, but he dropped to his knees and said, "What is your name, soldier?"

"Zeri," came the weak reply through tightly clenched teeth.

"Where were you bitten?"

"The bottom of my right foot."

"Well," the little man said in a hollow effort to lighten the mood, "if you're going to be stung by a scorpion, that's the best place—it's a long way from the heart." Reaching down, he untied the tourniquet on Zeri's leg. It was doing no good; the venom had long since bypassed the makeshift dam in the vein and was racing through his bloodstream with each beat of the boy's heart. Unstopping the spout of the goatskin water bag, the physician wet a small rag and began wiping Zeri's face and forehead with cool water. It was the only thing he could do.

Naaman turned to walk away but was stopped by Zeri's shout. "Captain, please don't leave me to die here."

Naaman halted in midstride, stepped back, and knelt beside the dying man. "I will not leave you on the Shalıba," he promised, patting the boy on the shoulder.

* * *

"What are you trying to tell me?" Naaman muttered again as he kicked at the pile of rocks with the toe of his sandal. There was no question that someone at some time had carefully and purposely stacked them there. He should have been ecstatic because in the two days since Zeri had been bitten, no one had seen a single monument. Naaman had blindly led the column of soldiers down one canyon after another, always going right except when the left fork descended more rapidly. And he had only backtracked once. Not because he was certain of a mistake but because they hit a dead end. They were boxed in with two-hundred-foot-tall sheer cliffs completely surrounding them. There was no way out except the way they had come, so they retraced their steps until they found another canyon to follow.

He stared at the rock monument in puzzlement. Why was it here? They were in the middle of a wide canyon; he could see for a mile ahead of him. Solid walls towered on both sides. There were no side canyons, not even any cracks or gaps in the walls large enough to pass through. "Why here?" he said out loud but to himself.

Malik looked down again at the stone monument. "The boy is nearly dead, and the men who have been carrying him are weary. There's no sense packing him farther. Let's just leave him here."

Naaman turned and glared at Malik. "No," he said forcefully. "Put him on my horse and tie him so he can't fall off.

"But, Captain—"

"Do it, Malik," Naaman commanded sternly. "I promised him I wouldn't leave him on the Shahba."

Malik spun on his heels and walked away, slowing only enough to grab the reins of the horse as he passed.

Naaman wiped his brow, stooped down in the sand, and picked up one of the rocks from the monument, idly tossing it in the air and catching it as his mind worked. Over and over the rock went into the air and landed in his hand—until the last time, when he let it fall past his hand and land back in the stack. Beneath the cloth that shielded his face, a smile spread across his lips. He had it! He had figured it out! "Malik," he yelled, "come quickly."

"What is it?" Malik said breathlessly as he ran up.

The dingy cloth puffed out as Naaman exclaimed, "I have it. I understand. The monument was a marker, a sign. Its only purpose was to confirm we're on the right path; I'm certain we're almost out of this forsaken place. Tell the men we move out immediately."

The change began slowly, almost imperceptibly. Two hours after leaving the marker, the men spotted a bird gliding in the sky, the first they had seen in five days. Then the sheer walls of the canyon began shrinking, getting shorter and less confining. By the third hour, the sand through which they trudged had turned from coarse black to dark grey and then a lighter shade of gray and finally tan and brown. Sparse little tuffs of brittle grass began appearing. By early evening the contingent was out of the Shahba and on the edge of the oak forests of Bashan.

Naaman called a halt beside a small stream of water where the dehydrated men dropped to their bellies and guzzled water alongside equally thirsty camels and horses. "We'll stop here for the night," Naaman told Malik. "Order the men to make camp."

"Gladly, Captain," Malik replied.

The mood among the men was lighthearted as Naaman made his way to the string of camels and horses, their sides puffed out from the gallons of water they had consumed. Camel drivers using long, thin staffs uttered a string of nonstop commands to encourage their recalcitrant beasts to kneel down so their packs could be unloaded. A lone horse stood tethered to a tree and strained at its rope trying to get at a clump of green grass just beyond its reach. Slumped over the saddle was a lifeless body.

"Easy, boy," Naaman said as he slowly approached the horse. It briefly raised its head in acknowledgement but quickly turned its attention back to the grass.

"He's dead," came a voice from behind Naaman. Naaman turned to see the small-framed physician striding toward him. "He breathed his last as we neared the trees."

"Will you help me untie him and remove him from the horse?" Naaman asked.

"Most certainly, Captain. But you needn't do this; I'll have others tend to it."

"No, I'd like to do it, but I would welcome your help."

"Whatever you say." The man walked to the other side of the horse and immediately began loosening the ropes that bound Zeri's arms and feet to the saddle.

With the knots untied and the ropes removed, Naaman reached up, grabbed the young soldier around the waist, and pulled him from the saddle. The lifeless body slid easily into his arms, and Naaman walked a short distance to a small oak tree and lowered the boy to the ground. Kneeling, Naaman looked into the dirt-and-dust covered face of the boy-soldier, taken aback to see Zeri staring back through open eyes. Though open, the eyes were unmoving and had no light in them. Naaman reached out with his hand and gently closed the eyelids. "May the gods of Syria allow you to rest peacefully," he said. Then placing the boy's hands on the lifeless chest, Naaman stood and walked to where the physician watched in silence. "See that he's buried there, beneath that small oak tree."

"Yes, Captain," the physician said. "And, Captain, thank you for leading us out of the volcanic fields."

Naaman smiled and nodded his head but said nothing as he turned and walked toward his tent, which a small group of soldiers had just finished putting up.

"I brought us food," Malik said as he strode up behind Naaman with a plate in each hand.

"Thank you," Naaman said as he took one of the plates, eyeing the dates, almonds, figs, and chunk of dried bread and goat cheese. "Come in, and we will discuss the raid on Ramoth-gilead."

The two men made themselves comfortable on the floor of the tent but said nothing as they began devouring the food, paying no heed to the gray-and-black mold on the cheese and bread. Naaman popped two almonds in his mouth and said, "We must attack quickly. If we delay, our presence might be detected, and this nightmare will have been for nothing."

Malik chewed rapidly as he nodded. "I think the men are up to it," he said taking a bite of cheese. "They're tired, but the fresh water and a day's rest in the coolness of these trees will revive them quickly."

"As soon as you finish eating, select a small group of men to spend tonight and tomorrow spying on the settlement. We will plan to attack at dawn the next day."

"Yes, Captain," Malik said as he shoveled the remaining food from his plate into his mouth.

* * *

The black of the early morning made vision difficult as Naaman swung his leg over the saddle and slipped his foot into the stirrup. Nudging his heels against the horse's ribs, he rode forward, weaving his way through the oak trees. There was no talking or chatter among the hundred Syrian soldiers as they silently dodged from tree to tree until they were huddled on the edge of the forest. Bowmen quietly reached into their quivers and deftly notched arrows in their bows. Spearmen cradled their smooth, wooden-shafted spears and ran their fingers over the bronze and iron tips, making sure they were secure. Everyone checked the straps on their helmets and breastplates one final time then settled down to wait for the first rays of the morning sunshine to spread over the eastern horizon.

"Malik, are the men in place and ready for the attack?" Naaman called softly as he cautiously walked his horse up beside Malik's.

"Yes, Captain. All is ready. We await only your command," he replied as he switched the reins to his left hand and drew his sword with his right.

"Is everyone clear on their orders? There are to be no survivors," Naaman said.

"Perfectly clear," Malik replied.

Naaman turned his horse around and spurred it to the edge of the trees just as the morning's first rays lighted the tile roofs of the unaware and innocent inhabitants of Ramoth-gilead.

"Sound the charge," Naaman yelled as he spurred his horse hard in the ribs, his sword held high over his head.

And the killing began.

Chapter Ten

Viewed through Gili's eyes, there was nothing miraculous about it, but the half dozen men and women standing around that bed would see it as nothing less.

The day began exactly the same as they had for as long as she could remember—which, given that she was only five years old, wasn't very long. As the golden streaks of the early morning sun forced the dark shadows of night into retreat, her mother's gentle voice called each of the children by name. "Uzzi, Hanan, Caleb, Gili, it's time to wake up." Her mother was only a room away, but in those hours of deep sleep, the voice sounded as if it came from another world.

The room in which the four children slept was small and teetered on being crowded. It would have been pushed over the edge had Uzzi not insisted on sleeping on a pile of straw covered by a few animal hides. "I'm a warrior," he proclaimed, "and warriors don't sleep in beds." The fact that he'd been sleeping like that every night for nearly two years amazed his parents and gave credibility to his words.

Eleven-year-old Uzzi kicked off the coarse camel-hair blanket and shot up from his bed, anxious to attack the day with the same enthusiasm with which he attacked everything. Hanan groaned and snuggled deeper into the soft sheepskin that encased him like a cocoon, his nine-year-old body craving a few more minutes of sleep. Caleb yawned and stretched his legs and arms to their full extent then, like a seven-year-old, kicked his feet mightily, sending his soft linen blanket flying through the air. It landed in a heap on the hard-packed clay floor.

In the far corner of the room, away from the door, two goat-hair blankets hung from the ceiling creating a room within a room. Little Gili, ensconced in her semiprivate corner, sat up on the edge of her feather-filled mattress for only the briefest moment before dropping to her knees beside her bed. In perfect innocence, she began her morning prayer in a voice only slightly louder than the beating of a butterfly's wings: "Friend, Jehovah," she began, as if she was speaking to her best friend in the village. "Thank you for letting us sleep safely last night. I love Daddy and Mommy and Uzzi, Hanan, and Caleb. Please keep us safe from soldiers and protect us today. Amen." The length of her simple prayer changed every day depending upon what was on her mind, but regardless of what other words she added or subtracted, the plea always included the phrase, "Please keep us safe from soldiers and protect us today."

* * *

It was a heartfelt request, born from a fear her young mind sensed but couldn't quite understand. It began a year earlier. Her mother had tucked her into bed, kissed her tenderly on the forehead, and repeated the same ancient Israelite phrase she always did: "A little sleep, a little slumber, for the strength to play and tumble."

Gili hugged her mother tightly around the neck. "Will you leave the oil lamp beside my bed for a while?"

A thin smile creased Miriam's lips. "Yes, but only for a few moments."

Gili wasn't afraid of snakes or unseen evil monsters; after all, Uzzi was on the floor to protect her. She wanted it because she loved watching the shadows as they danced on the walls, and she would drift to a world of dreams imagining wonderful adventures. But on this night, the dreams didn't come, and so she sheepishly slipped from her bed and crept toward the room where they ate their meals.

Stopping short of the soft yellow light emanating from the room, Gili stood silently, tight against the wall. Her father sat at the table, and her mother stood at the counter grinding wheat between two stones.

Gili looked on as Gideon leaned back in the chair and unlatched the leather armlets from his left forearm. "Jehieli said it was a complete massacre." Gideon placed the darkened leather on the table.

Miriam stopped grinding the stones together and turned to look at Gideon in horror. "All of them were killed?"

Gideon pressed his lips together and nodded somberly. "All of the men and women. A few of the older children were taken as slaves, but they killed all the younger children," he replied, struggling to undo the latches on the armlet on his right arm.

"But why? Why would they do such a thing?" Miriam asked.

"Because they can," Gideon said matter-of-factly. "And to make a point." He finally placed the second armlet on the table.

"But the children? What point does it make to kill innocent children?" Miriam asked incredulously.

Gideon looked pensively at Miriam. "Fifteen years ago, as a soldier, I could have answered your question and justified it perfectly. I participated in the invasion and annihilation of heathen cities—killing everyone in the city and then burning it to the ground." Shaking his head slowly, he added, "But now, as a father, the idea of killing children makes bile rise in my throat."

"Ramoth-gilead means nothing to the Syrians. It is a desolate little village," Miriam said. "How does that make sense?"

Gideon let out a deep sigh and rubbed his temples with the tips of his fingers. "Miriam, what are you feeling right now?"

Miriam looked at him in confusion. "What do you mean, what am I feeling right now?"

"Exactly that. What are you feeling right now after hearing what I just told you?"

"Fear!" she blurted out. "I'm afraid! I'm frightened for our lives, for all of us: you, me, and the children."

Gideon swiveled his muscular body to face her. "That is precisely why they did what they did. They want to cause fear. Ramoth-gilead is an easy journey from here, and if the Syrians attacked it, then they could easily do the same here. They want to intimidate us."

Miriam stared blankly at Gideon. "It's too much, Gideon. I can deal with the isolation, the endless work, even the poor living conditions. But I could not bear losing the children or you." Turning away from Gideon, Miriam set down the grinding stone and placed both hands on the small counter to brace herself. Her shoulders slumped, and her head dropped.

The muffled sobs gave way to uncontrolled crying as Gideon rose to his feet and gently placed his hands on her shoulders. Turning her around, he used his thumbs to wipe her tears away then hugged her tightly. "You have nothing to fear as long as I'm alive," he whispered quietly in her ear.

Miriam pushed free from his embrace and stared at him. "When we moved here," she said in a voice choked with anger and fear, "you told me that it was impossible for Syrian soldiers to cross that volcanic desert, the Sisibe . . ."

"The Shahba," Gideon corrected.

"Whatever it's called," she fired back, barely controlling her anger. "You told me our backs were protected. Now, you tell me a Syrian army has done the impossible and that I have nothing to worry about as long as you're alive. But what happens if they attack and you're dead? What then, Gideon? Is it death for the children and me? Or worse, will we be taken as slaves?"

The intense silence that saturated the room was broken by Gili. "Momma?" she said, stepping into the light.

Startled by the voice, Miriam and Gideon quickly turned. "Yes, sweetheart?" Miriam said softly as she quickly strode to where Gili stood. Scooping the girl in her arms, she asked, "What's the trouble, little one?"

"Who killed little children?"

Miriam shot Gideon an angry look and stammered a lie. "No one, sweetie. Daddy and I were just talking."

"Are soldiers going to hurt us?" Gili asked.

Gideon crossed to where they stood. Wrapping his arms around both Miriam and Gili, he said, "Everything is fine, Gili. No, soldiers are not going to hurt us."

Gili looked at Gideon. "But you just said—"

"No, Gili," Gideon said reassuringly. "There are no soldiers near here. Don't worry." Then giving her a quick peck on the cheek, he said, "Now it is time for you to go back to bed."

Gili offered an unconvinced smile. As Miriam started walking from the room with Gili in her arms, Gili anxiously asked, "Momma, what are slaves?"

* * *

Her morning prayer finished, Gili jumped to her feet and padded her way past a still-sleeping Hanan and walked down the short hallway. A smile spread across Gili's face. The rich aroma of freshly baked loaves of barley bread was getting stronger with each step. Every two days, her mother baked bread, and Gili loved the warm bread dipped in fresh goat milk, especially on those days when her mother was too rushed to skim off the thin layer of cream to make cheese.

Gili rubbed the last bit of sleep from her eyes as she rounded the corner into the main room of the house, dragging the tattered and dirty remains of a soft sheepskin blanket behind her. The sun had clawed its way higher into the cloudless sky and peeked over the low ridge of mountains behind the house. In not many minutes, the chill of the night would surrender to the heat of the day, and shimmering waves of heat would dance across the distant desert floor. But for now the few rays that spilled through the large window warmed the room and made it the perfect temperature.

Although larger than the other rooms in the house, it seemed smaller. A table, two chairs, and a long bench piled high with cushions and blankets gave the room a cramped feeling. Unlike all the other floors—which were bare clay that had been made hard and smooth from tramping, pounding and sweeping—this one had a large rug made from goat hides that had been tanned with the hair still attached. The hides had been cut in dozens of small perfect squares, and the white, red, black, and brown pieces were stitched together in an intricate symmetrical pattern. The rug and furniture combined to make this room an oasis in an otherwise monotonously colored place.

The elderly man sitting in the corner smiled warmly at Gili. He sat peacefully in the most comfortable chair in the house with his hands in his lap, his wrinkled fingers intertwined. His deep green eyes were the color of emeralds and radiated kindness as they peered from beneath eyebrows that seemed as white and fluffy as lamb's wool. His beard was white as the snow and stretched to the middle of his chest. The equally white hair was full and wavy; it cascaded off his head and mingled with his beard so that it was impossible to tell where one ended and the other began. He wore a deep blue robe, the color of the morning sky just before the sun rises, and the contrast with his hair and beard was striking. His cloak of the same color was draped over another chair beside him, and on top of that was a brilliant red mantle with fine threads of gold. His nearly worn-out sandals were laced in place, but Gili could see his feet still had a few muted sheen spots where the olive oil he had rubbed on them had not absorbed into his dry and calloused feet.

"Good morning, Gili," he said in a soft and pleasant voice.

"Hello," Gili said and abruptly altered her course away from the smell of the barley bread and toward him.

The kindly gentleman stretched out his arms in an invitation, and reaching his side, she tried to climb on his lap while clinging to her blanket. But her little arms and legs couldn't muster the strength, so he reached down and hoisted her up, wrapping her blanket snuggly around her in the process. He smiled warmly and gave her a gentle squeeze.

"Comfortable?" he asked with a chuckle as she fidgeted briefly before snuggling against him.

Gili rested her head against the man's chest, giving an almost imperceptible nod. She sat quietly watching the dust particles dance in the sunlight as it streamed through the window. She closed her eyes momentarily, not in sleepiness, but because she felt calm and peaceful in his presence.

"How have you been since I last saw you, my little friend?" the man asked softly.

"Good."

The man waited for her to expand her reply, and when it didn't happen, he said, "I'm glad for that," and gave her another slight hug.

"When did you come to my house?" Gili asked.

"Very late last night. Long after you were in bed asleep."

"Oh," she said, content with the answer.

They sat for several minutes enjoying the sunshine and the quiet before Gili broke the silence. "Prophet, I'm glad you're here," she said as she wrestled an arm from under her blanket and hugged him tightly around the neck.

* * *

Elisha smiled just as he did every time she addressed him. From the time she was old enough to talk, she had called him "Prophet." Others might use it as a title, but for her it was his name. It was more than a name though; she used it as a term of endearment. It was the only name she had ever called him. Millions of others in Israel's Northern Kingdom might call him the prophet or Prophet Elisha or Rabbi or Master, but she simply addressed him as Prophet. Though no ties of kinship bound them, he felt a closeness with the girl because, even at her young age, she had greater faith and trust than anyone he knew—child or adult. When he spoke, she believed.

The three years they had known each other had passed quickly for Prophet. The evils of the Kingdom of Israel weighed heavily on him, but the respite he found on his brief stays in this home rejuvenated him, primarily because of Gili.

Reaching out to the table beside him, Elisha picked up a small leather bag. "I brought something for you," he said as he handed her the small bag.

Gili looked at him in surprise. He had never given her anything before, and she was delighted with the small present. "What is it?" she asked in wonderment.

"Open the bag and see," he said smiling warmly.

Gili deftly untied the thin leather cords that held the bag closed and reached her fingers inside, extracting a beautiful stone the size of the fingernail on her little finger. "It's beautiful," she said as she held the small stone up and let the sunlight dance on its surface. "What is it called?" she asked as she twisted and studied the stone from every angle.

"Topaz," the prophet said softly.

"It's so clear I can almost see through it," she said, holding the stone so close to her eye that her long black eyelashes brushed against it.

"If you hold it just so," Elisha said as he gently twisted the stone in her hand, "it has a very slight pink color."

"Pink?" she said. "That's my very favorite color."

"I know." Elisha smiled.

"Is this really for me? And I can keep it? It's my very own?"

"Yes, yes, yes," Elisha answered with a mild chuckle.

Gili threw her arms around Prophet's neck and squeezed him with every bit of strength she had. "Thank you for my beautiful stone. I'll keep it forever."

Elisha returned the girl's hug. "I'm glad you like it."

"Let's go show my mother," Gili said as she slid to the floor.

"Of course," Elisha said.

Shifting her blanket under one arm, she clutched the stone tightly in one hand and reached up to grasp Prophet's hand with the other. With a slight tug, she began leading him toward the aroma of the fresh barley bread.

"Momma, look what Prophet gave me," Gili said, extending the stone.

Miriam set the plate of bread on the table and stooped to examine the small stone. "It's beautiful," she said as she twisted it in the sunlight streaming through the window. Rising, she looked at Elisha. "It truly is beautiful. And it was very kind of you to give it to her."

Elisha smiled and rested his hand lightly on Gili's shoulder. "She has amazing faith, this little one."

Miriam nodded her agreement and pointed to a chair. "Please, sit. We have fresh bread and honeycomb."

"Thank you. It smells delicious." Turning to the door, he added, "I'll join you in a few minutes, after my morning prayers. I won't be long."

After Elisha walked out the door, Miriam lifted Gili onto a chair, touched her lightly on the nose, and said, "Now, my joy, it's time to eat."

Gili alternated bites of warm bread with careful gazes at her pink stone. She had worked through one slice and started on a second when the distant sounds of a man's agonizing scream filled the home. It hadn't finished ricocheting off the walls when another scream filled the air, just as intense but from a younger person. The second scream died, only to be followed by hysterical yells of "Help!" and other indistinguishable words.

Chapter Eleven

Gili slid from her chair and raced toward the small home's door. Reaching it only a fraction of a second before Miriam, she grasped the leather latch and yanked hard. Stepping into the doorway, Gili collided with Uzzi, who had terror etched on his face.

"Come!" he shouted. "Father's hurt." Spinning on his heels, the boy sent dust and stones flying as he raced down the small dirt path toward a large enclosure of thorny brush, sticks, and cedar poles.

Miriam didn't hesitate. "Stay here, Gili," she commanded as she bolted through the door after Uzzi, her madly churning legs energized by fear and anxiety. In only a few strides, she passed her young son. Rounding a small bend in the path, she reached the mass of brush and poles that formed the enclosure that held their three cows, and she froze in revulsion. Hanging from the horn of a cow was an unconscious Gideon, his feet suspended six inches off the ground and his head and upper chest lying awkwardly over the cow. His right arm dangled lifeless across the beast's face, and his left arm hung limply beside its neck. He had been gored. The cow's long horn had entered Gideon's lower stomach, and four inches of it now protruded through his lower back.

Inside the fence, Elisha's servant, Gehazi, and another man stood motionless, as still as stones. Another man stood outside the small wooden gate, his eyes wide in horror. The large red cow stared at the ground directly in front of Gehazi and angrily blew a stream of snot from its nose. On the ground, inches from Gehazi's feet lay a newborn calf, still covered in mucus and fluids. The jerky flopping of its head and heaving of its sides told everyone, including its mother, that it was alive and needed attention.

It was a standoff. The protective cow wanted her newborn calf, and the people wanted Gideon, but no one, including the cow, was certain what to do next. One wrong move and the already enraged cow would go berserk, probably killing Gideon—if she hadn't already—and injuring others. The same thought raced through everyone's mind: how to free Gideon.

The man standing inside the enclosure beside Gehazi was the first to speak. In a calm voice, he said, "Gehazi, you must slowly back away from the calf. Make no sudden movements."

Gehazi nodded and backed away, first one foot and then the other. He had only taken two small steps backwards when the cow angrily pawed the ground and sent dirt flying. Gehazi froze. "You know, Bildad," Gehazi said to the other man from his motionless position, "if she charges me, I have no choice but to run for the gate, and you are directly in my path."

"I know that," Bildad replied. "But if you back away from her calf, she might calm down enough to lower her head and let Gideon fall to the ground. Then she'll probably run to her calf. When she does that, you and I can creep around the edge of the enclosure and drag Gideon to safety."

From outside the crude enclosure, the other man said, "Once she's near her calf, I don't believe she'll charge anyone. All she wants is her calf."

"That's easy for you to say, Nebat," Gehazi said. "You're not the one standing inside here. Now, open the gate and get ready."

With his eyes locked on the cow, Nebat slowly began pulling the gate open. Whether it was the squeak of the gate or Nebat's movement, the cow perceived a new threat and tossed her head savagely in the air, dislodging Gideon from her horn but causing him to land on the ground directly between her and her calf.

Free of her added weight, the cow raised her head high in the air and shook it vigorously, sending thin threads of saliva and snot flying through the air. Letting out a deep bellow, she lowered her head and charged toward Gehazi, mercilessly stomping on Gideon's stomach and chest as she did so.

Gehazi sprang sideways and lunged toward the gate running into Bildad in the process.

"No, Gehazi," Bildad shouted, grabbing him by his robes. "Not the gate. We must go for Gideon."

Gehazi looked at Bildad, the charging cow, the gate, and finally Gideon again. Pulling Bildad's hands from his robe, he bound for the partially opened gate. He didn't slow down to try and squeeze through the small opening; instead, he leaped over it as easily as a deer jumping a log.

Bildad spat on the ground. "You coward," he screamed at the fleeing Gehazi and ran at full speed to the side of the enclosure. Then running along the fence until he was exactly opposite of Gideon's crumpled body, he turned and raced the half dozen steps to where Gideon lay. Kneeling beside the limp body, he scooped Gideon up in his arms and stared at the cow.

The infuriated cow ran to her calf and stood over it, staring at Bildad and pawing the ground menacingly. It let out a series of throaty snorts and anxiously looked down at her calf and then back at Bildad but didn't move.

"You weigh more than I thought," Bildad said to the unconscious Gideon. "But not so much that I can't carry you."

Although several inches shorter than Gideon, Bildad was muscular and powerfully built. Holding Gideon in his arms, he slowly began backing away from the cow and away from the gate that was his only exit. It was a risky move. If the cow charged, there would be no escaping. He and Gideon would be pinned against the fence with no hope of getting away. The cow could butt, ram, and gore them repeatedly, and nobody would be able to come to their aid. But Bildad hoped that if he backed away, the cow would turn her attention to her calf and leave the men alone. Once he was as far away from the cow as he could get, his plan was to somehow hand Gideon over the thorny brush to the men on the outside and then climb out himself.

Bildad slowly retreated. With each step he took, the cow paid less attention to him and more attention to her calf. Except for the brief moment when he yelled his plan to Nebat and Gehazi, the cow didn't even look at him but concentrated on licking her calf and trying to nudge it to its feet.

Reaching the opposite side of the enclosure, Bildad managed to get Gideon's unconscious and battered body over the fence to Nebat and Gehazi. As Bildad gingerly climbed his way out of the enclosure, the other men carried Gideon to the shade of a tree and gently laid him on the ground.

Miriam ran the length of the enclosure, pushed Gehazi out of her way, and knelt beside her husband. As they all looked down at his body, no one believed he was alive. The front of his tunic was saturated with blood from his naval to his chest.

Cupping his head in her hands, Miriam turned his face towards her. "Don't you die!" she screamed in a voice that bordered on hysteria. "Do you hear me? You cannot die!" Then she leaned over him until her tear-streaked cheek nearly touched his nose. "He's still breathing," she said anxiously. "Carry him to the house."

Standing at his head and feet, Nebat and Gehazi exchanged questioning looks. The man may be alive, they seemed to say to one another, but he won't be for long. Why carry him to the house? Why make him suffer more? Let him die here in the shade of this cedar tree.

"Please," Miriam begged. "Carry him to the house. Now!"

Grabbing Gideon by the knees, Gehazi said to Nebat, "Pick him up under his arms. Hurry!"

Followed by Bildad and walking as fast as they could, the two men carried Gideon up the path to the house, passing Gili, Caleb, and Hanan as they went. Miriam called over her shoulder as she passed, "Hanan, draw a pot of water from the well. Caleb and Gili, sit beside the well and don't move. Do you hear me? Sit down beside the well and wait."

Miriam ran into the bedroom and pulled the bed into the middle of room where there was more light. She tossed the mattress aside to expose the flat, wooden surface of the bed frame. As hard and uncomfortable as the surface would be, it would be easier to work on Gideon's wounds without the mattress. Stepping back from the bed, she wiped the tears from her eyes with the sleeve of her robe and watched as Gehazi and Nebat laid Gideon on the wooden slab.

Without pausing she hurried over to a long white linen robe that hung from a peg, and she raced to the kitchen. Taking a sharp knife from a small cupboard, she cut the robe in long strips as she hurried back into the bedroom. Laying the strips aside, she slit open Gideon's tunic. She wasn't prepared for what she saw. The flesh of Gideon's stomach was torn from his navel to his ribcage. Blood oozed from the wound and dripped onto the wooden boards. Two broken ribs poked through the skin on his right side. Miriam looked at the battered body of her husband and recoiled in shock, dropping the knife. Both hands flew to her gaping mouth, and she let out an involuntary gasp.

* * *

Outside, Gili watched as Hanan tossed the bucket down the shaft of the well and listened for it to splash in the water. Sensing it was full, he grabbed the rope attached to the bucket's handle and pulled, hand over hand, as fast as he could. Lifting the bucket over the rock wall surrounding the well, he struggled to pour the cool liquid into a clay pot, but his eyes were so filled with tears that most of the water splashed on the dry dirt.

Picking up the half-filled pot, he ran for the door of the house, sloshing water as he went. "I'll take that," Bildad said to the boy when he was only halfway there. "Go and sit with your brother and sister by the well."

Hanan handed the pot to Bildad and watched as the man hurried to the door of the house. Then emerging again, Bildad closed the door and stood silently blocking the doorway.

His route to his father and mother blocked, Hanan looked toward the well but didn't move. Gili sat with Caleb, their backs against the cold stone surface of the well, their knees drawn up to their chests, and their arms wrapped tightly around their legs. "Hanan," Gili shouted. "Come here. Momma said we are to sit by the well." Hanan looked at Gili, then Bildad, and back at Gili. Slowly, he walked to where she was sitting and lowered himself beside her.

The three children sat in silence and stared at the door of the house, each desperately wishing their mother would come out and tell them everything would be all right. When she didn't appear, Caleb whimpered softly and lowered his head to his knees. Hanan stretched his legs out in front of him and absentmindedly fiddled with a small pebble between his fingers. Gili stretched her legs as well but slowly got to her feet and began walking away from the well.

"Where are you going?" Hanan asked with alarm in his voice.

"Away."

"Away, where?" Caleb asked curiously.

"Just away," Gili said without stopping.

"Momma told us to wait right here," Hanan said. "You better come back right now."

"I will come back, but I need to do something," Gili said.

Still clutching her tattered blanket, Gili cautiously picked her way up the path that led to a small knoll covered with towering and twisted cedar trees. The path was littered with sharp rocks and thorns that poked her bare feet. Twice she had to stop and reach down to pull the spine of a bush from her foot.

She wound her way through the trees to a grassy spot at the top of the knoll. It was her favorite place. It was quiet here . . . and peaceful. Her brothers preferred to play on the boulders and cliffs, so they never came here. From here she could sit on a small boulder and listen to the wind in the trees and watch her mother wash clothes by the well and her father work in the fields. It was her special place.

But this time little Gili didn't sit down. Brushing a twig and some small stones out of the way, she carefully laid her tattered sheepskin blanket on the ground, knelt down, and folded her arms across her chest. No tears dripped from her eyes or coursed down her cheeks. In the solitude of the trees, away from the commotion, fear, and unbelief of adults, she summoned the powers of heaven exactly as she had done every morning and night since her mother had taught her to pray.

Her prayer began as they always did. "Friend Jehovah," she said in a calm voice, "my daddy has been hurt by a mean cow. Mommy, Uzzi, Hanan, Caleb, and I need him to be made better. Please tell me what I can do to help. Amen."

Gili didn't immediately get up. Instead, she sat back on her haunches, deep in thought. After several minutes, she rose to her feet, knowing exactly what she needed to do—she went searching for the one person she knew could help.

Chapter Twelve

Gehazi gently put his arm around Miriam's shoulder. "Come, Miriam," he said softly. "Nebat has more experience with these things than any of us. Let him see what he can do for Gideon. It would be better if you waited outside."

Miriam looked at Gehazi through blank eyes. Without protest she let him guide her across the room to the door.

"Bildad," he said as he ushered Miriam outside, "will you please help Miriam while I assist Nebat?"

Bildad looked at Gehazi and then Miriam, searching their expressions for a clue that would tell him if Gideon was alive or dead. As he wrapped his arm around Miriam's shoulder, he wondered if he should speak words to console a grieving widow or encourage a struggling wife. Giving a weak smile to Gehazi, he nodded his head toward the water pot on the floor and said, "Take the water with you."

Picking up the pot, Gehazi walked into the room and stood beside Nebat. "Can you do anything for him?" he asked as he placed the pot of water on the bed frame.

"I've never seen wounds this serious," Nebat replied in complete honesty.

"But can you do anything?" Gehazi repeated somewhat more forcefully.

"Truthfully, no, I can't."

"What of Bildad? Does he have any skills?" Gehazi asked.

Nebat shook his head. "For all his strength and bravery, he knows nothing of treating injuries."

Gehazi's face mirrored his consternation as he considered Nebat's words. "So we are to let this man bleed to death without doing anything?"

Nebat looked directly at Gehazi, shrugged his shoulders, and held out his hands in a sign of unwilling defeat. There was no need for him to say anything. They both knew the facts, and there was nothing either of them could do to alter them.

The door opened with such force that it startled both men. Spinning around they watched as Elisha entered the room with Gili trailing in his wake. Three steps from where Gideon lay, Elisha stopped suddenly, his mouth gaping open as he looked at the horrific wounds. Turning around, he dropped to one knee and stretched out his arms, his cloak shielding Gideon's body from Gili's innocent eyes. "Gili, it would be best if you waited outside with your mother," he said firmly. Without waiting for a response, he called over his shoulder, "Gehazi, will you and Nebat please take Gili outside with you. I wish to be alone with Gideon."

"I want to stay with you, Prophet," Gili pleaded softly in protest.

Lowering his arms only enough to grasp Gili's shoulders, Elisha replied kindly, "My little friend, I promise you in the name of Jehovah that your father will be well, but you must leave us for a few moments."

Gili looked at him and seemed to be formulating a reply. Before she could say anything, Elisha added, "Do you trust me, Gili?"

"Yes!"

"Do you believe Jehovah can make your father whole and well?"

"If you say he can, then I believe it will be."

Elisha smiled warmly and drew Gili close in a hug. "Your faith is strong, little lamb. But you must leave me now."

Elisha rose to his feet, still using his body as a shield. Turning Gili toward the door, he beckoned to Gehazi. Placing Gili's hand in Gehazi's, Elisha gently herded the two men and the child out the door.

Miriam sat on the rock wall with her face in her hands. Tears dripped from her chin and landed on her robe, mingling freely with the blood that had already been absorbed by the robe's deep brown fibers. Clinging tightly to her were Hanan, Caleb, and Gili. Only Gili was not crying.

"You don't need to cry, Momma," Gili said as she moved a dirty strand of black hair out of her mother's face. "Prophet will heal Daddy."

Miriam pulled her hands from her face and sat upright. Looking at Gili through watery eyes, she smiled weakly and clutched her daughter close. She said nothing as she softly stroked her daughter's head, repeatedly running her fingers through the tangled hair in a vain attempt to straighten it. On the other side stood Hanan and Caleb. Despite constantly wiping his nose on his forearm, softhearted Hanan was unable to keep up with the continual flow of clear liquid dripping from his nose. Like his mother's, his eyes were bloodshot and swollen from crying. He wore no tunic—he never did—and his dirty bare chest was streaked where little rivers of tears had cascaded toward the belt around his waist.

Lines of fear and confusion were etched into Caleb's face as he looked at his mother, brother, and sister. Leaning his head against Miriam's arm, he closed his eyes and tried to stifle the sobs that shook his little body. After a moment, he opened his eyes, wiped tears from his cheek, and asked, "Where's Uzzi?"

Miriam suddenly stopped stroking Gili's hair and looked around. Panic gripped her, and she jumped to her feet, calling out as loudly as she could, "Uzzi!"

Turning in a circle, she scanned every direction, hoping to see the boy sitting on a rock or standing nearby.

"Has anyone seen Uzzi?" Miriam asked with clear panic in her voice.

Bildad, Nebat, and Gehazi all exchanged blank looks then quickly joined Miriam and the children at the well.

"I haven't seen him since we were down at the enclosure with the cows," said Nebat.

"Nor have I," injected Gehazi.

"He can't be far," Bildad said. "Miriam, you and the children wait here while we search for him." Turning to the other men, he said, "I'll check below at the cattle enclosure; you men should check the fields and hills." Without waiting for a response, Bildad turned and started jogging down the path toward the cattle enclosure.

The loose rocks on the sloping path made Bildad skid as he rounded the sharp corner. His sandaled foot slammed into a gnarled tree root with enough force that he lost his balance and tumbled down in a heap. Cursing, he dusted the grit from his scraped hands and knees and rose to his feet. An instant throb shot from two of his toes, and he crumpled back to the ground in pain. Reaching down he gently touched the two middle toes on his right foot and winced again in pain. "Broken or just sprained?" he muttered as he clenched his teeth.

Pushing himself to his feet, he hobbled the remaining distance down the path. For the second time that day, his jaw dropped open when he saw what awaited him inside the manure-covered enclosure.

Chapter Thirteen

As young Uzzi watched Bildad hoist his mangled father over the brush-and-pole fence to the arms of Nebat and Gehazi, he swore an oath to himself. Nothing, human or animal, would ever hurt anyone in his family without paying for it. As the men struggled up the hill with his father's limp body, Uzzi decided the cow would pay with its life for hurting and probably killing his father. He pushed the guilt from his mind—it was his own recklessness that had caused the cow to gore his father—and focused on what must be done. Vengeance would be sweet; the cow would die, and he knew exactly how he would do it.

Uzzi slipped behind a slender tree and watched the small group of people rush toward the house. Once they rounded the slight bend and were out of sight, he ran to the small shed in which grain and a few supplies were stored. Bursting through the door, he picked up a wobbly stool and set it on the ground directly beneath the doorway. Climbing on the stool, he reached high above the door and removed a powerful steel bow from the pegs on which it rested. Standing on the tips of his toes, he reached higher, grabbed the quiver of arrows, and stepped from the stool.

Leaning the quiver against the doorframe, he carefully examined the bow's graceful frame. Raising it in his left hand, he notched an imaginary arrow, took aim at the cow, and let the arrow fly. It was then he realized he had a problem: the bow was unstrung. One end of the catgut bowstring was attached to the upper tip of the bow, and the other end dangled in the air several inches from the other tip. After each use his father always unstrung the bow to preserve its spring, and now Uzzi would have to figure out a way to string it. His father could do it easily, but Uzzi lacked his massive arms and muscles; for him it would be a challenge.

Holding the bow and string as he had seen his father do on many occasions, Uzzi attempted the impossible and failed miserably. He tried again and again, but he lacked the strength to bend the bow far enough to loop the string over the tip. In disgust, he tossed the bow to the ground and dejectedly plopped down on the stool. It was all his fault—everything. If only he had listened to his father, none of this would have happened. And as he sat there crushed with remorse, his mind replayed the events.

On hearing his mother's call to wake up, he had raced outside, drawn water from the well, and splashed it on his face. Running his wet hands through his hair to dry them, Uzzi had looked up just in time to see his father leading three men down to the cattle enclosure. He immediately recognized Gehazi's slender frame, but he didn't know the other two. Fellow travelers with Gehazi, he thought, or perhaps they were here to buy grain.

With bare feet toughened from constant walking without sandals, he dashed down the path after the group, knowing they were going to check if the big red cow had calved. Uzzi ran up behind the men just as they came to a stop at the gate. Pushing against his father's leg, he peered through the slats to catch a glimpse of the cow.

She was by far the largest of their three cows, a monster by normal standards, and Gideon was always anxious to show her off to passing travelers. First, people's mouths gaped open, and then they would shake their heads in disbelief. She stood almost six feet tall at the shoulder, and Uzzi had listened to the men in the village estimate her weight at nearly one ton. Her broad head was topped with long horns, and when she shook them, which she did as a way of signaling her anger, the horns knifed wickedly through the air. She had a mean disposition in direct proportion to her size, and his father kept her for only two reasons: she produced very large calves, which he sold at a handsome profit, and she produced tremendous quantities of milk.

Uzzi looked at the cow then up at his father. "I can't see a calf. Has she had it yet?"

"Just barely," Gideon said, pointing to the newly born calf lying in the dirt in a corner of the enclosure.

Uzzi tried peeking over the top of the gate, but it was too tall. "I can't see the calf; is it a bull or a heifer?" he asked.

"I don't know," Gideon answered. "We'll check it later."

"Later?" Uzzi replied. "But I want to know now. You told me if it was a heifer, I could have it."

"You know this old cow, Uzzi. She is too mean and protective of her newborn calves to let us near now. We'll check it later," Gideon said with finality.

Turning to the men, Gideon pointed to a small shed behind them. "You came to buy grain, not see cows. Come, the grain is stored in the shed." He looked at Gehazi. "And while we're in there, let's also get some grain for that little donkey of the prophet's." Then with the wink of an eye, Gideon added, "Perhaps it wouldn't be so obstinate if you fed it a little better."

As Gideon guided the men to the shed, Uzzi pushed against the gate, hoping to create enough of a crack he could peer in at the new calf. "I can't see in," he muttered in disgust. Reaching up he unlatched the rope that secured the gate to a post and cautiously pulled the gate toward him. The bright early morning sunlight shone directly in his eyes, and he held his hand to his forehead to shield its glare. To his surprise, the cow had walked away from its calf and stood with its back to him.

Uzzi looked back over his shoulder and watched as the last of the men walked into the shed. Then he slowly opened the gate only wide enough for his slender frame to slip inside. If I'm quiet and fast, he thought, I can sneak in and out without disturbing the mother cow.

Stepping cautiously, Uzzi squeezed through the gate and crept along the edge of the enclosure to the corner where the calf lay. Pausing only long enough to make certain the cow still had her back to him, Uzzi squatted down and moved the calf's hind leg. At the touch of his hand, the newborn calf instinctively kicked at the unfamiliar sensation and let out a distressed moo. Startled by the calf's reaction, Uzzi rose up and began backpedaling as fast as he could away from the calf. In his haste, and not looking at the ground behind him, he stumbled over a long stick and lost his balance, falling onto his back midway between the calf and its mother. As he landed, an involuntary yelp escaped his lips, and the giant mother cow whirled to face her calf—and him.

The cow let out a loud bellow and raced toward her calf with head low, her horns only inches above the ground. At the same instant, Uzzi screamed, "Help! Father, help me!"

Gideon raced from the shed with the three men on his heels. In an instant, his mind took in the entire situation, and he pulled himself up and over the gate in a single motion. His entrance made the careening cow slide to a stop, uncertain which person was the greater threat to her calf.

"Uzzi," Gideon screamed, "run to me as fast as you can."

Without the slightest hesitation, Uzzi scampered to his feet and ran with all his might toward his father, yelling at the top of his lungs as he went. It was a valiant effort, but it would be too little, and Gideon knew it.

"Run for the gate," Gideon commanded as he himself charged toward the angry but confused cow. Perhaps if he could divert the animal long enough for Uzzi's short legs to cover the distance to the gate, he might save his son from injury.

His heart pumping and arms and legs thrashing, Uzzi propelled himself to the gate. With the same intensity, Gideon ran toward the cow waving his arms and screaming madly to intimidate the cow into changing course. It didn't work. The cow raced forward and lowered its head at the exact instant Gideon slipped on a pile of manure. Gideon let out a bloodcurdling scream as they collided.

The shortest and strongest of the three men watching the scene, Bildad, yanked open the gate with so much force that he nearly knocked Nebat, who was standing beside him, off his feet. Stepping into the enclosure, he grabbed Uzzi around the waist, flung him through the partially open gate in one swift motion, then turned toward the cow.

Miraculously, Uzzi landed on his feet, and with all the energy he could muster, he raced up the trail to the house screaming for help.

Now, less than an hour after it had happen, as he sat slump shouldered on the stool, he again told himself that it really was his fault—all of it—and if his father died, he was to blame. A crushing weight of sadness descended on him, and tears formed in the corners of each of his eyes. The little drops rolled down his cheeks and splattered on the edge of the steel bow that lay at his feet. Grief gave way to anger, and he kicked the bow, sending it clattering against the door. And that's when the idea came to him.

Rising quickly from the stool, he picked up the bow. Making sure the bowstring was securely on one end, he wedged one tip in the small space between the door and the frame. Using his body weight as leverage, he bent the bow toward him and looped the other end of the bowstring around the opposite tip. Smiling at his success, he took an arrow from the quiver. "Now you will die, cow," he mumbled to himself as he climbed into the enclosure and walked defiantly toward his intended target. Sidestepping to where he had an easy broadside shot at the cow, he raised the bow and arrow and took aim.

"Uzzi! What are you doing?" Bildad shouted as he limped to a stop outside the gate.

Startled at the sound of his name, Uzzi jerked his head toward the voice and accidently released the arrow, sending it flying harmlessly into the branches of a cedar tree. The bowstring zipped down the inside of Uzzi's left arm causing such a burning pain that he dropped the bow in a pile of manure.

The cow, which had been standing broadside to Uzzi, now turned to face him head on. It was instinct—pure, protective instinct—ingrained in every fiber of the cow's being that made her lower her head and thunder toward Uzzi.

"Run!" Bildad shouted. "Run toward the gate! Now!"

For the second time in less than an hour, Uzzi was being told to run for the safety of the gate. Had he obeyed and immediately started to run, there was a chance—a very small chance—he could have outrun the charging cow, but he hesitated. The bow was his father's prized possession, and Uzzi couldn't leave it lying there. Squatting down, he plunged his hand into the pile of manure and plucked the bow from the fresh brown goo. The split-second delay instantly evaporated whatever slim advantage he had.

Screaming at the top of his lungs, Bildad swung open the gate and raced, not toward the charging cow and Uzzi, but toward the cow's calf, which was standing midway along the length of the enclosure. It was a diversion, an effort to confuse the cow. The bewildered cow skidded to a stop, uncertain which person to charge. The confusion lasted long enough for Uzzi to scamper through the open gate and push it tightly closed behind him.

With his broken toes screaming in rebellion, Bildad clenched his teeth, raced past the calf, and ran the length of the enclosure to where he had lifted Gideon to safety. Knowing the poles and tangled mass of thorn-covered brush would entrap him if he failed, he gave a mighty yell as he leaped as high into the air as he could.

It wasn't the thorns that hurt; it was the landing. Flailing through the air in his adrenaline-charged flight, Bildad was almost clear of the thorn-and-brush enclosure when his robe, fluttering behind him like a flag in the wind, caught in a sturdy branch, stopping him as suddenly as if he had hit a wall. Bildad crashed to the ground in a heap, driving long thorns deep into his thighs and calves. His already-broken toes slammed into a small boulder, and he screamed in pain.

Uzzi ran up to Bildad and began pulling and yanking on tangled brush to help free the injured man.

"Don't!" Bildad yelled when Uzzi tugged at a heavy clump of brush. "You're driving the thorns deeper into my leg."

Uzzi relaxed his grip and meekly said, "Sorry."

No other words were exchanged during the two minutes it took to free Bildad.

"You saved my life," Uzzi said as Bildad hobbled to a small boulder and sat down. "Thank you."

The veins in Bildad's neck pulsated in anger, and he glared at the boy, with fire in his eyes. He sucked in a breath of air, preparing to lash out at Uzzi, but was stopped before he could get started.

"Bildad! Uzzi! Come quickly!" Nebat called from the path leading up to the house. Waving his arm frantically, he said, "You must come to the house now! Hurry!" Without waiting for a response, Nebat turned on his heels and disappeared as he ran back to the house.

Without hesitating, Uzzi walked not toward the house but to where Bildad sat on the small boulder, gingerly holding his broken toes in one hand and massaging his thorn-punctured thigh with the other. "Let me help you," he offered.

Bildad glared at Uzzi and wanted to refuse the boy's offer, but his foot and thigh throbbed so badly he wasn't sure he could negotiate the slope of the rock-strewn path alone. Instead he said firmly, but with a tinge of gratitude, "I'll need some help."

Chapter Fourteen

It took Bildad and Uzzi several minutes to work their way up the path to the house. With each step, Bildad wondered what he would find when they walked in the door. Would Miriam be kneeling beside Gideon's body, crying hysterically? Or would she be grieving in silence? He didn't know the woman, but judging from what he'd observed during the turmoil of the past hour, he felt certain she would be silent on the outside while a cauldron of emotion boiled inside.

As they passed beside the well, Bildad looked up to the house. He was mildly surprised to see the door partially open. He wasn't sure why, but it seemed more natural when mourning the dead to keep the door closed.

"Thank you for your help," Bildad said to Uzzi as he removed his arm from around the boy's shoulder. "I can walk from here by myself."

"Are you sure?"

Bildad shook his head. "I'm fine." He took the remaining steps toward the door. Hesitating only a fraction of a second, he drew a deep breath and braced himself. He gingerly pushed the door open with the tips of his fingers, and they both stepped inside.

Behind him, Uzzi stopped at the threshold, too frightened to enter.

At the first creak of the door's hinges, Gehazi spun around to see Bildad peer tentatively into the room. Waving his hand excitedly, Gehazi motioned to Bildad. "Come, come," he said, his voice a combination of relief, excitement, and reverence.

Bildad inched his way forward, unable to see anything more than the backs of Elisha, Gehazi, and Nebat as they crowded around the bed. As Bildad neared the bed, Gehazi and Nebat each stepped aside to give him an unobstructed view of Miriam sitting on the edge of the bed clutching Gideon's right hand to her lips. Hanan stood by her knees. He was leaning over the bed with his head resting on Gideon's shoulder. Caleb stood at Miriam's side with both small arms wrapped tightly around her waist and his head pressed tightly against her body, but he was looking into Gideon's face. On the opposite side of the bed stood Gili with a tooth-filled smile spread joyously across her face, her right hand gently stroking Gideon's matted hair and her left hand softly patting his mud-coated cheek.

Bildad stopped in his tracks with his mouth gaping, too startled to move or to say anything. Gideon slowly turned his head to Bildad and smiled warmly at the man who had rescued him. Withdrawing his hand from Miriam's grasp, Gideon extended it to Bildad. "I am in your debt, my friend. Thank you."

Bildad hobbled forward and clasped both of his hands around Gideon's. Totally confused, he uttered, "But . . ." Then as if his head was on a swivel, he looked from Gideon to Miriam and back to Gideon. Gideon shifted his gaze to Elisha and nodded. Upon seeing the nod, Bildad's confusion slowly turned to understanding: the prophet of God had called down the powers of heaven and restored a dying man to perfect health.

It was then that Gideon shifted his eyes from Bildad to the small figure who stood peering around the edge of the door, fright and uncertainty covering his face. "Uzzi," Gideon said in a strong and robust voice, "please come here. I want to hug you."

Whatever fear had previously held him back instantly vanished, and the boy bolted across the room as fast as his legs would carry him. Arms outstretched, he didn't slow down until he threw himself into the open and waiting arms of his father. Burying his face in the bloodstained and dirty tunic on his father's chest, the dam of pent-up emotion burst, and Uzzi sobbed great tears of relief.

Little Gili was the first to move. She crept around the foot of the bed to where Prophet stood. She said nothing as she raised both hands high above her head in a silent request to be picked up. The tall prophet bent down and lifted the girl in his arms. Without a second's hesitation, she threw both arms around his neck and hugged him as tightly as she could. Then with her nose only inches from his, she said sweetly, "Thank you, Prophet, for giving my daddy back to me. I knew you could do it."

Elisha encircled the little girl in a massive hug. "It was not me, but Jehovah," he said softly. "It was by His power that your father is healed and returned to life."

Gili looked at him through faith-filled eyes but said nothing more as she again hugged him tightly around his neck and rested her head on his shoulder.

Chapter Fifteen

Five years later

The first bright rays of the sun streaked across the sky, turning the thin layer of high clouds a delicate pink. Miriam paused along the stone path leading to the well as she surveyed the rugged hills on the eastern horizon. The clouds reminded her of the tails of horses running in the wind. In spite of the colorful sky, she was certain there would be no rain today; the clouds were too high and wispy.

Just as she'd done nearly every morning for the past ten years, she lowered the bucket into the black hole until she heard the familiar splash. After waiting a moment for it to fill with water, she raised the bucket, hand over hand, and set it on the edge of the well. She watched as water ran down the sides and coated the rocks with a thin layer of moisture.

The cool morning air felt luscious on her face, and she sat down next to the bucket, not caring that little rivulets of water would eventually find their way to the gray fabric of her robe. The sun painted the sky with its colors, and the air was so still not even the spiderweb in the bush beside her fluttered. Everything was peaceful, and she reveled in it. This was her favorite time of day—time for herself, time to reflect, but most importantly, a time to thank Jehovah for the miracles and blessings in her life.

In the five years since Gideon had been gored and Elisha had invoked the powers of heaven to heal him, not a single morning or evening passed that she didn't pause to give thanks to God for sparing her husband's life. And this day would be no different. Folding her hands in her lap, she bowed her head and said words that came from the very deepest reaches of her heart. They were simple words of gratitude and thanks. Always first was to thank Him for restoring Gideon's life, followed by thanks for her children. And somewhere in her words was the ever-present plea for protection and safety.

Lost in her devotion, she didn't hear the quiet footsteps behind her. Seeing her head bowed and hands folded, Gideon stopped a short distance away and stood motionless, not wanting to disturb her. A smile crossed his lips as he thought of the faith and strength of his wife. Protective and ferocious as a lioness when someone challenged her family, she was the essence of charity and kindness to those in need of help. It was an odd combination that made her ideally suited to life on the fringes of the Jewish frontier.

Miriam raised her head and took a deep breath of the sweet-smelling morning air.

"Good morning," Gideon said as he stepped to her, placed his hand on her shoulder, and kissed her lightly on top of her head.

Miriam reached up, took his hand in hers, and kissed it. "Good morning to you," she said. "Did you sleep well?"

"Too well, I'm afraid. I don't think I heard a sound once my head hit the pillow."

"I'd say that's true," she said with a smile. "And judging from how loudly you snored, I don't think you could have heard a pack of wolves if they had been howling outside our door."

"Why didn't you wake me up?"

"Oh, I nudged you—several times. And each time you rumbled about and immediately began snoring again."

"Sorry," he said, genuinely chagrined.

"I'm used to it. But one of these days, I'm going to send you to sleep with the sheep. No wolf or lion would dare come near with all the noise you make."

Gideon sat down beside her. "I think you should take a nap today to make up for all the lost sleep I caused."

"Oh, you do, do you? And who's going to wash your filthy robe and cook your meals and take care of our children while I'm napping? You?" she said teasingly.

"The children are old enough to take care of themselves, the dirt on my robe will be there tomorrow, and we can eat some goat cheese with the bread that you baked yesterday. See, it's easy; you can take a nap."

Miriam gave him a gentle shove. "Why didn't I think of that?" She paused. "Gideon," she said with a sudden seriousness, "will you tell me something honestly?"

"I've never lied to you."

"No, but sometimes you don't always tell me the whole truth either," she replied.

Gideon smiled at the remark. "What do you want to know?" he asked, inclining his head slightly toward his wife.

"What do you hear of the armies of Syria?"

The question caught him off guard, and he cautiously asked, "What do you mean?"

Miriam turned to face him and brushed a strand of hair out of her face. "Yesterday at the market, I stopped to buy figs from Hulda."

Gideon raised his eyebrows at the mention of Edrei's biggest rumor monger, but he said nothing.

"She said some of the other women have been told by their husbands about problems with Syria."

"What kind of problems?" Gideon asked without emotion.

"Not invasions but little skirmishes, instances where soldiers raid a house on the outskirts of a village and then disappear."

Gideon looked at Miriam and knew what was troubling her. Probably no one lived further on the outskirts of Edrei than they did, and Edrei was on the extreme edge of the Syrian and Jewish border. They were the most remote of the remote, and she knew it.

As they sat with the morning sun warming their backs, Gideon debated what to say. Should he tell her he knew all about the attacks and try to pacify her by telling her the stories were overblown? Or should he tell how he had bought three new steel bows and placed them strategically around the house and outbuildings? Would she like to know that he'd been making dozens of arrow shafts from the straight wood of the cedar trees surrounding their home and that he had traded some grain to the metalsmith in Edrei for bronze arrow tips and that he'd gathered chicken feathers for the fletching? And how would she react if she knew that, for weeks, he'd been teaching kindhearted Hanan, the boy who wouldn't kill a scorpion, how to shoot a bow with the thought that he might one day have to kill a man? And that while Caleb lacked the strength to draw the bows, he was becoming deadly accurate with a sling and had amassed a large supply of smooth, almost perfectly round stones.

It was impossible to hide Uzzi's skill with a bow; he practiced constantly and was always bringing home a roe deer or chucker he had killed. But would she find comfort knowing he could now outshoot Gideon? Just last week his son laughed when Gideon couldn't kill a darting rabbit at fifteen paces, and to prove he was a better shot, Uzzi waited until the rabbit was almost thirty paces away before he said, "I'll shoot him through the eye," and then did exactly that. Should he tell her that he had purchased a sword made of Damascus steel for Uzzi and that the boy could swing it with deadly force?

Finally he said, "Miriam, I've heard the stories. What can I tell you that will lessen your anxiety?"

Miriam quickly replied, "That we're moving to Jerusalem!"

The statement hit Gideon like a bucket of cold water. "Are you serious?" he asked. "Are you that frightened?"

Miriam turned her face from him and looked pensively down the valley toward Edrei. Letting out a slight sigh, she said, "Gideon, I nearly lost you once, and the thought almost made me want to die. I couldn't bear to lose you or the children." Waving her arm in a sweeping gesture, she said, "None of this—everything we've worked for—is worth what you and the children are to me. I've been wondering if we should leave here now before . . ." she hesitated, "before . . . anything happens."

An avalanche of thoughts swept through Gideon's mind. In the ten years they had lived in Edrei, their few sheep and goats had grown into a herd of more than a hundred. The two acres they had first planted and harvested had expanded to more than twenty acres. The house had been enlarged and furniture added. But more than all those things, their home had become a retreat for the prophet of God. Two or three times each year, the prophet came and stayed with them, sometimes for only a day but often for a week or more. His presence blessed their home and their lives in ways they could never count. It was not the idle rumors that floated about the marketplace that caused Gideon to prepare for possible Syrian attacks; it was the endless warnings Elisha gave to the people of the Northern Kingdoms. A hundred times Gideon had heard the man of God warn, "Repent or be destroyed." On those sacred occasions when Elisha came to their home, his very presence seemed to make the powers of heaven settle over them like a warm blanket. But there was another, deeper concern that entered Gideon's mind, and that was for Gili.

Gideon had watched his delicate little daughter grow from a child with innocent faith to a ten-year-old maiden whose faith knew no bounds, and he was certain it was because of her relationship with the prophet. There was a bond between the two that was deep and abiding. While the rest of them might tire of his teaching, Gili could and would sit at his feet for hours as he explained the things of God. She would ask questions and ponder his answers. For her, a move to Jerusalem or any of the cities in the south would mean severing ties with Elisha, and that would be heart-wrenchingly difficult. Gideon knew the reason he was still alive was because of her unquestioning faith in Elisha.

"If we move, what becomes of Gili and her relationship with Elisha?" Gideon asked.

Miriam brushed her hand through her hair. "It will be hard for her in the beginning, but she'll adjust."

Gideon folded his arms across his chest, looking out at the fields of wheat and the sheep grazing among the cedar trees. After a long silence, he looked at Miriam. "What if we don't decide now? We can wait until harvest and see how things are. If there continues to be unrest with Syria, then we'll leave. Will that be soon enough?"

Miriam mentally ticked off the three months before harvest time, and a sense of foreboding settled on her. "Can we leave sooner?"

"We can leave tomorrow if we want, but I'd prefer staying until harvest. That would give us more money. It would make more sense."

Miriam slowly shook her head as the oppressive feeling thickened about her. "I think we should leave sooner."

Gideon began thinking about the money they would lose by abandoning their wheat crop. He thought about the sheep and goat herds and knew it made more sense to sell them to people in Edrei rather than herd them to a new city. But doing so at this time of the year meant lower prices. He turned and studied Miriam's dark eyes and the stress lines in her face. Weighing it all in his mind, he licked his lips and said firmly, "Let's wait until harvest." And then in a gentler tone, he added, "I promise I'll be even more vigilant to the rumors about Syria. If at any time it seems that we might be attacked, we'll leave immediately."

Miriam slowly rose from the well and placed a large clay pot next to the full bucket of water. Lifting the bucket she dumped the water into the pot, spilling as much as made it into the pot. Turning to Gideon she said ominously, "I hope that's not too late." Then cradling the pot in her arms, she marched to the house without waiting for a response.

Chapter Sixteen

"Edrei, that's your destination," King Ben-Hadad said as he poked his finger at a small ink dot on the map. "You are to invade the village, capture as many as you can, and destroy houses, crops, and anything of value. Leave nothing behind."

Naaman pursed his lips and said in a neutral tone, "That will send a very loud message to the Israelites."

"That's exactly what I want to do," Ben-Hadad said, his jowls quivering. "I want them to know that Syria is a force that must be respected." Turning slightly to face Naaman, he asked, "How many men will you require to do this?"

Naaman straightened up and stretched the muscles in his back as he considered the question. "It's a sleepy village of only a few hundred people. They won't be expecting us, so they'll be undefended. The most difficult part will be bringing the captives back to Damascus."

Ben-Hadad looked hard at Naaman. "I agree; they can be unruly. How many men will you need?" he repeated more strongly.

Naaman took a quick breath and said, "Three hundred. I can do it with three hundred."

"Fine," Ben-Hadad said, nodding his head, which made his jowls shake even more. And almost as an afterthought, he added, "Take Adad with you as your second-in-command. He'll keep control of the captives when you come back."

Naaman shifted the sword that hung at his side and replied seriously, "I'd rather not."

Ben-Hadad raised his eyebrows at Naaman's mild refusal. "Why?" he said as he too straightened up and adjusted the large leather belt that encircled his ample girth.

"I don't like him; he's—"

"No one likes him," Ben-Hadad interrupted. "But he's my cousin's son, and I have to use him somewhere."

"I can send him on a different campaign with one of my other commanders," Naaman offered.

Ben-Hadad shook his head rapidly. "No, no. Naaman, I want you to take him. You're the commander of all my forces and the best leader I have. If anyone can control his anger, it's you."

"He's out of control."

Ben-Hadad raised both of his hands as if to stop any more words from coming. "Naaman, take Adad as your second-in-command. Train him. Teach him. Do what you can with him. But try not to get him killed—or to kill him yourself out of frustration," he added only partly in jest.

Naaman swallowed hard and clenched his teeth to stop the rising anger he was feeling. "When should we leave?" he asked in a voice that expressed his dissatisfaction about Adad.

"As soon as you can make all the necessary preparations," Ben-Hadad answered, barely a fraction of a second before a knock sounded on the door. "Enter," Ben-Hadad shouted.

An underfed servant noiselessly breezed into the room and bowed at the waist. "The vizier is here for his appointment with you."

"Show him in," Ben-Hadad said. He turned to Naaman. "May you have success in your campaign."

Still upset over having to deal with Adad, Naaman gave a halfhearted smile, gathered up the parchment map, and left the room.

* * *

The next several days preparing to raid Edrei would have gone much smoother had Naaman's new second-in-command not inserted himself in virtually every step of the process. Out of total frustration, Naaman created a long list of tedious tasks and told Adad not to come back until they were all completed. Free of the constant interruptions, Naaman eventually managed to get everything done and breathed a sigh of relief. Now he could finally spend some time with his wife before he must leave.

Leaning back against the plush purple cushions on the couch, Naaman stretched his legs in front of him. Looking across the room at his wife, he said, "Karinah, that meal was delicious. Thank you."

Karinah looked up from the roses she was arranging and smiled, but she could tell from the tone of his voice that there was more to the comment than complimenting her on a meal. Setting the roses on a small table, she walked across the tile floor with practiced elegance and gently sat beside her husband, drawing her feet up on the couch beside her.

"I'll be leaving tomorrow morning," he said as he used his fingernail to pick at a leftover fragment of lamb meat that was stuck between his teeth.

Although he hadn't said anything about his departure previously, the distracted way he spoke when they'd talked during the past several days told her this was coming. "Where?" Karinah asked as she smoothed wrinkles from her flowing pink robe, trying to sound only mildly interested while inwardly her stomach began churning.

"Places," Naaman replied.

"When will you return?"

"As soon as I can."

The conversation was nearly always the same. He never told her where he was going or when he would be back. It hadn't always been like that. He used to give her more details, but that changed after his march through the Shahba, mostly at her insistence. When he'd told her he was going through the Shahba, she knew how treacherous it would be, and every minute he was gone, she wondered if he was dead or alive. And when he didn't return when she'd expected, her worry turned to dread, almost incapacitating her with anxiety. Although she hated the ambiguity, she preferred it to the apprehension she endured by knowing where he was going and what he was doing.

Reaching up she brushed his dark hair away from his ear. "How much does it hurt?" she asked as her fingers skimmed the scaly white skin on his deformed earlobe.

"Not much, except when I touch it," he said with a smile, gently goading her for touching his leprosy-laden ear.

Karinah studied his ear carefully then pursed her lips. "It's getting worse, you know."

Naaman pulled his head away from her hand then quickly rose from the couch. Walking to the window, he leaned against the sill. The evening sun was hidden behind a thick layer of billowy white clouds that hung from the sky like a massive wool fleece, subduing the light and casting eerie shadows over the landscape. "I know it is," he growled as the hot midsummer breeze blasted his face.

Naaman lifted his right hand from the windowsill and rotated it in the fading light. The contrast between the darkly tanned skin on his arms and the stark white flesh of his hand was shocking even to him. For years the insidious disease had spread so slowly it was barely noticeable, but recently it was as if it had gained new life and gnawed at his flesh like a mouse eating cheese. All of his fingers were infected to his knuckles, and three of his fingernails had fallen off. Holding a sword was painful, and drawing a bow was impossible.

His left hand was only slightly better, and he now constantly wore carefully crafted leather gloves made of soft goatskin, regardless of the heat. It wasn't his hands, though, that caused him the greatest pain; it was his feet, especially his toes. They were almost always raw and bleeding. He walked now with a pronounced limp.

After tedious searching, he found a sandal maker in Damascus to whom he had paid a considerable amount of money to fabricate a sandal specifically to his order. The sole and straps of the sandal were of standard design, but abnormally, most of his foot was encased in soft deerskin. It annoyed him when bits of sand or pebbles worked their way inside, but it was far better than stubbing his unprotected toes on a rock. The leather was hot and made his feet sweat, so he devised a way to wrap them in linen cloth. Each night after he removed the sandals, he soaked his feet, still wrapped in the linen, in a pot of water to dissolve the dried blood on the cloth. Only then did he carefully unwrap his feet to reveal his decaying toes.

Karinah walked up behind him, wrapped her arms around his waist, and pressed her cheek against his back. "I love you," she said quietly, and she squeezed him.

Turning to face her, Naaman kissed her softly on top of her head with his irritated lips. "I love you too."

Chapter Seventeen

Naaman stepped into the chariot, gently stomping the dust from his feet, and turned back to study the three hundred foot soldiers stretched out behind him. Battle armor glistened in the sunlight, and twice his eyes involuntarily clenched shut when the light reflected off the breastplate of the man nearest him. The soldiers were formed in a long column, four abreast. The men in the outside columns had bows slung over their shoulders and quivers bulging with arrows. Short swords draped from their left sides and curved knives from their right.

The men in the middle columns held shields made of leather stretched tightly over wooden frames. They also carried long spears with heavy iron tips. From each man's left side hung a long sword, much longer than those of the bowmen, with blades that curved in a shallow arc. They all carried knives on their right side, tucked in the leather belts. Every man—archer and swordsman—had a goatskin bag filled with water, draped over a shoulder and held in place with wide leather straps.

At the rear of the column, two dozen camels grunted loudly as their drivers poked and yelled commands to urge them to their feet. The ponderous mounds of supplies swayed wildly as the beasts slowly unfolded their hind legs and then struggled to stand on their front legs. On their backs were containers of dried meat, figs, dates, almonds, cheese, and additional supplies of water that the men would consume over the week it would take them to reach the sleepy village of Edrei.

"Are the men ready to move out?" Naaman called to Adad, who was seated on a tall black horse that tossed its head and pranced nervously.

"They are, Commander," said Adad with an enthusiasm he could not hide. He thrived on the excitement and anticipation of battle.

Lifting the long leather lines that ran from the chariot to the bridles of the large black horses, Naaman gently slapped the beasts' rumps and commanded, "Forward!"

Adad instantly repeated, "Forward," in a booming voice and listened as four soldiers at the head of the column blared out the tones on their trumpets, signaling the contingent to move forward. Adad gently spurred his horse about and pranced forward. "You've become a legend, you know. Even after all this time, people talk of how you found a route through the Shahba without a guide."

Naaman pulled lightly on the reins to guide his horses around a clump of weeds. "I had help."

Adad waved his hand dismissively. "Yes, yes, the old soldiers talk of how it was the gods who guided you."

Naaman shot a sideways glance at Adad. "Syria's gods had nothing to do with it," he said curtly. "It was Bisha who got us through."

Adad reared back in his saddle. "Bisha? The merchant trader? The old man who died last year?"

Naaman gave a single nod.

"How could that old man have helped?" Adad sneered.

"It's a long story," Naaman replied abruptly, unwilling to continue the conversation. "But believe me, it will be much easier this time."

Over the years since the disastrous first expedition, Ben-Hadad had sent many scouts across the Shahba, and they had marked the trail. Although rarely used, the forsaken, desolate volcanic fields of the Shahba had been tamed, and crossing it was only slightly more difficult than any other route into Israelite territory.

King Ben-Hadad had once again chosen the rarely used route to launch the surprise attack on Edrei. But this time Naaman marched with different orders. When he attacked Ramoth-gilead, his orders were to kill every man, woman, and child, and then destroy the village. This time his orders were to kill those who resisted but take as many slaves as possible.

"I want to enlarge my palace and build new monuments," Ben-Hadad had told Naaman. "I need many new, strong slaves." Those that were fit enough would be kept in Syria; those that weren't would be sold to the Phoenicians or perhaps even the Egyptians.

* * *

By late afternoon of the third day, the soldiers were almost out of the Shahba. As he surveyed the changing scenery before him, Naaman let out a sigh of relief. The black volcanic sand had given way to dirt of varying shades of brown and gray, and in the distance he could see pockets of green cedar trees dotting the hillside. The worst was behind them. They had crossed it without death, sickness, or setbacks.

Adad rode up beside him and reined to a stop. “It was much easier this time, eh, Captain?”

Naaman nodded his head. “Much. Still, it was three long days filled with nothing, and I’m glad to have it behind us.”

“And me as well.”

Naaman pointed in the distance. “We’ll camp at the same place we did last time and prepare to attack. Edrei is an easy day’s march from here. Two days from now, it will all be over, and we’ll be marching back to Damascus.”

Chapter Eighteen

Gili walked softly to the door of her parents' bedroom and lifted the latch as quietly as she could. Inching the door open, she stared intently at the bed where her parents lay sleeping. The moonlight streamed through the windows of the room behind her and perfectly silhouetted her in the doorframe. She stood motionless, and except for the barely audible whimpers, she could have been a statue.

Miriam rustled ever so slightly in the bed and said softly, "What's the matter, Gili?"

It was all the invitation Gili needed, and she scurried across the floor to half sit and half lie on the bed. She threw her arms around her mother, hugging her tightly.

Miriam eased her hand from beneath the wool blanket and gently ran her fingers through the girl's long hair. "It's okay, little lamb," she whispered. "Everything is all right."

This was nothing new. Countless times over Gili's ten years, a vivid dream of one sort or another would cause the little girl to flee from her room in the middle of the night, seeking the security of her mother's arms. Sometimes she would be sobbing, but most often, like tonight, she would whimper softly, needing the reassurance that her mother was near.

Through a sleep-fogged mind and with eyes still closed, Miriam asked, "What's troubling you tonight, my joy?"

Gili shook her head and snuggled more closely against the warmth and security of her mother.

The two of them lay quietly, Miriam drifting in and out of sleep and Gili completely awake. Gili slowly reached up and softly stroked her mother's cheek. "Momma, are you awake?" she whispered.

"Uh huh," Miriam answered groggily, more asleep than awake.

"There were soldiers," Gili said softly as she continued stroking Miriam's cheek. "Many of them."

Miriam shifted slightly, and Gili immediately took advantage of the added space to wriggle more deeply into the bed and slide her cool feet against Miriam's legs.

"Soldiers?" Miriam mumbled, as the forces of sleep and consciousness waged war in her head.

"They were everywhere," Gili said a little louder than a whisper. "Here, in Edrei," she said, patting Miriam on the cheek as if to make sure her mother was awake and listening.

Sleep fled, and Miriam's eyes opened. Her stomach tightened in a knot, and a sense of dread washed over her. On many occasions since Gideon had been gored, the little girl had been given promptings and impressions that the others never felt. Miriam had thought about it repeatedly over the years, wondering if her daughter's sensitivity was a result of her closeness to Elisha or if she was drawn to the prophet because of her natural spiritual capacity. Either way, Miriam had learned to listen carefully to Gili's utterances about future events.

Gideon rolled over and groaned as Miriam pushed herself upright in bed. In as calm a voice as possible, she said, "Do you want to tell me about the soldiers, honey?"

Gili didn't sit up but instead pulled the blanket tightly around her shoulders and nestled more tightly against Miriam. In a voice betraying her distraught emotion, Gili said, "It was terrible. My dream was terrible."

Sensing Gili's anxiety, Miriam reached over and gently shook Gideon's shoulder. "Wake up," she said softly but firmly.

Unlike Miriam's slow awakening, Gideon immediately sat up with his senses scrambling to analyze if there was a threat and what it was. "What is it? What's wrong?" he asked rapidly.

Miriam patted his shoulder. "Be calm. Gili had a bad dream and wants to talk about it."

The tension drained from Gideon as he looked at Gili snuggled tightly against Miriam. "Oh." As he leaned his back against the bed's headboard, he said soothingly, "Hi, precious," and patted the bed in the space between him and Miriam.

Gili tossed the blanket aside, scurried over Miriam's legs, and wrapped her arms around Gideon's neck. Clinging with all her might, she blurted out, "They killed you, Daddy. The soldiers killed you and—" That was as far as she got before the rest of her words were washed away in a burst of tears and unintelligible mumbles.

Gideon hugged Gili tightly and kissed her lightly on the side of her head. "It's all right, Gili," he comforted as he patted her gently on the back. "Nothing is going to happen to me."

Although Gideon couldn't see her clearly in the dark, he could sense Miriam staring at him, and he could only imagine the look of panic on her face. As much for Miriam's benefit as Gili's, he said, "Everything is fine. You just had a bad dream. In the morning, things will be just like they always are. When morning comes, you'll—"

"No, it won't, Daddy," Gili insisted, pushing herself slightly away from Gideon. "You don't understand. Everything won't be fine."

Gideon reached up and grasped each of Gili's arms. With his face only inches from hers, he said calmly and reassuringly, "Gili, you had a very bad dream. You'll see—things will be better in the morning."

"NO!" she screamed defiantly as the tears flooded down her cheeks and dripped on the blanket. "Tell him, Momma," she sobbed, looking over at Miriam. "Tell him that everything won't be fine." She lunged over into the arms of her mother.

Miriam clung onto Gili in alarm. Never, ever, had the child been so distraught or inconsolable. "Gili, Gili, Gili," Miriam repeated softly as she held the girl tightly and gently swayed side to side to calm her, all the time staring through the black of the night at Gideon, who had now twisted sideways in the bed to face them.

Gili wrapped her arms around Miriam and began squeezing so tightly that Miriam struggled to take a lungful of air. Clinging to her mother as if she would never let go, Gili continued, "And then they took me. The soldiers took me away from you."

Miriam tightened her embrace momentarily before reaching up with one hand and stroking Gili's hair reassuringly. After a long moment with only the sound of Gili's sobs, Miriam looked to Gideon and said, "We should listen to the child." Making no effort to conceal her fear and anxiety, she added, "We should leave this place—now—before something bad happens."

Gideon looked first at his sobbing daughter and then his wife. Reaching out he patted Gili lightly on the back and then gently stroked Miriam's cheek with the tips of his rough fingers. Nodding his head slightly, he said, "You're right. We should leave."

Miriam's mouth dropped open, and she leaned back in total surprise. Swallowing quickly she asked, "You agree we should leave? We're going to Jerusalem?"

Gideon threw the covers off his legs and rose from the bed. "Yes, we should leave—but not for Jerusalem."

"Where will we go?" Miriam asked anxiously as she shifted Gili in her arms.

Gideon didn't respond. He walked quickly to the door and shouted, "Uzzi, Hanan, Caleb, wake up and come here." Walking into the large room, he picked up a smoldering stick of wood from the fireplace and fanned it to a flame. He went back into the bedroom and lit an oil lamp on a table beside the bed and another one hanging from the wall.

Uzzi ran through the bedroom doorway, fully awake, and asked loudly, "What's the matter?"

Before Gideon could reply, Hanan and Caleb staggered in, each of them only slightly more awake than asleep. Hanan said nothing, and Caleb croaked out a groggy, "What?"

"Listen to me very carefully, and I want you to do exactly as I say. Do you understand?"

The seriousness and force with which Gideon spoke instantly galvanized the boys' attention. Whatever sleep clouded their minds was replaced with perfect attention. All three boys looked at Gideon and nodded their heads in unison.

"Uzzi, go to your room. Get your bow and quiver and put them by the fireplace. Then go down to the shed and get the bow and quiver hanging over the doorway. Bring them back here as quickly as you can."

Without a second's hesitation, Uzzi ran from the room, put on his sandals, and was out the front door of the house in a dead run.

Looking at Hanan, Gideon said, "I want you to run to the shed where we store the wool. In the corner of the shed, you'll find a large wooden box under a sheepskin. Inside the box are three leather quivers filled with fifty arrows each. Bring them here at once."

"Why?" Hanan asked.

"I don't have time to explain; just do it," Gideon demanded.

Hanan shrugged his shoulders, walked back to his room, slowly tied on his sandals, then walked out the door.

"Caleb," Gideon said, "where is your sling and supply of rocks?"

"Beneath my bed," the boy replied.

"Did you finish making the leather pouches to hold the rocks as I asked?"

"Three are finished, but I haven't finished the flap on the fourth one yet," Caleb answered.

"It will have to do. Get everything, and put it all by the fireplace," Gideon ordered.

Caleb's eyes glowed in uneasy excitement, and he shot from the room to do as he'd been asked.

Gili had stopped crying as soon as Gideon lit the oil lamps. She and Miriam now sat arm-in-arm on the bed with dumbfounded looks on their face. They watched Gideon as he knelt down on his hands and knees and pulled a dirty goatskin from a space between the headboard and the wall. Placing the goatskin on the table beside the bed, he unfolded it to reveal a powerful-looking steel bow and the hilt of a sword sticking from a long metal scabbard. As Gideon pulled the sword from the scabbard, the sound of metal against metal made Gili cringe, and she gripped her mother's arm. The long blade glistened as Gideon tested its sharpness with his thumb. The merchant who'd sold him the sword laughed when Gideon said he would hone the blade to an even keener edge. "It's Damascus steel, straight from a dead Syrian. It can't get any sharper." Gideon hoped the man was right because he hadn't sharpened the blade, and now he was out of time.

Looking at the surprised expression on Miriam's face, Gideon said, "I may die, but not without a fight." And then his voice softened. "It would be very helpful if both of you would each get dressed in your very warmest robes, and then gather together six wool blankets and place them by the fireplace."

"Warmest robes?" Miriam asked skeptically. "It's summer and hot outside. We won't need robes to travel."

Gideon smiled slightly and repeated, "Your warmest robes. It's quite cool where we're going. When the boys return, tell them to do the same." Then walking toward the door, he said, "I'll be back in a few minutes, but we must hurry."

Chapter Nineteen

Naaman moved his arms out from beneath his blanket. Folding them across his chest, he looked out at the black night sky through the flaps in the tent. He had no notion of what time it was, but ever since lying down, he had watched the sliver of a moon slowly march across the sky. The time for war was near.

A brilliant light streaked across the sky directly above him, and he wasn't sure whether to take the falling star as an omen for good or ill. Neither, he finally decided. It was just what it was—the star had outlived its usefulness, and the gods had hurled it from the heavens.

The uneven, hard ground combined with the throbbing in his hands and feet to make sleep impossible. He was feeling old, old and tired, or at least tired of battle. The nights when he'd lain awake before a battle in eager anticipation were gone, long gone. His thoughts were now of Karinah, his home, and more and more often, his leprosy.

Naaman placed his hands behind his head and loosely intertwined his fingers, but he immediately separated his hands and returned them to his chest. A stab of pain from his damaged fingers reminded him that even simple tasks were becoming difficult. His chest rose as he sucked in a lungful of air and let it whistle slowly out his nose. This would be his last campaign. He was finished. A younger man could step into his position. There would be no disgrace in quitting now. He had risen to the top; no man stood between him and the king. He would stay on as a commander, but it would be an advisory role. No more bloody battles, no more screams from dying men, no more looking into the sad eyes of grieving widows and fatherless children. When the leprosy got too bad, he would simply quit altogether and quietly slip into an obscure life, out of sight of everyone but Karinah and those closest to him.

King Ben-Hadad would probably object, but Naaman could deal with that as well. He was certain Ben-Hadad knew of the leprosy, but he hadn't ever said anything. At the appropriate moment, Naaman would tell—no, show—the king his hands and feet. Then he would be willing, maybe even happy, to let Naaman relinquish his command.

"Commander," a voice said softly from outside the tent, "it's time to awake."

"Thank you, Adad," Naaman said as he tossed his blanket aside. His back ached, and his joints rebelled as he gingerly worked himself to a sitting position. He slowly began moving his fingers back and forth and wiggling his toes. They hurt, all of them, and he had to force himself to get the blood moving more freely. He could hear the crackle of campfires coming to life and the hushed voices of men all around him, preparing for a day of agony and death.

With his feet wrapped in linen and gently slipped into his odd sandals, Naaman put on his gloves and walked out of his tent to find Adad and several lesser commanders huddled around a small fire.

Greetings were exchanged, and Naaman turned to Adad. "Have the spies returned from Edrei?"

"Yes, Commander."

"What is their report?"

"The village is totally unprepared for an attack of any kind."

"No guards, no lookouts, nothing to warn of our advance?"

Adad grinned and shook his head. "Nothing! We'll be able to slaughter them without any effort."

Naaman shot a disapproving look at Adad and said, "Slaughter isn't why we're here. The king wants slaves."

Adad shrugged his shoulders and replied, "They're Israelites—not much better than cattle. The world will be better if we kill some in the process."

Naaman considered issuing a stinging rebuke but thought better of it. He didn't want to correct his second-in-command in front of lesser officers; he would save that for a private moment. Looking at each of the men surrounding the fire, Naaman said with an authoritative voice, "Our orders from our king are to overrun the village. We kill those who offer resistance and take as many captives as we can." Looking at Adad, he said, "The king wants slaves, not corpses." Then looking at each man, Naaman added, "Is that clear?"

Mumbled responses of "Yes, Commander," and "Yes, sir," came from each of them.

"Make certain your men understand these orders very clearly," Naaman said sternly.

"What about women or children who put up a fight?" Adad asked. "How shall we treat them? I don't want to get an arrow in my back because I let some youth or woman live."

Naaman sighed and gave his head a slight shake. "A child isn't going to shoot you with an arrow, nor is an old woman. Use your best judgment."

"Nits make lice," Adad said defiantly.

Naaman glared at him. "I'll only say this one more time: we are here for slaves. Keep as many alive as you can."

Each of the men in the circle shifted his weight, kicking at imaginary objects or staring blankly into the dark sky, clearly uneasy at the censure Adad had received. Adad was unaffected; it was as if nothing happened. Those in the circle who knew him best knew he would mostly follow orders, but they also knew that things could become confused in the heat of a battle, and Adad was not above intentionally adding to the confusion when it suited his purposes.

Naaman turned to Adad and asked, "How long will it be before we can break camp and begin our march?"

"One hour, no longer."

"And how long do the spies estimate it will take us to march to Edrei from here?"

Adad hesitated and looked at one of his subordinates. The man shifted his breastplate and cleared his throat. "Five hours," he said.

Naaman pursed his lips and thought for a moment. "That will put us there late in the morning, perhaps even more toward midday. Can we move faster?"

"I don't believe so, commander, unless you want to sacrifice the element of surprise. If we were only going to Ramoth-gilead, it would be easy, but the terrain from here to Edrei is more difficult."

"So be it," Naaman sighed. "Pass the word that we leave in one hour."

Each of the men saluted Naaman and walked off into the darkness. "Adad," Naaman called, "I want to speak with you."

Adad turned around and walked back to where Naaman stood with the orange glow of the fire reflecting from his skin. "Yes, Commander?" he said.

"Is there any question in your mind about our orders?" Naaman asked sternly.

"No, sir."

"Are you very certain?"

Adad clenched his jaw and looked Naaman in the eyes. "I'm certain. You can be assured I will follow the king's order as closely as possible."

"See that you do, Adad," Naaman said slowly and warningly. "That is all. You may leave."

Adad gave a quick salute and walked off without saying anything.

Naaman turned from the fire, limped back into his tent, and eased himself down on a small chest resting in the corner. Reaching down beside him, he lifted the ornate scabbard with his sword tucked firmly inside. Drawing the sword, he ran his fingers over the intricately carved designs that decorated the blade. It was time for him to quit this business. Later today, husbands, fathers, and sons would die in battle, and the thought saddened him.

What should have been a five-hour march stretched into six, and the hot sun had taken its toll on the soldiers. Now standing and sitting in the hills above Edrei, the men were tired and hungry, not rested and eager for the fight. The last few miles had been the most difficult. The trees on the hillside that hid their advance also prevented them from walking in an orderly column. They'd had to weave their way between live trees, step over dead and rotting ones, and bypass large clearings.

Naaman's leprosy-eaten toes screamed in pain each time the wheels of his chariot bounced over a downed tree or slammed into a protruding rock. His team of horses had bolted once, when one of them was stung by a wasp. Even with his glove-covered hands, yanking back on the leather lines caused his fingers to bleed and ache. When he finally inched his way up to the crest of the hill overlooking Edrei, he was grateful for the chance to rest for a few minutes. Reining his horses to a stop, he tied off the lines and stepped down from his chariot. Limping a few steps to a small rock, he sat down to survey the sight in front of him.

The waves of heat coming off the ground danced in the air and made it difficult to see details of the village of Edrei in the narrow valley below. He could see little flashes of motion and assumed it was soon-to-be slaves going about their midday activities. In a few hours, these poor people's lives would change forever. The freedom they knew would be yanked from them, and their lives would become a miserable day-to-day struggle. They would be beaten, starved, and worked until they dropped dead from exhaustion. Naaman smiled to himself. Perhaps the lucky ones would be those who died this day.

Adad rode up beside him and reined his horse to a stop. "Commander," he said breathlessly, "our spies report the village is quiet. The soldiers are in line and ready to attack on your command."

Naaman rose from the rock, stepped into his chariot, and grasped the lines to his team. He had never entered a battle when his heart didn't race and his stomach didn't churn in knots. This time was no different. Taking a deep breath, he said, "Have the trumpeters sound the order to charge."

Chapter Twenty

Uzzi was the first to return to the house, followed quickly by Hanan and then Caleb. The boys laid their respective burdens by the fireplace and looked at Miriam and Gili in surprise.

Hanan scrunched up his face and asked, "Why are you dressed like that?"

"Because your father told us to," Miriam replied. "He wants you to do the same—dress in your warmest robes."

"Why?" Caleb asked curiously. "Where are we going?"

"I don't know," Miriam replied. "All I know is that you must hurry."

The surprised and startled look on Uzzi's face suddenly changed, and his eyes got wide with excitement. "I know where we're going!"

The confusion on Hanan's face changed to incredulity. "You do?" he asked.

Uzzi nodded his head. "To the caves."

Caleb looked at Uzzi with even more confusion on his face than before. "Why?" he asked.

At that instant Gideon burst through the door and frowned at seeing the boys still dressed in light linen tunics. "Boys, you must hurry and get on your warmest robes. Go now!"

Uzzi was out of the room almost before Gideon finished talking, but Hanan and Caleb didn't move. It was Hanan who asked, almost pleadingly, "Where are we going, Father?"

"To the caves. I'll explain more as we walk, but you must hurry."

"Why must we leave now, in the middle of the night?" Hanan complained.

Gideon clenched his jaw to control his irritation. "Hanan, go and get your robe now! There is no time for discussion."

Hanan was about to object when Caleb pushed him and said, "Come on. Let's go change into our robes."

Hanan swatted Caleb's arms away. "I—"

"Go, Hanan," Gideon interrupted. "I'll explain as we walk."

Hanan scowled, shrugged his shoulders, and trudged from the room without saying anything more.

Gideon looked at Miriam and could see the confusion in her eyes. Before she could say anything, he said, "Thank you for changing. The caves aren't cold, but they are much cooler than we're accustomed to." Then kneeling on one knee in front of Gili, he wrapped a strong hand gently around each of her arms. "Are you doing okay, little lamb?" he asked.

Gili gave a slight smile and nodded her head. "Yes." Then looking deep into her father's eyes, she added, "They're coming now, aren't they?" They were the first words she had spoken since she had stopped crying uncontrollably in the bed. The words were spoken calmly and evenly, without fear, and not so much a question as a statement.

Gideon encircled his young daughter in his arms and hugged her close. "I'm not sure," he said honestly, "but if they are, we're going to be in a safer place."

Miriam's mind was whirling at a frantic pace, trying to sort everything out. "Safer?" she asked. "How?"

At that moment, Uzzi, Hanan, and Caleb hurried into the room, each dressed in heavy, black woolen robes that could keep out the chill of a winter day. In addition, they had each put on a heavy cloak. "We're going to roast dressed like this," Hanan complained, holding his arms out from his side.

Gideon smiled at the remark as he looked at each of his sons. Uzzi was the brave one, afraid of no one and nothing. At sixteen he was already big and strong, agile as a cat and coordinated. Things requiring physical strength or dexterity came naturally to him.

Caleb was the smart one. He possessed native intelligence that allowed him to size up a situation and practically and methodically sort things out. Whatever he did was done with as much efficiency as his twelve-year-old mind could fashion, which was frequently more than most men.

And Hanan. He was as kindhearted and gentle as he was strong willed, the one who would carefully set a baby sparrow back in its nest. At fourteen he still choked back tears when a lamb died and would console anyone who was hurt or distressed. He could spend hours sketching a flower or plant and was far more at ease reading a papyrus scroll than shooting a bow. They were different, each with his strengths and weaknesses.

Gideon rose from his spot next to Gili and walked to where the bows, arrows, slings, and stones lay in front of the fireplace. He had debated how best to say what he was about to say and had finally decided to be as honest and straightforward as he could.

"We're going to the caves in Edrei," he said.

Miriam looked at him in dismay and fired back, "Why? What will we eat and drink?"

"It's all there," Gideon replied, "except for what I've just loaded on the donkey."

Miriam looked at him quizzically and was about to say something when Gideon said, "Trust me, Miriam, it's all there—everything we need to live for a month, if we need to. I even have some clothing for each of us but nothing warm like you're wearing now. Please, I'll explain as we go, but we can't lose any more time." Then turning to the boys, he pointed to the pile of items on the floor. "Pick all this up; we must walk quickly."

The boys loaded everything in their arms and walked out the door without looking back. Miriam reached down and took Gili's hand but didn't move a step. As the small yellow flame from the olive oil lamp flickered and danced, she looked at the rugs on the floor, the chairs and couch with their brightly colored pillows tucked neatly against the walls, and she felt a rush of sadness blanket her.

Gideon strode to the table on which the lamp rested and took a breath to blow out the flame. He hesitated when he saw Miriam pensively examining the room. "I think I'll leave the lamp burning," he said gently, "so we'll be able to find our way back when this is over."

Miriam smiled at him; it was a symbolic gesture. She knew the oil in the lamp would burn out before they even reached the caves, and the home would be lost in the darkness. Tugging slightly on Gili's hand, Miriam said, "Come, sweetheart, we must leave."

Gili pulled her hand from Miriam's; said, "I'll be right back"; and ran quickly from the room. A moment later she came back holding a small leather pouch. "I couldn't leave Prophet's topaz here," she said with a smile, tucking the pouch inside the folds of her robe. Then slipping her hand back in Miriam's, Gili smiled and said, "Now, I'm ready to leave."

The two of them walked out of the soft light and stepped into the darkness of the night. Gideon followed closely behind, and after taking one last look, he closed the door and walked to his waiting family.

Uzzi, bow slung over his shoulder, led the way down the narrow, stony path. He was followed closely by Caleb and Hanan. Miriam and Gili, walking hand in hand, came next. Gideon was last, leading the small donkey packed high with small sacks of grain, skins filled with goat milk, three flasks of olive oil, fresh goat cheese, and two madly squawking chickens tied securely to the uppermost sack so they couldn't fly away. Two dogs trailed behind, panting lightly and tongues hanging out from chasing each other. The soft white light of the pale moon sliver flooded the countryside, silhouetting the little column of figures as they walked down the trail to the main road into Edrei. They walked single file or two abreast. Except for the occasional outburst when a sandal-clad toe jammed against a rock, each person walked in silence, too confused and uncertain to know if they should be excited, frightened, or both.

As they stepped from the winding trail that led to their house and onto the main road into Edrei, they all stopped. Hanan plopped down on a nearby rock and removed his sandals, brushing the accumulated sand and tiny rocks from the bottoms of his feet. Replacing one sandal he asked, "Father, will you please tell us why we're doing this?"

With every footstep he'd taken over the past hour, Gideon had turned over in his mind exactly what he was going to say and how to say it. He wanted them to have enough information to be satisfied but not so much they would be alarmed. He chuckled to himself when he thought about not alarming them—everything he'd said or done in the past few hours had done nothing but alarm them. At this point, anything would be anticlimactic. In the end, he decided he would be honest but brief. He would give them the facts and then answer their questions.

"Yes, Hanan, I will tell you, but before I do, I want to thank you for being so obedient. You've followed my instructions without complaining and without knowing why." Although the darkness made it impossible to clearly see any of their faces, he knew they were all looking at him with questioning and eager eyes.

"Many months ago while selling sheep to an old trader in the village of Aphek, I ran into a small contingent of Israelite soldiers. Their leader was a man I served with when I was in the army. I asked him why he was so far from his post in Samaria, and he told me there were rumors the

Syrians were making plans to invade outposts in Israel. His company was spying on them to know if it was true."

"Was it?" Uzzi interrupted.

Gideon nodded his head. "Yes. And he warned me that I should be alert for signs or hints of Syrian activity around Edrei, that it might be one of the first villages they attacked."

"Is that why you bought bows and swords?" Uzzi interjected again.

"Uzzi, be quiet and let Father talk," Caleb said with some exasperation.

"Partly," Gideon said in response to Uzzi's question. "Some time after my conversation with him, I was in Edrei having a plow repaired by the blacksmith. A group of nomads stopped to have him repair something for them. It was very hot, so we all sat and talked while we drank cool water. They said they had just left a small valley twenty miles north of here because their goats had eaten all the grass, so they were moving on. But while they were there, a small group of Syrian soldiers stumbled into their camp. The soldiers were nearly dead from lack of water and in need of food, so these men had helped. Because they never see soldiers so far in the desert, the nomads asked many questions. One of the soldiers let it slip that they had gotten lost on their way to Edrei to check its defenses."

"They were coming to Edrei?" Uzzi said anxiously as he adjusted the bow on his shoulder.

"Yes," Gideon answered.

"Is that when you bought the bows?" Uzzi asked.

Gideon shook his head. "I'd already bought the bows and swords by then, but that's when I started making arrows and preparing other things."

"What other things?" Caleb asked.

Gideon ignored the question and went on. Looking at Hanan he said, "Remember last week when you couldn't find one ewe and her lamb?"

"Yes," Hanan answered.

"After you told me, I went out searching for them," Gideon said. "About dusk I was up in the cedars and the oak trees on the ridge behind our house. The wind was blowing lightly, and I could hear voices on the breeze. No one should have been there, so I began creeping toward the voices. I almost stepped on them before I could get a good look at them. There were six Syrian soldiers."

Miriam let out a small gasp. "Syrians? Behind our house?"

Gideon looked over at Miriam, though he couldn't see her clearly in the darkness. "Fortunately, they all had their backs to me, and they were paying close attention to one of them who was drawing in the sand with a stick. I eased away from them slightly and dropped on my belly behind a fallen log. They were too far away for me to hear what they were saying, but after only a few minutes, they stood up and crept away.

"Where did they go?" Caleb asked.

"They went north and east, back toward Syrian territory. I followed them until it was too dark; I was afraid they might stop and I'd run into them, so I turned around and went back home. Early the next morning, I went back to where I first saw them and looked at the drawing they had made on the ground."

"What was it?" Uzzi asked excitedly.

Gideon let out a long, slow sigh. "I believe it was a plan for invading Edrei. It's impossible to tell for certain, but they had clearly drawn symbols showing the village and the hills." Then Gideon stopped. After a pause he added, "They even had a mark that I believe represented our house."

Miriam's hand flew to her mouth, and she stifled a gasp. But before she could say anything, Gideon continued, "Since then I've been making plans and figuring out what to do."

"Why didn't you say something?" Miriam said with rising anger in her voice. "We could have left. We could have gone somewhere."

"Where? Where could we have gone?" Gideon asked defensively. "All the nearby villages are as vulnerable as we are."

"We could have gone anywhere," she fired back. "We could have even gone back to that disgusting shack we lived in years ago."

Gideon didn't want to debate the issue in front of the children, but he knew they would all be waiting for his response. "How? We couldn't take all the animals; there are too many for us to herd, and that miserable plot of ground wouldn't support them all even if we could get them there. And we couldn't sell them at this time of year; no one has any money. And what about the grain? It's a beautiful crop."

"We could have left it all, Gideon," Miriam said tersely. "We could have walked away."

"And just leave everything we have, everything we've worked for?" Gideon replied.

"We may have been poor, but we would be alive! I hope you haven't sentenced us to death or, worse, to slavery!" Miriam said, unable to control the fear-laden anger building inside her.

An awkward silence fell over the family, and nobody moved. After several minutes had passed, Gideon said, "Over the past few days, I have been taking food, clothing, and other supplies to one of the caverns in the cliffs outside Edrei. It has a small stream of flowing water, a vent up to the outside, and plenty of fresh air flowing through it."

"Which one?" Uzzi and Caleb asked at almost the same time. "We know them all." It was true. The boys had spent countless hours exploring the twisting turns and large chambers that was once a city in the rocks.

"Near the extreme far end, the—"

Without any more of a description than that, Uzzi said, "I know the one you mean. It's perfect! The best one in all the cliffs. Let's go."

And they did. Miriam grabbed Gili by the hand and led the way down the road. She had no idea where she was going, but she felt an overwhelming sense of urgency to get moving.

* * *

Two hours later as the sun was rising over the eastern hills, Gideon poured oil into three lamps and lighted them. Handing one lamp to Miriam and another to Uzzi, Gideon instructed them to get into a single line and follow him through the entrance to the cave and down the long, sloping tunnel into the large cavern.

Chapter Twenty-One

Not a particle of sunlight permeated the black rock of the cavern, and Miriam waited for her eyes to adjust to the dim light of the lamps. She couldn't see the small stream on the far side of the cave, but she could hear the water trickling over small rocks. She held her lamp high above her head, expanding the fragile circle of light to reveal black walls and a domed ceiling twenty feet above her. The room was roughly rectangular, much wider than deep, and larger than she expected. It was probably three or four times the size of the home they had just left. A slight draft kissed the back of her neck, and she watched the small flame of the lamp dance to confirm there was air moving through the darkness.

She shuffled cautiously toward the back of the cave until the light illuminated the rear wall. Piles of rock were strewn against the lower portions of the wall, but above them she was surprised to see what resembled a series of chiseled steps that disappeared up into the darkness. "That's our back door," Gideon said from the shadows. "Climb up those steps, and you'll find a narrow shaft leading outside."

The thought of a second way out of the cave was somehow reassuring to her. "How large is the shaft?" she asked.

"You can get through it easily, Mother," came Uzzi's voice.

"How do you know?" Miriam asked.

Uzzi chuckled. "Hanan, Caleb, and I have explored all these caves many, many times. We know them all, and this is by far the best."

"What makes it the best?" Gili asked innocently. "To me it's dark and scary."

"Well," Uzzi said, suddenly proud to be an authority on the caves, "first of all, it has not two but three ways out." He walked forward with his lamp until its pale yellow light shone on a dark hole into which the small stream disappeared. "If you don't mind getting a little wet, you can scoot on your back into the next cave. It's too small to belly-crawl; you must go on your back. You're in total darkness, but it's only about thirty feet. Inside the next cave is a small opening in the roof, and you can climb a pile of rocks and get outside."

"You've done that?" Miriam felt a sense of claustrophobia sweep over her at the thought of inching her way through a tunnel in total darkness, on her back, with her nose and shoulders only inches from solid rock.

"Oh sure," Uzzi replied, "we all have."

"What else makes this ideal?" Miriam asked.

"You can't see it and no sunlight comes in, but there's a natural vent in the ceiling. When you light a fire in just the right place, the smoke rises in a column and goes outside."

"How do you know that?" Miriam asked in amazement.

Caleb let out a short exasperated sigh. "Because we've done it," he said. "What do you think we did when we came down to these caves, just walked around?"

Turning in a slow circle, she saw one wall of the cave was lined with bags, pots, and jars. "What's all that?" she asked.

"Food, cooking supplies, oil for the lamps, some clothes, and even some soap," Gideon replied. "Walk a little closer and you'll see a large stack of wood, enough to last for a month."

"Father," Hanan said from the blackness, "are we going to tell anyone else about the raid?"

It was a serious question, one Gideon had wrestled with constantly over the past few days. One he had not answered.

"I don't know. To be honest, Hanan, I don't know what I would say to someone."

"You could tell them exactly what you've told us," he replied.

"And what if I'm wrong? What if there is no attack?"

"But what if there is? Shouldn't we warn our neighbors?" Hanan replied.

"Who would you warn, Hanan?" Gideon asked with slight irritation in his voice.

"Micah and his family," Hanan shot back without a second's hesitation.

"Ooo," Caleb teased, "you just want Samara to be here with you."

Miriam and Gideon's mouths dropped open at the same instant, and they both looked into the darkness where Hanan was sitting. When there was no rebuttal from Hanan, Miriam said, "I didn't know you liked Samara."

"We're friends," Hanan said defensively. "That's all."

"Sure it is," Caleb said. "If that's true, why didn't you mention Jabesh, Gaal, Ebed, and their families?"

Sensing Hanan's awkward situation, Gideon said, "She's a pretty girl, Hanan, and very talented at playing the lute."

"Should we talk to them?" Hanan asked.

Gideon thought for a moment and then said, "How about this: After we get everything situated and we eat our midday meal, I'll go into town. If I learn of more danger, we can talk to them then. They only live a short distance from here, and we could bring them quickly."

Hanan sat quietly in the darkness and brooded over what his father had just said. Years of experience told him there would be no benefit in arguing with the man. He had decided, and there would be no further discussion. "Whatever you think, Father," and he said no more.

"Come, boys," Gideon called. "Let's go unload the donkey."

While Gideon, Uzzi, and Hanan unloaded the donkey, Caleb built a small fire. Even with the flickering flames lighting most of the room, it was well past noon before Miriam was satisfied with how things were organized. Then she fixed a small meal of goat cheese, bread with honey, almonds, and dates.

"Come, everyone," she said. "Let us give thanks to Jehovah and eat."

The boys attacked the food like starving wolves. They had eaten no breakfast and were famished. Gili nibbled at her food but almost immediately said she was sleepy and asked if she could lie down. Gideon nervously picked at his food and finally said, "I think I'll walk into the village to see what I can learn. I should be back within an hour or two." Turning to the three boys, he said, "Help your mother clean up, and then you can sleep as well."

Taking a small stick from the fire, Gideon lit a lamp and walked up the tunnel. The brightness of the midday sun almost blinded him, and he raised his hand to shield his eyes while they slowly adjusted from the dark of the cave. Placing the lamp on the ground at the cave's entrance, he thought about extinguishing the flame but changed his mind; he didn't have any way to light it upon his return.

His eyes fully adjusted, Gideon began walking the half mile to the center of Edrei, but his eyes were focused on the hills to the east of the village, out toward his home. He wasn't sure what first drew his attention to the small clumps of trees a mile beyond the village. Perhaps it was a quick reflection of sunlight off metal or the birds he could see circling in the air, but as he swept the distance with his eyes, he continually returned to the trees.

Stopping in the middle of the road, he raised both hands to his forehead and strained to make out the odd shapes clustered unnaturally beneath the limbs. It was then he saw an army of men begin running from the trees with swords and spears. The wind was at his back, so he could hear nothing, but he was certain there were trumpets sounding and screams coming from the mouths of each of the attackers.

Chapter Twenty-Two

His first impulse was to turn and run for the protection of the cave, but Hanan's words about warning others flashed through his brain. He began running as fast as he could for the center of the village. Screaming a warning of attack, he burst through the blacksmith's door, startling the half dozen men lounging inside. "Syrians are attacking from the east!" he screamed. "Get your weapons!" Without waiting for a response or giving them time to ask questions, he bolted from the door and raced for the cave.

The dusty streets came alive as he ran through them, pounding on doors and shouting through windows. His heart pounded, not only from running but out of fear. Adrenaline pumped through his body, charging his legs but slightly fogging his mind. Had he been thinking clearly, he would have taken the extra few minutes and detoured to Micah's house and warned him and his family. As it was, the thought never crossed his mind.

The last quarter mile to the cave was the most difficult. Uneven ground, boulders, and no clearly defined path meant he could go no faster than a slow trot, and each passing second caused him anxiety. What if the attackers saw him duck into the cave? It would all be for nothing. Scrambling to the entrance, he scooped up the oil lamp and silently thanked Jehovah that the wind had not doused the flame.

Shielding the lamp's flame with his hand, he skidded and slid down the incline to the cavern calling out, "Miriam, are you here?"

His heart beat faster when there was no reply, and as he raced into the large cavern, he discovered why. A small fire was burning, and everyone was sleeping peacefully on their beds of sheep and goat skins.

Stumbling to Miriam's side, he shook her forcefully on the shoulder, "Wake up," he said breathlessly. "The village is under attack." Then raising his voice, he called out, "Everyone wake up. The village is under attack."

As the little family slowly came to life, Gideon raced to the corner of the room where they'd placed the weapons. Taking his bow he quickly fastened the string and did the same with each of the others. "Uzzi," he called, "get your bow and two quivers of arrows. Hanan, you do the same."

Uzzi leaped from his bed and was at Gideon's side in an instant. After slipping a long dagger under his belt, he slung a quiver filled with arrows over each shoulder and picked up his bow.

Caleb reached for his sling and all of his pouches filled with stones. He slipped one after another over his shoulders.

"Hanan, come quickly," Gideon called over his shoulder. "You must get your bow and arrows."

There was no movement in Hanan's bed, and Gideon picked up the lamp and strode over. Reaching down he grabbed the heavy woolen blanket. "Hanan, get up." He gave the blanket a toss. There was no Hanan, only a rolled-up goat skin.

Gideon turned around and yelled, "Where is Hanan?"

Miriam reached for a lamp and replied, "I don't know." And then with alarm in her voice, she added, "He was here when I went to sleep."

"Hanan!" Gideon shouted loudly, but the name bounced off the dark walls of the cave and went unanswered.

Miriam spun in circles looking at every nook and cranny and then, in desperation and panic, screamed, "Hanan! Where are you?" But there was no answer.

Gideon dashed across the cave, picked up a lamp, and was heading for the tunnel when Gili softly said, "I know where he is."

Gideon whirled around to see her standing on the opposite side of the cave, barely within the circle of light from the fire. "Where?" Gideon demanded far more forcefully than he intended.

Gili bit at her bottom lip and said, "He made me promise not to tell."

"Tell me," Gideon yelled. "Now!"

"Gideon!" Miriam screamed as she ran to Gili's side and put her arms around the frightened child. "Don't yell at her like that."

Gideon sucked in a huge breath and said only slightly more calmly, "I'm sorry. But, please, Gili. You must tell me."

Gili looked up at her mother and said almost tearfully, "He made me promise!"

Miriam knelt on her knees in front of Gili and gripped her lightly on each shoulder. "Gili," she said as calmly as she could, "I understand he asked you not to tell, but his life might be in danger. If you know where he is, please tell us."

The little girl lowered her head and said softly, "He went to Samara's house. He said he wanted to warn her."

Still kneeling Miriam quickly turned and looked across the dimly lit cavern to where Gideon had been standing, but he was gone. From the darkness of the path, his voice called, "Everyone stay here. I will return."

Uzzi grabbed another lamp and knelt by the fire to light it. "I'm going with Father!" he said as the oil in the lamp took the flame.

"No!" Miriam said forcefully. "You must stay here; we may need you."

"But—"

"No, Uzzi. You must stay here!"

Uzzi let out a frustrated sigh and reached for his bow. "I can't be of any use in here. I'm going up the tunnel to the entrance."

"We'll all go," Miriam said as she rose to her feet. "We'll stay hidden, but we'll watch for Father."

Uzzi led the way as the four of them cautiously walked up the inclining path. They stopped well short of the entrance and allowed their eyes to gradually adjust to the brightness of the afternoon sun. "Wait here," Uzzi said quietly and crept farther on his hands and knees. Inching forward he heard and smelled the deadly business of war long before he saw it.

It was the noise—the screams of men and women, the sound of buildings crumbling, and the crackle of fire—that made him drop to his belly before he reached the mouth of the cave. As he lay there with his chin almost touching the pebble-covered dirt, the faint smell of fire drifted into this nose. The gray-brown cloud of smoke began climbing into the sky and filtering the sunlight, and he knew houses and fields of ripe grain were burning.

Using his elbows and toes, Uzzi inched forward until he could peer over the lip of the entrance. It was the perfect vantage point. From here he could look down the gradually sloping hillside to the streets and houses of the village. It was only a quarter mile from the cave to the nearest street of the village, but it was a challenging distance. Aside from the upward rise of the uneven terrain, there were rocks—some as big as a house—a few scraggly trees, and countless clumps of brush that had to be negotiated. The last hundred yards to the entrance was open ground that offered no hiding places. Watching from here, Uzzi found another reason why his father had chosen this cave—not only was it farther away from the village, but anyone attacking would have no protection as they neared the entrance. It could be easily defended.

Uzzi looked beyond the rows of rock and mud houses that made up Edrei to the wheat fields. A wall of bright orange flames stoked by the wind leaped twenty feet in the air and devoured the stalks of wheat like a fire-breathing monster. Thick plumes of dark-gray smoke rose hundreds of feet in the air and then spread horizontally as if trapped by some unseen hand that would let them go no higher. The thickening smoke hung in the air, turning the bright yellow sun a sickening red.

Uzzi shifted slightly so he could look down at the main road leading out of Edrei. He watched a man frantically pulling on the lead rope of a donkey. A woman sat on the donkey's back, and Uzzi could tell she was clutching a small child in her arms. She kicked at the small animal with her heels and swatted at it with a willow stick, but the stubborn creature simply would go no faster than a casual walk. Ahead of them two men were running hard, their robes flapping wildly with each step. Uzzi watched as they overtook and raced passed a man and woman clutching the hands of four little children, being pulled along faster than their little legs could churn. Uzzi slowly shook his head and wished he could warn all of them. What the fleeing people could not see was that a quarter mile beyond them, half a dozen Syrian soldiers with bows and spears stood shoulder to shoulder across the road. The frightened villagers were fleeing into the waiting arms of the enemy. There would be no escape.

Panic reigned in the streets of Edrei. Uzzi watched as women dashed into houses and slammed shutters shut. Men were crouched on rooftops with bows in hand, awaiting the advancing attackers. But the attack wasn't orderly, street by street or house by house. Instead, it came from all sides almost at once. The soldiers were like mad ants as they rushed from house to house, killing those who resisted. Women and children were dragged into the middle of the streets and forced to sit on the ground with their hands on their heads. Uzzi watched a woman leap to her feet and rush toward a young man who lay with an arrow protruding from his back. As she ran, a soldier on a black horse rode up beside her and violently kicked her in her back. The woman stumbled to the ground and fell under the horse's wildly stomping feet. The rider never looked back at the motionless woman lying in a heap. Uzzi rose on one knee, methodically reached over his shoulder, and pulled an arrow from his quiver, notching it in his bow. "Come within range of my bow," Uzzi snarled as he looked at the horseman, "and you will die."

Uzzi caught the movement out of the corner of his eye and instantly dropped back to the ground. Scanning the boulder-strewn landscape below, he watched two figures darting hand in hand from one large boulder to the next. Although he couldn't see the faces, there was no mistaking Hanan's black-and-white striped tunic. The other person, with long hair trailing behind her, was Samara.

His first instinct was to shout out to Hanan to stay where he was. Running would only attract the attention of the soldiers, and the two of them could easily hide among the boulders and trees until dark. But he knew Hanan. His brother was probably frightened out of his wits right now, and darkness held even more terror.

It was only after he watched the young couple scurry twice more from rock to rock that he noticed a third person. This new figure was hiding in the shadows of an old shed, his back pressed tightly against the dilapidated structure, a bow in his hand. One hundred feet beyond him, three soldiers were cautiously working their way toward the man, darting from the protective cover of one hiding place to the next, obviously in pursuit. "Father?" he mumbled in quiet alarm as he recognized the tunic of the man beside the shed.

Standing beside the shed, Gideon pulled an arrow from his quiver and notched it in his bow as he watched Hanan and Samara duck behind a boulder. He shook his head. If only they would stay still. Each time they moved, they ran the risk of attracting the attention of a soldier.

He could neither hear nor see the soldiers, but he knew they were nearby. They had been chasing him ever since they'd caught sight of him leaving Samara's ransacked and empty house. There had been four, but when one of them had stumbled on Gideon and charged with his sword drawn, Gideon deftly shot an arrow just below the man's body armor. The soldier dropped to his knees but bleated a warning before he fell forward on his face in a lifeless heap.

Uzzi looked down the hillside as Hanan and Samara dropped down behind the last large boulder before they'd have to cross the open ground. He knew what Hanan was going to do, and somehow he had to get his brother's attention to stop him. If the soldiers saw them run across the open ground to the cave, they would jeopardize everyone's safety by revealing their hiding place. Rising cautiously to one knee, Uzzi took careful aim with his bow and let an arrow fly. The arrow arced through the air and slammed into the rock about six inches above Hanan's head, splintering into a dozen pieces.

At the sound of the arrow striking the rock, Hanan ducked down and covered his head with his arms. After a moment he slowly raised his head and looked up the incline to where Uzzi was crouching. Uzzi held up both arms and emphatically motioned for him to stay where he was. Hanan shook his head. He pointed to Samara and himself, then he pointed up the incline to where Uzzi was. Uzzi shook his head angrily and more adamantly motioned for Hanan to remain behind the rock and pointed down the hillside toward Gideon and the soldiers.

Hanan didn't even bother to look. He shook his head, grabbed Samara by the hand, and together the two of them rose and began running across the open ground.

Hanan's black-and-white striped tunic and Samara's off-white robe contrasted perfectly with the black dirt. They looked like flags waving in the breeze as they ran.

Gideon looked up the hillside and watched in shock as the couple began their dash across the open ground, knowing that their movement and brightly colored clothing would instantly attract the attention of not only the three soldiers pursuing him, but dozens more nearby. The couple had run fewer than a dozen steps when Gideon heard a soldier yell, "There, up in the clearing just above the rocks!"

In a split second, Gideon made his decision. Running out from behind the shed, he yelled at the top of his lungs, "You Syrian dogs!" and charged forward, letting his arrow fly. It was intentionally a wild shot, meant to distract, not injure or kill, and it worked. All three soldiers instantly ducked for cover, as did Gideon when he reached another, smaller shed.

Uzzi watched in horror as his father charged from his hiding place and sent the arrow through the air. He didn't see him drop behind the second shed because at that exact moment, Hanan and Samara charged to the cave's entrance and dropped to the ground beside him.

"We made it," Hanan exclaimed breathlessly to Samara. "We made it!"

"And probably killed Father in the process," Uzzi hissed angrily.

"What are you talking about?" Hanan said.

Uzzi grabbed Hanan by the cheeks and turned his head down the hill so he could clearly see Gideon valiantly trying to fend off the three soldiers creeping toward him.

"I didn't know he was there," Hanan said defensively.

"Why do you think I was warning you to stay hidden?"

Hanan started to say something, but Uzzi was already on his feet and racing down the hillside toward the boulder from which Hanan and Samara had just run.

Chapter Twenty-Three

Naaman clung to the sides of his chariot and tried to steady himself as it bounced over the uneven ground. Each jolt sent a fresh stab of pain into his already throbbing feet, and he anxiously measured the distance until he would be out of the trees and onto the roads of Edrei. Adad raced ahead of him, his black horse almost white with lather; stretched out behind them were hundreds of yelling soldiers.

The attackers poured out of the trees and down the hillside like a horde of cockroaches after a crumb of bread. Naaman could see the first contingents were already at the outskirts of the village, and he knew others would be blocking the roads to stop any who might try to escape. In the distance he could see the first plumes of smoke rising above the fields as soldiers set fire to the ripe wheat. By the time they finished, even the dogs and wolves would not want to live in Edrei.

Lashing out at the team of exhausted horses pulling his chariot, he pulled onto the smooth main road into Edrei and breathed a sigh of relief. Ahead of him a confused group of would-be Edrei defenders were being mercilessly cut down, first by volleys of arrows then by swordsmen slashing and hacking. He grimaced at the sight but couldn't help thinking those poor men might be the lucky ones. Death was better than slavery.

"Commander," Adad said as he wheeled his horse alongside the chariot, "there has been very little resistance. It will be a huge victory."

Naaman looked at his second-in-command and scowled to himself. From a military standpoint, there was little to be proud of for storming an unsuspecting and virtually defenseless village. "When the people are out of their homes, order the troops to begin setting fire to each house," Naaman commanded. "But do not burn a house until you're certain everyone is out. Do you understand?"

"Can the men take things of value for themselves?" Adad asked as he fought to keep the prancing horse under control.

Naaman eyed the ramshackle houses lining the streets. "Yes, whatever they find is theirs."

"Excellent," Adad said, spurring his horse and charging onto a side street crowded with frightened Israelites who had been routed from their houses. "You may keep anything of value you can find, but burn the houses to the ground," Adad commanded as the horse trotted along the line of people. Without warning a young boy—no older than ten or eleven—jumped up from the ground and charged at a soldier about to set fire to a house.

"No," the boy screamed. "My sick grandmother is still in that house."

Without a second thought, Adad slapped the horse's rump and raced forward with his sword high in the air. Overtaking the boy at almost a full gallop, Adad brought the sword down on the boy with a sickening thump, sneering as the child crumpled to the ground in a heap.

The soldier holding the torch gasped in horror. "He was but a boy!" he yelled at Adad.

"He was about to kill you," Adad shouted in return.

"He was defenseless."

"I saved your life." Adad said as he sidestepped the horse away from the lifeless body. "Now torch the house!"

"The boy said there's a sick old woman inside," the soldier said.

"I don't care. Torch the house!"

The soldier stared at Adad and flung the torch to the ground. "Do it yourself," he said and walked away.

"I'll see you dead," shouted Adad, jumping from the saddle. Snatching the torch, he kicked open the door and tossed the flame inside, ignoring the plea of help from a frail woman lying on a makeshift bed of straw. Climbing back on his horse, he continued down the street, shouting the same order to loot and burn.

* * *

Naaman stepped down from his chariot and walked toward a group of a dozen men sitting in the dirt in front of the smith's shop. They sat with their hands on top of their heads and their legs crossed in front of them. Six soldiers encircled them with bows drawn, and two more stood outside the circle with swords unsheathed.

"What are those caves up there?" Naaman said as he strode forward, pointing to the small openings in the black cliffs in the distance.

The men sitting in the dirt looked at Naaman and then at each other, but no one said a word.

"It really makes no difference whether you tell us or not; we're going to investigate them anyway," Naaman said matter-of-factly. "I simply want to know their purpose."

Except for blinking eyes and shallow breathing, the men sat as still as stone statues. Beneath the calm exterior, each man's heart raced wildly, and they seethed with a combination of fear and anger. The same thought raced through each man's mind, and each of them hoped against all hope that their wife and children had somehow managed to find their way to the safety of the caves.

Naaman turned from the men as the sound of pounding horse hooves reached his ears. Adad rode up again and jumped from the saddle as the horse skidded to a stop only inches from where Naaman stood.

"Commander," Adad said in a voice hoarse from constant yelling, "we've captured most of the people on the far side of the town and have started burning the houses. In another hour, we'll have worked our way through most of the village."

"Excellent, Adad," Naaman said. "See those caves in the cliffs beyond the village? What did our scouts tell you of them?"

Adad looked to where Naaman was pointing. "Our scouts reported nothing of them to me."

Naaman shook his head. "I think it's unlikely anyone made it up into them, but take a contingent of men and begin searching them."

Chapter Twenty-Four

Uzzi ran down the slope as fast as his muscular legs could propel him and dropped, unseen, behind the protective cover of the first boulder he came to. There were too many trees and rocks to see either his father or the soldiers, so he cautiously began working his way to where he could get a clear shot at the soldiers. If he could kill at least one, that would even the odds.

He had run, crept, and crawled what he thought was half the distance to where he'd last seen the soldiers when he suddenly froze in his tracks. No more than fifty feet ahead of him stood a soldier with his back to Uzzi. The soldier was motioning frantically to someone Uzzi couldn't see. He wasn't motioning for the unseen man to come to where he was, but for the other man to take a different course.

Crouching behind a large rock, Uzzi silently pulled an arrow from his quiver and notched it in his bow. Standing up to his full height, he whistled softly. As the soldier spun around to face the noise, he instinctively raised his own bow and let fly a poorly aimed arrow. But Uzzi's arrow had begun its deadly flight long before the soldier's arrow had even left its bowstring. Countless hours shooting at darting rabbits and spiders walking up tree trunks assured the arrow would find its target, but before the arrow had even lodged in the man's chest, Uzzi pulled a second from his quiver and took aim. It was an unnecessary action, for the man was dead before his knees buckled.

The thought that he had just ended another man's life briefly entered Uzzi's mind, spun around for a split second, and was immediately cast out. "No one hurts my family," Uzzi breathed out as he stepped silently closer to where he thought his father would be.

* * *

Gideon squatted down as low as he could and listened as the arrows zinged past his head. He was trapped. The two soldiers were doing exactly what he would have done, and they were doing it well. One would shoot while the other advanced, and their rhythm was such that Gideon couldn't even raise his head let alone take aim and fire a return arrow. Judging from the shrill whine the arrows made as they passed, he knew they must be closing the distance and were probably less than thirty feet away. He had only two options. He could stay where he was, jump to his feet, take quick aim, and hope to hit one of the soldiers, or he could run for the better protection of the larger shed behind him. Either way, he was likely to get hit with one, possibly two arrows.

He churned both options over in his mind. Whatever he was going to do, he must do it quickly or he would surely die. He had barely positioned his legs under him when he heard, "Father," yelled from the rocks far to his left.

Keeping his head low, Gideon shifted around to see Uzzi looking at him from behind a boulder the size of a house. Gideon flashed a huge grin; the odds had now changed. As if on cue, Gideon rose to his feet at the same instant Uzzi rolled out from behind the rock. Each took aim at the totally unprotected soldiers standing thirty feet away and released their arrows.

Gideon's was the first to find its target. It entered the soldier's chest just below the sternum and passed through his body, lodging in the man's backbone. Uzzi's arrow sliced into the same man's chest, an inch below Gideon's, and passed through his heart.

Gideon and Uzzi looked at each other in stunned disbelief. Neither of them had thought for a second that they might both choose the same target. The remaining soldier was the quickest of the three to process the situation, and he held a slight advantage—he already had an arrow in his bow. In a split second, he chose his target, aimed, and released.

It was as if time suddenly slowed to a crawl. The perfectly smooth wooden shaft with its two red feathers and one white feather slowly rotated as it left the bowstring on its violent mission. The razor-sharp steel tip sliced silently through the air until it pierced a woolen tunic, then flesh, and imbedded itself in heart tissue.

The soldier had no time to revel in his well-placed shot, for his arrow had no sooner found its target than another arrow passed through his throat, severing windpipe and artery as it went. "No one hurts my family," Uzzi hissed as he lowered his bow and ran to his father's side.

* * *

Looking down from the cave's entrance, Miriam gasped in horror and screamed as she watched her husband slump to the ground, the arrow protruding from his chest like a pin from a cushion. Frantic with fear and panic, she clawed her way from her stomach to her feet to run to Gideon. She had only taken half a step before two hands quickly reached out and gripped her ankles, tripping her flatly to the ground.

"You can't go down there, Mother," Caleb said as he scooted forward and wrapped his arms tightly around her.

"Let me go!" Miriam screamed as she struggled and twisted to free herself from his ironclad hold.

"No! You can't go!" he said fiercely as the two of them thrashed in the dirt.

Miriam struggled for only a moment before her body relaxed, and she began sobbing uncontrollably. Only then did Caleb release his viselike hold on her. Turning to Hanan, he said, "You must take Mother back inside the cave."

Hanan didn't move. He was on his hands and knees, his mouth gaping open and his eyes firmly fixed on the unmoving body of his father lying in the dirt below.

"Hanan!" Caleb shouted. "Take Mother inside the cave."

"Is he dead?" Hanan mumbled, still not moving.

Gili and Samara moved at almost the same instant. In an effort to remain unseen, they crawled forward and ushered a sobbing Miriam back to the obscurity of the cave.

"Get down," Caleb hissed to Hanan who was still on his hands and knees. Pointing in the distance, he said, "Soldiers are coming up toward the caves."

And indeed they were. Dozens of soldiers streamed from the village streets with swords and spears. They trudged up the hillside toward the black cliffs riddled with caves, but they were concentrated far from where Caleb and Hanan were watching Uzzi.

Uzzi knelt down and gently cradled his father's head in his arms as tears dripped from his eyes onto the dead man's face. After a moment, Uzzi wiped his eyes and looked up the hill to where Hanan and Caleb peered down at him. He could see Caleb motion with his arm, and he instantly knew that soldiers were combing the caves.

Laying Gideon's head gently on the ground, Uzzi pushed strands of hair from his father's face. "I love you, Father," he said as he tenderly patted Gideon's cheek.

Rising to his feet, Uzzi wiped his eyes on the shoulders of his tunic. Picking up his bow, he began stealthily dodging from rock to rock and tree to tree as he made his way up the hillside. Before he moved from one hiding place to the next, he carefully scanned ahead and to both sides, searching for any movement or glint of metal that might warn him of a soldier. It had taken much longer than normal, and now the only thing that stood between him and the security of the cave was three hundred feet of open terrain.

An hour earlier he had considered this open patch of ground to be a blessing. It was impossible for anyone to approach the entrance to their cave without crossing this stretch of ground. With its few blades of dried grass and rocks no larger than oranges, the area offered no cover behind which advancing forces could hide. Any fanatic foolish enough to rush the cave would easily be riddled with arrows. But now the blessing had turned to a curse. As fast as Uzzi might run, he would be exposed to the eyes of any soldier giving even half a glance in this direction.

Uzzi considered his options, but the decision was already made for him. Caleb was watching Uzzi when Hanan tapped him on the arm and pointed, "Look, down by Father!" he exclaimed.

Caleb watched as a large black horse worked its way between houses. Its rider guided it cautiously to the shed where Gideon lay in the dirt. "Where did they come from?" Caleb said mostly to himself. Behind the man walked six soldiers, two with bows and three with swords and spears. Although he could hear nothing, Caleb knew the horseman had issued an order because the three bowmen immediately drew arrows from their almost-empty quivers and notched them on their bowstrings. The rider raised his sword and gave a quick motion; the spearmen fanned out as if searching for someone. The rider turned his horse slightly, and Caleb and Hanan watched as he began methodically scanning the hillside.

"We must warn Uzzi," Hanan said as he rose from his stomach to his knees and frantically began waving his arms to draw Uzzi's attention. Uzzi immediately saw Hanan waving, but so did the rider on the black horse.

"Get down!" Caleb shouted.

Hanan dropped to his belly and said, "I hope Uzzi saw me!"

Caleb didn't hear the remark; he was staring not at Uzzi but at the horseman. The next actions would tell it all. Caleb's heart sank when the rider stood up in his stirrups and pointed the tip of his sword directly at where Hanan and Caleb were hiding. A fraction of a second later, the rider and all six men began cautiously ascending the hillside.

From his precarious position, Uzzi watched the approaching men and considered the only two options he could think of: running across the barren ground to the cave or fighting them from where he stood. If he stayed, he could almost certainly kill some of the soldiers, but it would only be a matter of time before they managed to get reinforcements and overpower him. And that's when a third alternative hit him.

Uzzi cautiously lowered himself and began half crawling and half running to a small gully less than twenty feet away. It was a tangled mass of dead cedar trees, rocks, sand, and prickly weeds. Oblivious to the pain from the sharp needle-like spines, he began pulling and stomping on the weeds until he created an opening large enough for him to hide in. Tossing his bow in the makeshift burrow, he eased himself in and pulled a layer of weeds over the hole. It was far from perfect, but he hoped the men would be so focused on the cave that they wouldn't see him.

Hanan and Caleb watched Uzzi's odd preparation in wonderment. "What's he doing?" Hanan asked in anxious confusion.

Caleb's mind whirled, and then he stammered, "I think . . . I think he's going to hide until they pass."

"What, and then run away? What about us? Is he going to leave us?"

"That's something you might do but not Uzzi," Caleb fired back angrily. And then he immediately said, "I'm sorry, Hanan. I didn't mean that."

Hanan's soft brown eyes registered the rebuke. "I know," he replied softly and gave a weak smile.

Caleb looked back down at Uzzi's strange hiding spot and shook his head in bewilderment, but then he suddenly understood. "He's going to ambush them from behind! And we need to attack from the front!" Easing himself away from the opening, he said, "Stay here, and keep careful watch. I'm going into the cave to warn Mother and get the other bow and my sling."

Caleb scrabbled down the sloping tunnel, stumbling in the darkness until he saw the glow from the fire in the main cavern. "Mother, the soldiers are coming, and we must be prepared," he said loudly, well before he could even see in the dim light.

Miriam, Samara, and Gili were huddled together on the far side of the cavern, barely within the fire's circle of light. Miriam and Samara sat on small sacks of wheat, and Samara had her arm around Miriam's shoulder. Miriam sat with her hands in her lap, twisting a small, white linen cloth in ever-tightening knots. Gili stood at Miriam's side and tenderly patted the bereaved woman on the hands. It was an odd sight: the young comforting the old.

Walking rapidly over to them, he reached down and touched his mother's hands. "Mother, you must leave this cave."

Miriam looked up through tear-drenched eyes but said nothing.

"She's in shock," Samara said softly.

Caleb looked lovingly at his mother and suddenly felt very alone. Letting out a deep sigh, he looked alternately at Samara and Gili. "A small group of soldiers is coming up the hill to the cave. We're going to try overpowering them, but we can't risk having you trapped in here." Turning to Gili he said, "Do you remember how to get out of this cave?"

"Yes, we walk out the front."

"No, no, I mean the other ways out of the cave. Do you remember the other way out that we told you about?"

"I think . . . maybe," she said uncertainly.

She said it so tentatively Caleb shook his head and looked at Samara. "I don't have much time, so you must listen carefully." Pointing into the blackness behind them, he said, "The back wall of the cave is mostly a jumbled mass of rocks and boulders. Walk to where the side wall and the back wall meet—it's near where the stream seeps into the cave. Climb up the pile of rocks, staying close to the wall. When you reach the top of the pile, look carefully with the lamp, and you'll find steps that have been cut into the wall. You must climb up the steps; they lead to a narrow ledge near the roof of the cave. As you crawl along the ledge, you'll begin to feel a rush of air. Follow that air until you come to a narrow passage. It's really nothing more than a split in the rock. It'll be a tight fit, but stand as straight as you can and inch yourself sideways into that split."

"How will we carry a lamp?" Samara asked. "We won't be able to see."

Caleb looked at Samara with slight irritation. He was in a hurry, and her questions were delaying him. "You can't carry a lamp; leave it on the ledge. You'll be in total darkness from the moment you enter the split," he said with more agitation than he intended. "Now listen, carefully. You must inch sideways for thirty or forty feet until you can go no farther. Look up and slightly to your right, and you'll see a small sliver of sunlight above your head. That's a smooth shaft that will lead you to the outside. You'll think it is a great distance, but that's just because the shaft is so narrow. It's only a few feet above your head."

"But how will we get out?" Samara asked with some concern.

"Use the rope!" Caleb responded as if she should know what he was talking about.

"What rope?"

Caleb let out another sigh. "There's a rope dangling down the shaft—you'll be able to see it in the light. By pulling with your arms and pushing with your toes, you can wiggle your way up the shaft. Do you understand?"

Samara nodded but said nothing.

"Once you're out of the shaft, you'll be in the bottom of a narrow ravine. Work your way up the ravine, and you'll come out on top of a large, flat plain that overlooks Edrei. It's only a few miles from there to our house." Looking at Samara and then Miriam, who was now far more alert, he continued, "It's important that Gili goes last. She's not tall enough to reach the rope, and it will take both of you to lift her out. One of you must reach down into the opening headfirst while the other holds onto her legs. That's the only way you'll be able to get Gili out."

Miriam's eyes widened in alarm. "I won't allow Gili to go last. What if something happens to her?"

"Mother, please," Caleb pleaded. "It will be difficult enough for you and Samara to get her out with both of you helping. It is impossible for her to get out by herself; the rope simply isn't long enough for her to reach it. You must help her from the topside."

"And what about you, Hanan, and Uzzi?" Miriam asked. "How will you escape?"

Caleb smiled smugly at his mother. "Don't worry about us, Mother. We'll fight long enough for you to escape, then we'll follow you. Uzzi, Hanan, and I know these caves very well. The Syrians will never find us." He said all this with complete confidence, never doubting their ability. "Don't go directly back to the house," he warned. "Stay in the ravine for at least two days to be sure the soldiers are gone." Hurrying over to a bag, he withdrew two loaves of unleavened bread and some goat cheese. "Stuff this in your robes. There's a small trickle of water in the ravine but no food. We'll meet you at the house in two days."

Leaning over he gave his mother a kiss on the cheek and hugged Gili. "Now go, quickly," he said. He ran over and picked up the bow, quiver, sling, and pouches of rocks and then headed for the cave's entrance.

Chapter Twenty-Five

The two archers passed so close to Uzzi's makeshift burrow that he could see their sandals sink in the loose sand as the men struggled up the hillside. Uzzi offered a silent prayer of thanks to Jehovah that they were concentrating so intently on what was ahead of them that they didn't see what lay at their feet. After a long minute of trying to keep his racing heart in control, he cautiously pushed aside some of the thorny brush and eased his head out of his makeshift burrow in time to see the soldiers split up. One raced up the hillside and disappeared into a congested mass of boulders and trees. The second had stopped fifty yards ahead of Uzzi and was leaning against a tree, rubbing the muscles in his leg. Taking his bow in hand, Uzzi eased from under the debris, notched an arrow, and began creeping forward.

Except for a quick, high-pitched zing as Uzzi released his arrow, there was no noise. The arrow covered the twenty-foot distance to the soldier in a split second, entering his back and tearing through his body with such force that the tip protruded out his chest. The soldier crumpled to the ground without a sound. Uzzi silently moved to where the man lay, made certain he was dead, and began stalking the second archer with the same stealth he stalked a deer.

* * *

Caleb struggled to the cave's entrance and dropped down beside Hanan. "Here, take these," he said, shoving the bow and two quivers filled with arrows toward his brother. "What has happened?"

"The man on the horse is directly below us, in the trees and rocks. Four of the soldiers are hiding behind those rocks to the right," he said, pointing down the hillside. "I don't know where the other two men are. I haven't seen them since they started up into the rocks and trees on the left. What do we do now?"

Caleb shook his head. "I don't know, Hanan. I guess we wait."

"Wait for what?"

Caleb shrugged. "For them to attack?" It was a question not a statement.

* * *

Adad looked up the hillside at the cave's entrance then weaved his horse around rocks and trees to where the four soldiers had taken cover behind rocks. "I saw only one person—a boy, I think," he shouted from astride his horse. "Spread out, and be prepared to rush the cave."

The four soldiers exchanged nervous glances. One of them pointed toward the cave and said, "Beyond here there's no cover. If he has a bow, we'll be easy targets. What of our archers? Where are they?"

"They're working their way through the trees on our right flank. Once they see us begin our assault, they'll race in from their position. Now get ready. On my command, we charge."

* * *

Except for the snap of a dry twig, Uzzi could have dispatched the second archer as easily as the first. The man was resting against a large cedar tree, panting heavily from the strain of climbing the steep hillside.

When Uzzi was still forty feet away, he eased his foot over a decaying log and stepped on an unseen branch, snapping it in two. In the quiet of the tree-covered hillside, the snap echoed like thunder.

In one swift movement the soldier spun around, launched an arrow, and ducked behind the tree. The shot was poorly aimed, and the arrow glanced off a rock beside Uzzi, landing harmlessly in the dirt.

At the same instant the soldier shot, Uzzi released his arrow, but the soldier's quick movement saved him. Rather than strike in the chest, where Uzzi had aimed, the arrow pierced the soldier's left bicep, lodging in the bone as he ducked behind the tree. Seeing his botched shot, Uzzi yanked another arrow from his quiver and notched it in his bow.

As Uzzi sidestepped his way toward the tree, he watched the soldier grasp the shaft and gingerly give it a slight tug. The arrow didn't move; it was lodged too deeply in the bone. His left arm useless, the man dropped his bow and pulled his long Damascus sword from its scabbard. Lurching from behind the tree, he took only two steps before Uzzi's second arrow struck him solidly in the chest, dropping the soldier to his knees.

Uzzi looked on in horror as the man struggled to his feet—first one leg and then the other—and charged, yelling as he came. Uzzi drew another arrow from his quiver and let it fly. The impact of the arrow in the man's chest stopped him in his tracks. He swayed slightly and fell onto his back, staring blankly at the blue sky.

Uncertain what to expect, Uzzi notched another arrow on the bowstring and took aim at the dying man. Walking forward, Uzzi kicked the sword from the man's hand and watched as blood dripped from the corner of his mouth. The archer stared at Uzzi through pain-filled eyes.

Uzzi backed away as his stomach suddenly grew queasy. In less than an hour, he had killed two men, and now a third was about to die. Killing an animal for food was one thing, but as Uzzi watched the man's labored breathing, the finality of taking another human life sank deep in his soul. Then, in the only way he could justify his actions, he said to the dying man, "You should never have tried to hurt my family, and I wouldn't have come after you." Lowering his aim and relaxing the tension on the bowstring, Uzzi turned around and began working his way up the hillside.

* * *

Hanan stared down at the rocks on the far side of the clearing and asked nervously, "Caleb, do you think they'll attack us slowly or rush up the hillside?"

Caleb swiveled his head around. The expression on Hanan's face was one of pure panic. In a false sense of calmness, Caleb replied, "If it was me, I would creep up the hillside."

"Why?" Hanan asked nervously.

"I don't know." Caleb shrugged. "That's just what I'd do."

Scanning the hillside below him, Hanan shook his head. "Not me; I'd charge up all at once."

Caleb was about to ask why when he saw a lone figure step out from the trees, far to their left. Shaking Hanan's arm, he said, "It's Uzzi."

"Where?" Hanan asked, raising himself on his elbows.

"Over there, to our left," Caleb said and immediately followed it forcefully with, "Keep down."

Standing to the side of a tree that shielded him from the view of Adad and the remaining soldiers, Uzzi raised both hands high above his head twice in rapid succession, paused, and then did it again.

"Why's he doing that?" Hanan asked in total confusion.

"I don't know," Caleb said equally perplexed.

"Do you think he—"

"I've got it," Caleb interrupted. "He's telling us he's taken care of the two soldiers that we couldn't see."

Hanan raised his eyebrows. "You think so?"

"That must be it. Why else would he be standing out there like that?"

* * *

At that precise moment, Adad spurred his horse in the ribs and shouted, "Charge them!"

In a military sense, it wasn't much of a charge. At the unexpected gouge of the spurs, the horse reared upward rather than forward. Although he clamped his legs around the horse's ribcage, Adad couldn't maintain his seat and tumbled backwards. Doing a complete somersault, he landed on his back, the jolt knocking the air completely out of his lungs. He lay on the ground, thrashing about trying to breathe.

Seeing their leader thrown to the ground, the four foot soldiers came to a stop only two steps into the charge and stood with their swords at their sides. They stared at their unhorsed leader in bewilderment.

"Get my horse!" Adad coughed out as he struggled to his knees. But by the time he gave the command, the horse was running at a full gallop through the rocks and trees like a deer bounding through a forest. All five men watched the black horse dart and weave until it disappeared from sight.

Disgusted at the turn of events, Adad shouted angrily, "Charge them, you fools!"

The first few strides the soldiers made were quick and intensive, but the steep slope and the long march earlier in the day took their toll. The running quickly turned to fast walking followed almost immediately by strained plodding. Advancing as slowly as they were, with no bowmen to provide cover, the five men were easy targets.

* * *

Uzzi shouted with glee as Adad fell from his horse. Instantly slipping back into the protective cover of the rocks and trees, he began running.

If he could get within bowshot of the five soldiers and yet remain in the trees, they would be trapped in the clearing between himself and Hanan and Caleb. It would be five hardened soldiers against three inexperienced youth, but he and his brothers would have the advantage of cover. With legs racing and heart pounding, Uzzi raced through the maze of boulders and trees, oblivious to the tree branches slapping him in the face as well as to the rocks and stones that gouged his sandal-clad feet.

Stopping behind a large rock, Uzzi slid to the ground and leaned against the sun-warmed boulder. He was in the perfect position to end this nightmare in the next few minutes. Taking several deep breaths, he wiped sweat from his brow with the palm of his hand and then wiped his palm on the front of his dirty, bloodstained robe. The sight of his father's blood unleashed a firestorm of sorrow, anger, frustration, fear, and hope, colliding in an unyielding battle. Reaching over his shoulder, Uzzi withdrew an arrow from the quiver and notched it solidly on the bowstring. Rising cautiously he peered over the top of the rock. "A few more steps," he mumbled to himself. "Wait until they're a little closer to Hanan and Caleb." He wanted them trapped at an equal distance between any cover.

Standing behind the rock, Uzzi took careful aim at the back of the soldier nearest to him. The arrow had barely cleared the bow before Uzzi dropped behind the rock, reaching once more into his quiver. He didn't need to see to know the arrow had found its mark. The loud scream of pain followed by shouting and yelling told him another man was dead. Confusion was setting in.

Drawing the bow to its fullest, Uzzi rose from behind the rock and instantly picked his next target. This one, facing directly toward him, died with a look of complete confusion on his face as the arrow ripped through his leather tunic just above his breastplate. As he watched the man sink to his knees, Uzzi pulled another arrow from his quiver and picked his next target: the man who had been astride the horse.

* * *

Hanan rose to his feet and slipped an arrow on his bowstring as Uzzi's second arrow found its mark. Looking down, he watched as the soldiers suddenly abandoned their charge and searched for cover. Drawing the bow as much as he could, Hanan aimed at one of the soldiers, closed his eyes, and released the bowstring. The arrow sailed through the air in a glorious arc, flying high above the heads of the confused soldiers and landing almost at Uzzi's feet. As the arrow flew harmlessly overhead, the three soldiers trapped in the clearing immediately knew which way offered their best chance of survival. With fear and adrenaline charging their legs, they rushed up the hill.

Putting another arrow in his bow, Uzzi raced from behind the rock and into the clearing. The men were moving beyond the effective range of his bow, and he had to close the gap.

Slowing to a walk, Uzzi drew the bow, fired, and watched as the arrow fell a dozen feet behind the nearest man. Pulling another arrow from the quiver, he notched it on the bowstring while he ran forward. Knowing he needed accuracy, he stopped, sucked in a deep breath, and took careful aim. The arrow's razor-sharp point sliced through the thick leather tunic of the nearest fleeing soldier and lodged itself deep between the man's shoulder blades. The soldier dropped to the ground, futilely pawing at the arrow in his back before he stopped moving. Only two left, Uzzi thought to himself as he again set an arrow on his bowstring. Inhaling, exhaling, then inhaling once more, Uzzi held his breath and drew his bow to its maximum pull. But just then, Adad unexpectedly turned to face him.

* * *

Caleb watched Hanan's poorly aimed arrow land harmlessly in the dirt. "Lower your aim," he said as Hanan pulled another arrow from the quiver.

Hanan didn't acknowledge the comment. He was fighting to control his trembling hands so he could notch an arrow on the bowstring. With the arrow in place, he rose to his feet, pulled back on the string, and froze. "Caleb, look!" he screamed as he accidently released the arrow, which whistled through the air and struck the dirt only twenty feet in front of him.

Caleb scrambled to his feet and stared down the hillside. Adad and the remaining soldier had climbed most of the way across the open ground. In a desperate attempt to get within bowshot, Uzzi had raced after them and was standing unprotected in the middle of the clearing with his bow drawn. Beyond Uzzi, half a dozen soldiers with bows and a dozen more brandishing swords were emerging from the trees and bolting up the hillside. Far beyond, beside the shed where Gideon's body lay, stood a man in a chariot.

Hanan and Caleb stood, mouths agape and their hands hanging limply at their sides. They watched in total helplessness as the first of three soldiers let fly with an arrow. The arrow slammed into Uzzi's upper leg, knocking him off balance and spinning him to face his attackers. The second arrow sliced into the muscle and tissue of Uzzi's left shoulder, but only after the boy had instinctively released his own arrow. As the third archer released his arrow into the hot afternoon air, Uzzi's own arrow was on its mission of death. The two arrived at their intended targets at exactly the same moment. Uzzi's arrow entered the third archer's open mouth, tore through his throat, and lodged in his spine. As the soldier helplessly pawed at the arrow in his throat, Uzzi rocked sideways with the momentum of an arrow that had buried itself in his left side just below his ribcage. Uzzi dropped to the ground in a lifeless heap.

"Hurry, Hanan, into the cave!" Caleb screamed, but the fourteen-year-old boy stood transfixed, looking at the motionless, arrow-riddled body of his older brother. "Now!" Caleb grabbed the sleeve on Hanan's robe and pulled his brother down the slight decline of the tunnel toward the cave's main chamber.

Without a lamp to light their way, the two boys stumbled in the darkness of the long shaft. They felt their way along the tunnel's damp walls until the dim light of the still-burning fire came into view. "Praise Jehovah the fire is still burning," Caleb said, trotting toward the main chamber with Hanan close behind.

Slowing only enough to snatch a stick of burning wood from the fire, Caleb hurried to the back of the cave where the small stream of water disappeared into a small opening less than a foot tall and eighteen inches wide. "Come, Hanan, we must escape this way," Caleb said.

Hanan stood by the fire shaking his head. "No, Caleb, I'm not going that way. I'm going out through the roof, out to where Samara is."

Caleb's eyes widened in disbelief. "Are you crazy? You'll never make it up the steps let alone through the split before the soldiers get here."

Hanan shook his head. "I have plenty of time," he replied with a shaky voice. "They'll never come in here without a torch, and by the time they get one, I'll be gone."

"Please, Hanan, you won't have time. Come with me."

"No, I'm going to where Samara is."

Caleb let out a sigh and shook his head in dismay. Then on impulse, Caleb ran back to where Hanan was standing and hugged him tightly. "Jehovah be with you."

"And with you as well," Hanan replied.

"I'll hide out in the caves for two days, and then I'll meet you back at the house," Caleb said and then added, "Tell Mother and Gili that I love them."

Hanan nodded his head, and the two brothers wrapped their arms around each other in a final quick embrace.

Without saying another word, Caleb trotted back to the stream. Lying on his back in the cold, trickling water, he inched into the small opening. Looking back at Hanan one last time, he listened to the brief hiss of the small flame as he doused the stick in the water and began pushing with his heels and wriggling his body into the total darkness of the opening.

Chapter Twenty-Six

With a deep breath, Miriam filled her lungs with air then slowly let it escape through her nose. She closed her eyes and turned her face upward, letting the sunshine flood her skin with warmth and light. "I'm so glad to be free of that narrow passage," she said as she pulled Samara up the last couple feet of the shaft.

"It feels wonderful," Samara agreed as she brushed her long hair from her face with her scraped and bleeding fingers.

Miriam knelt beside the narrow shaft and called down, "Gili, are you okay?"

"Yes, Mother, I'm fine," the soft voice purred out.

"I'm going to lie on my stomach, and Samara is going to hold my legs and lower me down. You need to reach as high as you can and grasp my hands. Do you understand?"

There was no response.

"Gili, do you understand what I said?"

There was another longer pause and then, "Mother," Gili said with alarm in her voice, "I've forgotten my stone."

Miriam's mind raced, but she didn't understand. "What stone?"

"The pretty one, the stone Prophet gave me."

Miriam's eyes suddenly widened as a wave of anxiety swept over her. Before Miriam could say anything, the small voice at the bottom of the shaft said, "I must go back for it."

"No!" Miriam screamed in panic. "You must not."

"I left it beside my sheepskin pillow in the cave."

Miriam pushed herself forward and leaned over the edge of the shaft, her head and arms dangling in the air below her. "Gili, you must not go back. Reach up and grab my hands, NOW!"

"Mother, I can't leave my stone here. I must go get it."

"Gili, I'll get you another stone, but please, please take my hand," she begged. "Please!"

"Mother, it will be all right," the girl said, sounding as if she were an adult. "I'll take the lamp, hurry down, and get my stone. I know exactly where I left it. I'll be back in just a minute."

"GILI!" Miriam screamed. "Don't go!" She shoved herself forward in a desperate attempt to grab her daughter.

It was only Samara's quick action that stopped Miriam from plummeting headfirst down the shaft. At the same instant Miriam grabbed for Gili, Samara lunged forward and grasped Miriam's ankles. With her sandals skidding in the loose gravel and sand, Samara fought to stop Miriam's headlong plunge. Slowly, she tugged and pulled a sobbing Miriam from the shaft.

"Let me go," Miriam demanded, twisting around. "I must go down there."

Samara grabbed Miriam around the shoulders and held her tightly. "How?" she asked. "Even if you could lower yourself back down the shaft, Gili will have the only lamp, if it's even still burning. You'd be in total darkness."

"I can feel my way along the split in the rocks until I get to the steps," Miriam fired back through her tears. "I don't need a lamp."

It was folly, and both women knew it. Inching through the narrow split without a light had been terrifying enough, but it would be impossible to get down steps without one.

"Just wait here," Samara said soothingly. "Gili will be able to find her way. She'll be back in a couple minutes."

* * *

Gili inched her way back through the narrow split and let out a quiet sigh when she saw the lamp's small flickering flame. She picked up the lamp, eased onto the uppermost step, and took a quick breath. "I can do this," she said softly.

Holding the lamp in front of her, she lowered herself down the first uneven step and then the next, descending into the blackness below. Halfway down, she froze. Coming up the steps was the small flame of an oil lamp. "Who is that?"

"Gili?" came the almost instant reply. "Is that you?"

"Hanan!" she exclaimed in delight and scampered down the steps that separated them.

"What are you doing here?" Hanan asked with worry.

"I came back to get the stone Prophet gave me."

"There isn't time; the soldiers are coming."

"Hanan, I must get it," she said as she brushed by him on the narrow steps.

"Gili, you don't understand," he called after her. "I've heard their voices. They're going to be here any minute."

Hanan watched the little light from the lamp as his sister descended the remaining steps. The flame was so pitifully small he could see nothing more of Gili than her hand. The delicate yellow light seemed to float like a butterfly in the black cavern.

"Hurry, Gili," Hanan called out urgently.

"I can't find it," Gili said in frustration and anxiety. "It's so dark I can't even find my pillow."

The lapse of silence was shattered by the muffled voices of men.

"Gili, the soldiers are in the tunnel. You must come back now! Forget the stone."

"Just a minute," she pled.

"No, Gili, now!"

"I found it!" Gili exclaimed from the darkness. "I'm coming."

But so were the soldiers. Hanan watched in panic as a faint light from the tunnel began growing brighter. In seconds the soldiers would be turning the corner. "Run, Gili! Run!" he hissed.

Just as Gili leaped on the first step, the golden yellow light of a burning torch spilled into the main cavern. "Be cautious," a deep voice warned.

"Douse your flame so they can't see it," Hanan whispered quietly to Gili as she stepped up beside him. Pushing her ahead of him, he instructed, "Go as quietly as you can up the steps."

"But I can't see," she whispered so softly that Hanan could barely distinguish what she was saying.

"Use your hands. You must feel your way along."

How far ahead of him Gili was, he couldn't be certain, but Hanan had only managed to move up a few steps before another torch entered the room, doubling the amount of light. With the added light of a second torch, Hanan strained to see Gili, but it was simply too dark. Looking down, he could tell he still had more than half the distance to go before he reached the top of the steps. "The split, that's all we need. Then we'll be safe," Hanan whispered as he eased forward.

"Well, well," a disembodied voice said. "What is all this?"

Even with the distance and in the poor light, Hanan recognized the speaker as the horseless leader and immediately crouched down so that he was nearly lying on the steps. As he did, the toe of his sandal caught on a small rock and sent it bouncing down the steps below him.

The soldiers' reaction was instinctive and instantaneous. Bowmen pulled back on their bows, pointing arrows in the general direction of the sound, ready to let fly at the slightest provocation.

"The torch," the leader shouted. "Take the torch to the back of the cave." The two soldiers bearing the torches hesitantly inched their way toward Hanan.

In the light of the torches, Hanan's black and white tunic fairly glowed, and a dozen arrows, swords and spears instantly pointed at his cowering body.

"If you value your life, you will not move quickly," the leader's voice warned ominously.

Not only did Hanan not move quickly, he did not move at all.

"Very slowly sit upright, and place your hands on top of your head."

Hanan swallowed hard and did exactly as he was told. "Now I want you to very carefully come down here. Do not make any sudden movements, or you will die."

Hanan eased himself down from the steps and cautiously walked to where the man stood. In the light of the torch, the leader looked carefully at Hanan and sneered. "I recognize you. You're the one who can't shoot an arrow." Hanan looked at the man and said nothing. "There were two of you. Where's the other one?" the man demanded.

Hanan swallowed hard and tried to steady his shaking hands. Squaring his shoulders he said, "I'm the only one here. There weren't two."

In the poor light, Hanan never knew what hit him. The man's fist hit the boy's jaw hard enough to dislocate it and send the boy crashing to the ground. In a slow, even voice, the man said, "I asked you where the other person is," and then he added menacingly, "and I won't ask again."

"I'm here!" Gili shouted from the protection of the split in the rock. "I'm right here, and I'll come down."

"No, Gili," Hanan shouted. "You should—"

He couldn't finish the sentence. The leader kicked him so violently in the ribs that it knocked the air from his lungs. Hanan wrapped his arms around his stomach and writhed in pain.

"I can't see. I need more light!" Gili shouted.

The leader waved his hand at one of the soldiers carrying a torch, who walked partway up the steps. As Gili reached the floor, she pushed her way through the group of soldiers and dropped down on the ground beside Hanan.

The leader looked down at Gili and said incredulously, "You're only a young maiden." Then turning to the soldiers, he commanded, "Get them out of here."

Gili leaned over to help Hanan to his feet and was grabbed on the shoulder by a soldier. "Let go of me," she yelled and pulled away from the man. Squatting down she grasped Hanan's arm and did her best to support him as he rose to his feet.

"Walk," the leader commanded, shoving Hanan in the back and causing the boy to stumble forward.

"Please stop that!" Gili shouted. "Can't you see my brother's hurt?"

"Walk, both of you, or he'll be hurting worse than he is right now."

With the torchbearers leading the way, the group slowly walked from the main cavern and up the tunnel leading to the outside world. "My side hurts, and I can't breathe," Hanan struggled to tell Gili through his dislocated jaw. "I think I may have a broken rib."

"Silence, Hebrew," a soldier spit out as he prodded Hanan with the point of his sword. "Walk in silence!"

Stepping into the sunlight, Hanan painfully raised his hand to shield his eyes from the intense brightness. He surveyed the scene below, and a look of confusion spread over his face. There were dead soldiers lying in the clearing—the result of Uzzi's attack—but where was Uzzi? His body was no longer lying where he had fallen only minutes before. Leaning over slightly, Hanan whispered to Gili, "I think Uzzi might still be alive."

Gili looked at him perplexed and asked, "Was he dead?

For some reason, Hanan found humor in the remark and smiled. "I thought so but not anymore."

"What happened to him?"

Hanan didn't have a chance to reply. Pointing to two soldiers with bows, the leader said, "You two come with me. The rest of you take this

Israelite down to the other captives." Walking up beside Gili, he grabbed her by the shoulder. "You're coming with me."

Twisting from the leader's grip, Gili shouted, "I'm going with my brother! He's hurt, and he needs me."

The leader lunged forward, grabbed a handful of Gili's hair, and yanked her forcefully to his side. "You're coming with me," he repeated angrily and started walking rapidly down the hillside toward the man in the chariot.

"Hanan!" Gili screamed as she stumbled along, fighting against the hand that yanked her hair.

Hanan leaped forward to wrest Gili from the man's grip but was knocked to the ground in midstride by the violent thrust of a soldier. Looking down at Hanan's prostrate body, the soldier said, "Get up!" in a sinister voice. "And if you do it very slowly, you may live to make it to the other captives."

Hanan lay on the ground clutching his already battered side and watched as Gili was led away, struggling against the unrelenting pulling of her hair. Spitting dirt from his mouth, he slowly rose to his hands and knees. He was about to push himself to his feet when an awkward flash of movement in the rocks far below caught his eye. Half crawling and half dragging himself to the protective cover of a large rock was Uzzi, bow over his shoulder and quiver of arrows on his back. Hanan smiled to himself. If the man dragging Gili stayed on his same course, he would pass within Uzzi's easy bowshot.

"Get up now!" the soldier said, grabbing Hanan by his hair and pulling the boy to his feet. Hanan only smiled as he rose, and with a look of defiance, he spit in the man's face. It was Hanan's last act on this earth. The soldier's shock was instantly replaced with anger, and in a lightning-fast movement, he ran the Damascus steel blade of his sword into Hanan's body, thrashing it back and forth before he slowly pulled it out. Hanan dropped to the ground with his head facing down the hill. As his eyes slowly closed for their last time, a faint smile formed on his blood- and dirt-caked lips as he watched Uzzi place an arrow on his bowstring.

* * *

Two soldiers with bows walked ahead of the leader in single file, one trailing slightly behind the other. Being led by the hair, it was impossible for Gili's short legs to keep pace with the men, and she repeatedly fell to her knees, only to be viciously yanked to her feet again.

As the little group left the clearing and entered the tree-strewn hillside, the leader paused briefly. He had been pulling Gili behind him, but now as they entered the convoluted trail through the rocks, he yanked her forcefully in front of him. Letting go of her hair, he reached out and grabbed her robe at the nape of her neck. "Walk," he said roughly as he shoved her forward.

Uzzi watched the first arrow speed silently through the air and enter the leader's body with devastating velocity at the base of his skull. The force of the impact knocked him forward, and he fell on top of Gili without making a sound. The second arrow slammed into the back of the rearmost bowman, and his scream of pain caused the lead bowman to spin around in time to catch an arrow in his chest. In less than ten seconds, three men lay dead.

* * *

Gili could see streaks of blood on the boulder when Uzzi's legs sagged and he slowly sank to the ground. He sat unnaturally, one leg stretched in front of him the other curled back awkwardly, an arrow protruding from his hamstring. His left arm hung limply at his side, blood saturating his filthy tunic as it seeped from his wounded shoulder. His right arm lay across his stomach, his hand loosely wrapped around the arrow embedded in his side. The barely imperceptible rise and fall of his chest was obliterated when damaged nerves suddenly wracked his body with a spasm, held his muscles taunt for a brief second, then relaxed their grip. Slowly, Uzzi's arrow-riddled body slumped to the dirt.

Gili screamed as she fought to free herself from the body that had fallen on her. Kicking free, she struggled to her feet and ran to where Uzzi lay.

Dropping to her knees, Gili reached out, lifted Uzzi's head, and brushed dirt from his cheek. "Uzzi?"

As Gili held Uzzi's head, a gloved hand reached over her shoulder and forced Uzzi's left eyelid open. A fraction of a second later, a deep male voice said, "He's dead."

Chapter Twenty-Seven

"Something's happened," Miriam said in an emotion-choked voice as she nervously tucked loose strands of dirty, sweat-saturated hair behind each ear. "I just know it has."

"Everything is fine," Samara replied, but the words were hollow and without conviction.

Miriam fired an intense gaze at Samara. "Everything is not fine! My sons and daughter are not here with me. Something's happened."

Samara cowered, shocked at the intensity in Miriam's reply. "You're right, everything is not fine." And after a long pause, she added forcefully, "I don't know if my father and mother are dead or alive; I watched my younger brother get bludgeoned to death; my older sister, my brother-in-law, and my young nieces and nephews were herded like animals down a street, and I don't know what's become of them; and I know nothing of Hanan. So you're right, everything is not fine."

The intensity drained from Miriam's face as she listened to Samara, and suddenly she felt very ashamed. Rising to her feet, she quietly walked over to where Samara was leaning against a rock and hugged the girl tightly. "I am so sorry. Please forgive my selfishness. I've been so caught up with my own troubles I didn't stop to think about you."

Samara gave an understanding smile but said nothing; she let her head drop against Miriam's shoulder and began sobbing uncontrollably. Miriam reached up, gently wiping the tears from the girl's cheek and smoothing Samara's matted and tangled hair. Over and over, Miriam repeated the motion while quietly cooing words of comfort.

As the tears slowed and then stopped, Samara lifted her head and wiped her dripping nose with the sleeve of her once-white robe. "Thank you, Miriam," she said. Her gaze fell on the large wet spot her tears had made on Miriam's robe. Then with a slight chuckle, she said, "I think your shoulder's wet."

For some unknown reason, the remark sparked a sense of relief, and Miriam gave a warm smile and pulled at the sides of her robe. "I wanted to wash this old rag today, but I just haven't had a chance." Both women smiled and instinctively reached out to give each other a gentle hug.

"What do you think we should do?" Samara asked with slightly renewed confidence.

Miriam let out a deep sigh. "I don't know."

"Do you think Gili, Hanan, and Caleb were captured?"

"I don't know," Miriam said shaking her head. "But something has gone wrong or they would have returned long before now."

Looking down at the shaft in the ground, Samara asked, "Do you think there's any possibility the soldiers could find their way up here?"

A startled look spread across Miriam's face. "I don't know. I hadn't thought about that." She too looked over at the narrow opening in the ground. Then almost on impulse, she walked over to the rope that was hanging down the shaft and pulled it up. Looking over at Samara, she wiped her hands back and forth against each other and said, "There. If they do manage to find their way, there isn't any way they can get up."

"But what if Hanan and the others come?" Samara asked.

Looking up at the sun in the sky, she said with resignation, "It's getting late, and it'll be getting dark soon. Would you be agreeable to staying here tonight? If they are able to make their way to the shaft, they would certainly call out, and we can drop the rope to them."

"Yes, we can do that, but can we find the little stream and get a drink? I'm very thirsty."

The stream was, in reality, little more than a tiny trickle of water, but they each found a place where the water had pooled, allowing them a few swallows of clean water. As the sun slipped behind the towering edges of the ravine, the scorching heat of the day released its grip, and the cool evening air brought a sense of relaxation to the two women. They sat with their backs against a flat rock, idly letting the fine gray dirt trickle between their fingers. As dusk turned to night, a thousand stars peppered the black sky, and the air turned uncomfortably cold. "Snuggle up next to me," Miriam said as she wrapped her arm around Samara's shoulder. "Maybe by being close, we'll at least have a little warmth."

After some time in the darkness, Miriam felt Samara's body relax as sleep overtook her. Miriam closed her own eyes, not in sleep but in prayer. "Please, God," she begged, "keep my children safe." And then later, much later, after quiet tears had been shed for Gideon, sleep blissfully came to Miriam.

* * *

It was the warmth of the sun on her face that first caused Samara to stir. Slowly her eyes opened. The fog lifted from her brain, and she remembered where she was. It was then that she sat up with a start and looked around her. She was alone. "Miriam," she shouted. "Miriam, where are you?" Jumping to her feet, she ran to the shaft and saw the rope was again hanging down inside.

"Samara," she heard a voice call from below, "I'm down here, but I'm coming up."

Samara watched as Miriam slowly inched her way up the rope. "I didn't know where you were!" Samara exclaimed in a panicked voice.

"You were right. It is too dark and difficult to see without a lamp. I think I managed to find my way to where the split opens into the main cavern, but it's too dark so I came back."

Samara let out a deep sigh of relief but said nothing as her heart returned to a normal pace.

"I had to try, Samara. I couldn't leave here without at least trying to find out if my children were still there."

Samara nodded her head. "I understand. But what do we do now?"

"We go."

"Where?"

"Up the ravine, just as Caleb instructed us. We'll do exactly as he said until we find our way home."

Chapter Twenty-Eight

The total darkness was thick and black as Caleb pushed, wiggled, and inched forward on his back. The icy water in the streambed had saturated his robe, and as he'd pushed frantically, grains of sand and bits of volcanic cinders had worked their way over the collar of his robe and down his back, scratching and tearing at the flesh on his shoulders and backbone. He had no idea how much of the confining tunnel he'd crawled through, but after three minutes he was exhausted and stopped to rest.

The back of his head was cold and wet, and he raised it only to slam his forehead into the sharp rock two inches above the tip of his nose. He dropped his head back into the water and instinctively tried to extend first his right arm and then his left to rub the hurt on his forehead, but he couldn't. His underground escape route was narrow, and his arms could only move a few inches before hitting solid rock on either side.

In spite of the cold water, Caleb's palms were sweating and his heart racing. Panic clawed at his throat, and he opened his eyes wide, blinking repeatedly in a desperate attempt to see something, but there was nothing but blackness—total, complete, impenetrable blackness. Fear swept over him, and forgetting the cold of the water and constricting confines, he closed his eyes and frantically thrashed so rapidly his head and shoulders were well into a large cavern before he realized it. Only then did he open his eyes to see the narrow shaft of sunlight almost directly above his head.

The thin beam of sunlight streaming down through the roof of the cavern forced the fingers of panic to relax their tenacious grip. Still lying in the streambed, Caleb reached up with both hands to rub his forehead and eyes. Then slowly, he rolled out of the streambed and onto the cold dirt floor of the cave. Rising to his knees, he took a deep breath. Except for the thin shaft of sunlight, the monstrously huge cave was dark, but he didn't mind. He'd been in this cave many times and knew exactly where he was. Better yet, he knew exactly how to get out.

He carefully rose to his feet and slid first one foot and then the other forward until he felt the cold water of the stream trickling over his feet. With his arms fully extended in front of him, Caleb began shuffling forward, keeping one foot in the water so he didn't become disoriented, until he felt a hard stone wall. Turning to his left, he inched his way forward, his right hand on the wall of the cave and his left hand stretched out in front of him. Shortly he would feel the cave's wall make a sharp turn to the right. When it did, he would be in another tunnel that would take him to daylight.

It was then Caleb heard the first muffled sound of men's voices. Freezing in midstride, he felt his heartbeat quicken as the talking grew louder and more distinct. Turning around he retraced his steps along the cave's wall until he stepped into the stream. His first thought was to slosh up the stream and hide in the small tunnel from which he had just escaped. But the volume of the voices told him he'd never make it. Not knowing what else to do, he lay facedown in the stream.

Only a moment later, the blackness of the cave was pierced by the yellow glow of a burning torch.

"How many of these disgusting black holes in the rock have we searched?" a deep voice bellowed.

"Too many," the second man said. Holding out the torch to the first man, he said, "And it's your turn to walk around while I wait here."

"It's not my turn," the first man complained. "It's yours. Besides, my legs are too tired.

"Mine are as well, but it's still your turn."

"I've a better idea," the first man said with a faint smile on his face. "We've searched a dozen of these caves and found no one. Why don't we take a short nap—an hour, no more."

There was silence as the man holding the torch considered the suggestion.

Sensing a glimmer of willingness in his comrade's hesitancy, the first man added, "No one will know. Besides, we've been searching these caves all afternoon. We deserve a rest."

Shifting his weight back and forth, the second man finally gave in. "You're right, but not here. If our torch burns out, we'd be trapped. Let's go nearer the entrance."

"Agreed," the first man said. "Now let's get out of this place."

"Aren't we going to search the cave?"

"What for?" came the confident reply. "There's nobody here. Let's go back and sleep."

Caleb slowly raised his head and watched as the glow of the torch dimmed and then disappeared. Rising from the stream, a shiver coursed through him as the water from his now-drenched robe dripped off him. Stepping from the stream, he again inched his way along the wall of the cave for a few feet. Then, bracing his back against the wall, he slowly sank to the ground and waited.

As he sat in the darkness of the cave, he couldn't stop his mind from replaying the horror of the last few hours. The vision of his father and Uzzi lying on the ground haunted him. Tears formed in his eyes and streamed down his cheeks. He leaned his head back against the wall and cried, the muffled sound of his sobs echoing against the unseen walls of the cave. As the dark gloominess of despair reached the same blackness as the cave, Caleb thought of his mother, Gili, Hanan, and Samara, and a small ray of hope flickered in his mind. Surely they had all made it out and were now hiding safely, waiting for him to join them. The thought gave him a brief shot of courage, and he wiped his tears.

Uncertain how much time had passed, Caleb rose to his feet and began feeling his way along the wall until he came to what he was sure was the sharp right turn into the tunnel that would lead him into the light. He strained to remember the distance from where he stood to the entrance of the cave. What of the soldiers? he thought. Were they still asleep or had they moved on?

Caleb's ears answered the question long before his eyes. Stepping as silently as he could, he worked his way noiselessly forward until the unmistakable sounds of snoring reverberated through the tunnel and stopped him. Dropping to his knees, he inched his way around a bend in the tunnel and stopped. Far down the tunnel, he could see the small, flickering flame of a torch that had been propped up with rocks and was about to burn itself out. A hundred feet beyond that, soft rays of yellow sunlight filtered into the darkness and revealed the entrance of the tunnel. Dropping to his stomach, Caleb propped himself up on his elbows and waited.

As the flame on the torch flickered its last, one of the soldiers jerked with a start. Running his hand through his beard and opening and closing his mouth to dispel the unpleasant flavor, the man licked his lips and kicked his sleeping companion in the foot. "Wake up!"

The second man awoke with a start and instinctively reached for his sword. "What's the matter?" he said, his mind whirling at being startled from a deep sleep.

"We must go."

Letting out a deep sigh, the second man removed his hand from the hilt of his sword and rubbed his eyes. "All right." He struggled to his feet and stretched his aching muscles.

"Take the torch."

"Why? It's burned out."

"So we can show the others that we searched until our torch burned out," he said with a chuckle.

The man picked up the torch, and without another word, both men stumbled along the tunnel and out of the cave.

Waiting long enough to ensure they were gone, Caleb rose to his feet and, hugging the wall tightly, walked cautiously forward until he was several feet from the entrance. Then lowering to his stomach, he silently pulled himself over the rocks and peered outside.

Smoke filled the sky and filtered the late-afternoon sun. Although there was little movement that he could actually see, faint shouts and screams from the village floated to his ears and gave a sense of commotion. A few hundred feet to his left, Caleb could see the entrance to the cave where only a few hours earlier he and Hanan had made their less-than-valiant stand against the soldiers. He slowly shook his head as he considered how little they had done to stop the advance of only a few men. And then he saw it, the black-and-white tunic and the body it encased lying in a crumpled heap on the ground.

In dismay, Caleb's mouth dropped open, and he inched closer, as if a few more inches would somehow change the image. There was no mistaking it: Hanan's body lay still and lifeless. Caleb was partway to his feet when movement far down the hill drove him to the ground again. He watched as a soldier rose and stepped back away from another body. Sinking down lower, Caleb blinked several times. Still kneeling beside the second body was Gili. He watched as two other soldiers, spears in hand, trotted up beside the man and offered a salute. A few words were exchanged, and then the first man—Caleb was sure he was the commander—pointed to Gili and then to the town. One of the soldiers stepped forward, took Gili by the arm, and pulled her away from the body. Although the distance was too great to hear, Caleb could see she was crying. Gili turned and kicked the man in the leg. Breaking free, she ran back and threw her arms around the body. It was then that Caleb recognized Uzzi's robe.

Caleb rose up on his elbows and watched as the commander stepped forward, said a few words to Gili, then reached down and pulled her away from Uzzi's body. Faint screams made their way to Caleb's ears as he watched the commander shove Gili into the viselike grip of the soldier. "No!" Caleb shouted as the soldier began walking away with a kicking, screaming, and twisting Gili in his arms.

"No, no, no," Caleb uttered helplessly as the commander turned and awkwardly limped between boulders and trees, followed by the soldier carrying Gili and the third soldier, who now carried a spear in each hand.

Caleb's head dropped to the dirt, and as a fresh flow of tears began, he pounded his fist angrily in the sand. Nothing he did could save Gili; he was helpless to do anything, and he knew it. Pushing himself to his knees, he raised both hands and yelled, "Gili!" as loudly as he could. Then standing up, he quickly wiped each tear-filled eye with his dirty hands and yelled again, "Gili!" But his screams were lost in the noise of the wind and squeaking wheels of a chariot as the commander whipped his horses and rolled away, the soldier carrying Gili following behind.

Chapter Twenty-Nine

Samara darted from behind the cedar tree, sprinted to a small clump of bushes, and dropped down beside Miriam.

Miriam gave her an approving look. "When we get to the top of this hill, we'll be able to look down on my house," she whispered.

"Then how far is it to the house?"

"Not far, maybe a few hundred yards."

Samara looked around her. It was only a hundred feet to the crest of the hill, and the thick trunks of the cedar trees would provide excellent hiding places the entire distance, something they had not always had over the past several hours. Smiling at Miriam, she said brightly, "This should be easy compared to what we've been through."

Although the house was only a few miles from Edrei, it had taken the women two days to get where they were. The walk out of the ravine had taken a savage toll on their feet, hands, and legs. Bushes thick with thorns and burrs clogged the bottom of the ravine in search of the few drops of rainwater that occasionally formed a stream. The women had no choice but to claw their way over or through it, puncturing and scratching their skin with each step. For a time they had attempted to stay higher on the sides, climbing over rocks as large as houses, but abandoned that effort when they were faced with rocks too big to climb.

The small trickle of water that Caleb had told them was in the bottom of the ravine had long since dried up. The first day the fugitives drank water from a puddle with green slime around the edges. Drinking all they could, they soaked up what was left with their scarves and draped them over their heads to ward off the heat from the sun reflecting off the ravine's stark walls. When the heat and scorching sun became too oppressive, the women sought shade under a small rock overhang, which they shared with spiders and a mound of ants. When the bites from the ants became unbearable, the women abandoned the shade and pushed on until it was too dark to see where they were going.

Two hours after sunrise on the second day, Miriam and Samara worked their way out of the ravine and found themselves on a barren plateau overlooking Edrei. For all their effort, they had only traveled a couple miles. Crouching down so as not to silhouette themselves against the skyline, they crept to the edge of the plateau. Edrei lay in smoldering ruins, deserted, but the road leading from the village was congested with men, women, and children being herded between two columns of soldiers. Leading the group was a man in a chariot.

Miriam's head sank as she looked down on the pitiful mass of people. Although more than a mile away from the captives, Samara studied the backs of each person in hope of seeing the familiar colors of her mother's robe or the ambling gate of her father. But they were simply too far away, and her eyes were too teary to see clearly.

The two women knelt on bleeding knees and watched in silence as individual people merged to form an indistinguishable mass which then descended a hill and disappeared from view. The screech of a red-tailed hawk drew Miriam from a world of thoughts, and she reached out and put her arm around Samara's shoulders. The two women looked at each other and then embraced.

After more long minutes, Miriam said, "I see no reason to go back into that forsaken ravine. No one is here."

"What if they left soldiers behind to capture any stragglers? As hard as it is, I would feel more secure hiding in the ravine," Samara said.

Miriam raised her eyebrows and nodded her head. "I didn't think about that. Perhaps you're right. Let's go back. We'll stay in the ravine through the day, and then as evening comes, we'll find a place to climb out. By then we'll be much closer to home."

The rest of that day was as punishing as the first had been, but with countless cuts and scrapes and with their robes snagged and torn, the ragged pair emerged as the sun began slipping down in the west.

"Wait here, and I'll go to where I can look down on the house," Miriam said. "I'll wave at you if everything is okay, and then you can come up to where I am."

Samara smiled faintly. "Fine. But it'll be dark soon, so we must hurry."

"I'll be quick," Miriam said as she began running toward the crest of the hill and the protection of the cedar trees.

In the early-evening sunlight, Samara watched Miriam as she swiftly walked to a tree and looked intently in every direction. Satisfied everything was safe, the older woman hurried to the next and did the same. Over and over, she zigzagged her way from tree to tree or clump of brush until she was at the crest of the hill. She crouched down behind the charred remains of a massive old cedar that looked as if it had been struck by lightning years ago. Samara watched Miriam peer over the hulking black tree trunk and waited for the signal to join her.

After five minutes, Samara wasn't sure what to do. Miriam had looked to her left and right but hadn't turned back to look at Samara or wave her hand. After another minute, Samara rose to her feet and followed the same trail Miriam had used until she too could look down the hill. But unlike Miriam, she didn't crouch down behind the fallen cedar. There was no need.

One hundred yards below her, Samara could see the fine wisps of smoke rising from smoldering ruins of what had been Miriam's home. Nothing was left. Once-sturdy roof timbers were little more than charred sticks. The block walls had been pushed over or had fallen on their own, and nothing but black and gray ash remained of chairs, beds, and clothing. Beyond the scorched earth of the house lay the black remains of a shed that had been filled with grain and wool—all of it gone, burned in the fire. Only the rocks that formed the walls of the well remained standing, although black smudges streaked the light-colored rock.

Samara lightly placed her hand on Miriam's shoulder. "I'm so sorry."

Miriam looked up, forced a smile, then turned her gaze back to what had once been her home.

"Come, Miriam, it's getting dark, and we cannot stay here," Samara said as she reached down, slipped her hands under Miriam's armpits, and pulled the stunned woman to her feet.

"Is there someplace close by that will provide shelter?" Samara asked. "Or should we find a place under the trees?"

Miriam acted as if she hadn't heard and said only, "I'm thirsty."

Samara gave her a tender smile and said, "We'll go down to the well." Samara gently guided Miriam around the fallen tree, and as the sun slipped behind the western hills, the two slowly descended the hillside.

Chapter Thirty

Caleb sank to his knees and let his head fall to his chest. The tears streamed from his eyes and washed little paths in dirt-stained cheeks before dropping to his filthy robe. From the center of Edrei, the harsh sounds of a trumpet permeated the air and caused fear to grip his heart. With his father and two brothers dead, his sister taken as a slave, and probably his mother captured as well, he didn't care if anyone saw him. He watched in dismay as soldiers emerged from caves, rocks, and the few remaining homes, flocking toward the sound of the trumpet like ants returning to their mound.

"I'm still here!" Caleb shouted defiantly, but none of them looked in his direction.

Lowering himself to the ground, he suddenly felt very alone. He sat back, staring at black pebbles as his emotions raced in a vicious circle between grief, pity, anger, and fear. Drained of tears, he stood up and began walking toward the nearest member of his family: Hanan.

Stepping over rocks and small clumps of brown grass, Caleb made his way to the black-and-white tunic of his brother. Caleb lovingly knelt beside the body, lifting his brother's head and patting his cheek. Then the tears began anew. Wiping his dripping nose on his sleeve, he slowly adjusted legs and arms so that Hanan was lying on his back, legs stretched out and arms folded on his chest. Caleb had no idea why he did it, only that he felt Hanan would somehow be more comfortable. That done, Caleb stood up and walked down the hill to where his father lay.

At the sight of the arrow protruding from his father's body, the grief Caleb felt was washed away with a flood of anger. He suddenly hated the life-depriving arrow and the faceless men who had taken his father from him. Caleb reached down and violently tugged on the shaft. The arrow eventually yielded to the pull, and Caleb snapped it in two over his knee and tossed the pieces as far away as he could.

Kneeling beside his father, Caleb's tears once again welled up. "I don't know what to do, Father," he choked out between sobs. "What do I do now?" he cried as he picked up his father's stiffening hand and held it tightly.

Once more wiping his eyes and nose, Caleb gently arranged his father's legs and arms as he had Hanan's; then he took a deep breath. Looking down he said, "I'll return and bury you properly, Father, but now I must go to Uzzi." Turning, he slowly began trudging up the hill to where the third body lay.

Caleb cautiously wound his way to where Uzzi lay on the ground. Unlike Hanan or Gideon, his body was in a more natural position, and he looked far more peaceful in spite of the three arrows protruding from his body.

Kneeling down, Caleb lifted his brother's shoulders and head, hugging them to his chest and, with genuine affection, choked out, "Thank you, Uzzi, for protecting us. You were always the brave one." Holding Uzzi's head in the crook of one arm, Caleb looked down and lovingly wiped dirt from his older brother's forehead and cheeks. With the tip of his finger, Caleb gently dabbed the tiny teardrops that were nestled in the corners of each of Uzzi's eyes. "Don't cry, big brother. They can't hurt you anymore," he said softly as he rocked back and forth.

Only when cramps began in his legs did Caleb gently lay Uzzi's head and shoulders on the ground. Sitting down beside the still form, Caleb stretched his legs out in front of him and sat in silence for several minutes, looking at the smoke-filled sky. Then as if speaking to Uzzi, Caleb said stoically, "Father is dead; Hanan is dead; Gili has been taken by soldiers; and I don't know what has become of Mother, but she's either dead or taken as a slave." Turning his head to look down at Uzzi's face, he added, "You would know what to do, but—" and he stopped in midsentence. There was another tear in the corner of each of Uzzi's eyes.

Caleb reached beneath his own robe and pulled out a corner of the linen tunic. Finding the cleanest piece of cloth he could, he carefully dabbed the little drops and watched. Slowly, another clear drop of liquid formed in the corner of each eye, and again he wicked up the tears with the edge of the cloth. As yet more tears formed, Caleb excitedly scrambled around and placed his ear on Uzzi's chest and listened. Nothing. The rough wool of Uzzi's tunic tickled Caleb's ear so he withdrew his head, rubbed his ear, and quickly put his head back down. But there was still no beating of a heart.

Looking at Uzzi's closed eyes, where yet another tear had formed, Caleb reached up with his dirty thumb and gently raised an eyelid. He wasn't sure what he would see, but instead of the brilliant green eyes that always sparkled with excitement, there was only white.

Letting the eyelid slide back into place, Caleb carefully undid Uzzi's tunic and took a deep breath. Disregarding Uzzi's blood streaked chest, Caleb lowered his head and placed his ear directly over where he thought Uzzi's heart should be, straining to hear the sound of a beating heart. For a brief second, he thought he heard something, but the longer he listened, the less certain he became.

Caleb leaned back and stared at Uzzi's bare chest. If his heart was beating, surely his chest would be rising and falling as he breathed, but there was nothing. And then he did the only thing he could think to do: he talked. "Uzzi," he said with guarded excitement, "I don't know if you are alive and if you can hear me, but if you can, move your finger."

Dropping to his elbows so his nose was only a few inches from Uzzi's hand, Caleb studied every finger watching for movement. What he was expecting was a finger to wiggle wildly; what he got was an almost imperceptible twitch of a little finger.

"Praise Jehovah!" he shouted at the top of his lungs. "Uzzi's alive!" He jumped to his feet and began leaping in the air. After three leaps he dropped to his knees, clasped Uzzi's face between his hands, and shouted again, "You're alive!" But when Uzzi neither moved nor blinked, the jubilation disintegrated as rapidly as it came, and suddenly Caleb was overwhelmed by the thought of what to do next. He was twelve. He had no skills or training. His mind raced in a thousand different directions and arrived at the same destination—confusion. He didn't know what to do. And then he thought of Gili being torn from Uzzi's side. What would his spiritually inclined young sister do?

Taking Uzzi's limp hand in both of his, he bowed his head and prayed: "Oh, great Jehovah," he began, "I have not the faith of Gili or of the prophet Elisha, but I need help. I have tried to keep the Law and follow the prophets, and I pray that you will look down on me with favor this day. My brother Uzzi is wounded and is almost dead, and I don't know how to help him. Please preserve his life and help me know what to do to take care of him." And then, not knowing what else to say, he simply uttered, "Thanks be to Jehovah."

Caleb knelt somberly in silence, staring at the arrows' smooth wooden shafts. He knew they had to come out, and quickly, but he had no idea how. Seeing the knife hanging from Uzzi's belt, Caleb withdrew it from its sheath and carefully cut away Uzzi's leather tunic and robe. Sitting back, he examined each wound.

Of the three arrows, the one in Uzzi's side was buried the deepest, and Caleb cringed at the thought of pulling it out. The arrow in the shoulder wasn't deep, but Caleb could see it was embedded in muscle. Then he looked at the arrow sticking out of Uzzi's thigh and decided that was where he would begin.

The arrowhead had entered the front of Uzzi's thigh, and as Caleb lifted his brother's leg, he could see the tip of it was already protruding out the back side. Using the knife, Caleb cut off the shaft below the feathers, leaving about six inches protruding. Propping Uzzi's leg off the ground with his own, Caleb placed the flat blade of the knife on top of the stubby shaft and in one quick movement shoved down. The bloody arrowhead popped through the underside of Uzzi's leg. Tossing the shaft aside, Caleb wadded up some of Uzzi's robe and placed it under the freely bleeding hole.

Caleb let out a deep sigh and looked at Uzzi, who hadn't moved or made a sound as the arrow was removed. "Sleep, brother," he said out loud. "Then you won't feel any pain."

Caleb twisted around to face his two remaining opponents. Reaching up he tugged lightly on the arrow buried in Uzzi's shoulder. Solid. Having watched his father and Uzzi remove arrows from deer and grouse, Caleb knew he would do far more damage trying to extract the arrow the same way it went in. As he pondered this, a flood of thoughts streamed into his mind, and he knew what he needed to do.

Jumping to his feet, he ran to the closest fallen soldier and sliced long strips of cloth from the edge of the man's cape. Next, Caleb ran down the trail to the shed where his father had hidden from the approaching soldiers. Taking a bucket, Caleb filled it full of water and hurried back to where Uzzi lay.

"Brother," he said as if Uzzi could hear, "I'm going to wash you up a little." He dipped a strip of cloth in the bucket and began washing the bloody thigh. Satisfied it was as clean as he could make it, at least for now,

Caleb folded two of the strips and placed them on either side of Uzzi's bleeding thigh. Using a third piece, he wrapped Uzzi's leg to hold the other two pieces in place and tied it securely.

With one wound cleaned and bandaged, he ran back to the dead soldier and quickly cut off the remaining cloak, rolling it up as he walked back to Uzzi. Lifting his brother's shoulder, he stuffed the cloak under it so Uzzi was slightly off the ground. Using the knife, Caleb cut the arrow's shaft, leaving it much longer than the first. Holding the arrow firmly in place with his left hand, he picked up a flat-sided rock in his right. After taking careful aim, he swung the rock and hit the end of the arrow. After the second blow, the arrowhead popped through the backside of Uzzi's shoulder, and after the third, enough of the shaft protruded for Caleb to pull it completely out. Tossing the arrow aside, Caleb washed both sides of the wound and stuffed a small corner of a cloth into both wounds to staunch the bleeding.

Without slowing, Caleb rolled Uzzi onto his side, removed the third arrow, and quickly washed and bandaged the wound. Dipping his hands in the little remaining water in the bucket, Caleb washed away the dirt and blood and sank back against a rock, completely exhausted. He closed his eyes, not in sleep but in prayer. "I've done everything I know to do and more," he said quietly. "I need him; please don't let him die."

Chapter Thirty-One

Miriam and Samara sat in the small shed beside the cattle enclosure chewing on kernels of wheat and sipping cow's milk. "I don't know how this escaped the soldiers' torches," Samara said as she looked about the small shed with its stacks of wheat and barley.

"Probably because it was down the hill and out of sight," Miriam replied with a shrug of her shoulders. "They destroyed everything else, so if they had seen it, they would have torched it as well—and killed the cows."

"I'm grateful they didn't find it. At least we have water from the well, milk from the cows, and wheat and barley, even if the grain is full of weevil." Samara lightly blew away the weevil from another handful of wheat before putting it in her mouth. It was the first thing they'd eaten in two days, and in spite of the tiny insects, they voraciously ate.

The sound of rocks sliding down the path behind them made both women exchange alarmed glances and instantly dash across the shed and beneath a pile of flea-infested sheepskins on the floor. With hands pressed to their lips to muffle their shallow breathing, the women closed their eyes and offered silent prayers that whoever entered would somehow overlook the fresh milk in the two earthen cups that sat on the shelf.

The sound of sandaled feet rapidly entering the shed caused both the women to involuntarily suck in a breath of air and hold it. In the semidarkness, Miriam could hear the sound of a stool—the very stool on which she had been sitting only a moment before—being dragged across the hard-packed dirt floor until it stopped only inches from the sheepskin under which she was hiding. At that instant, a small flea dropped from the sheepskin onto her cheek. It worked its way across her upper lip and into her nostril. The sensation of the pest's tiny feet in her nose tickled, and she involuntarily blew a snort of air through her nose in an attempt to dislodge the bug. Alarmed at the noise she'd made, she silently inhaled another breath and listened carefully, hoping the thick pile of sheepskins had completely muffled the sound. Soon she heard one foot and then another step on the stool. Someone was rummaging through containers on the shelf almost directly above her head.

A slight sense of relief swept over Miriam as she heard the sandaled feet step down from the stool and walk back to the door. Holding her breath again, she listened as the unseen scavenger stopped. And then she heard the unmistakable sound of one of their milk-filled cups being lifted from the shelf on which she had placed it. After a brief pause, she heard it being set almost noiselessly back down.

The sound of the sandals walking across the room toward the pile of sheepskins made Miriam's heart race uncontrollably, and her palms grew even more moist. The feet stopped so close to where she was she was certain that if she lifted the corner of the sheepskin, she would see every detail of the person's toenails. And then, without warning, the feet abruptly turned around and hurried from the shed.

Miriam and Samara breathed a collective sigh of relief, but neither flinched nor moved; except for shallow breaths, the women were as silent and motionless as stone for several more minutes. When they could hear no other sounds, Miriam cautiously lifted the edge of the sheepskin ever so slightly and peeked out. From where she lay, all she could see was the floor, but not seeing any feet or legs, she whispered, "I think they've gone. Stay here, and I'll check."

Easing herself from beneath the sheepskin, she crawled to the center of the shed and looked out the doorway. Seeing no one, she cautiously inched her way toward the door and stuck her head outside.

"Mother!" Caleb shouted as he jumped up from his hiding place behind a bush just outside the door. Before Miriam could overcome her shock, Caleb raced toward her. Miriam managed to rise from a crawling to a kneeling position before Caleb crashed into her and wrapped his arms so tightly around her that she couldn't breathe. "You're alive. You're alive," he repeated over and over as he clung to her.

Small tears formed in Miriam's closed eyes as she hugged her youngest son close to her. Blinking repeatedly she managed to ask, "Are you hurt?"

"No," Caleb said as he relaxed his hug and stepped back slightly. "I'm fine. And you? What about you?" he asked.

"We are well," Miriam said.

Samara crawled out from under the sheepskins. "Is Hanan with you?"

Caleb looked first at Samara and then Miriam and back at Samara as he slowly shook his head back and forth.

"Where is he?" the two women said at almost the same instant, one with anxiety and the other with hope.

Caleb let out a deep sigh and said softly, "He is . . . dead."

Samara's hopeful smile vanished only a fraction of a second before both of her hands flew to her mouth to hide her quivering lip, but she said nothing.

Rising to her feet, Miriam gripped Caleb's arms in her hands. "No, he can't be!"

Except for a slow nod, Caleb stood motionless looking into his mother's grief-stricken eyes. In an even voice, lacking any emotion, he said, "I found him yesterday morning near the entrance to the cave."

Miriam felt her knees go weak, and she slumped down on a half-filled bag of wheat and dropped her head to her chest.

"Yesterday morning?" Samara asked.

"Yes," Caleb replied. "I had—"

"What of Gili and Uzzi?" Miriam interrupted. "Do you know anything of them?"

Caleb looked at his mother's dirty face with its drawn and pale skin and considered what to say. Her natural cheeriness was gone, replaced with sadness and despair. Her hair was matted against her head, and she looked much older than she was. A dull emptiness had replaced the bright sparkle that usually radiated from her deep brown eyes, and every fiber of her seemed to yearn for some thread of hope to cling to. "Uzzi is alive," he said with genuine enthusiasm.

It was the right thing to say. The gloom on Miriam's face was suddenly swept away and replaced by a small sense of relief. "Alive? Where is he?" she asked.

"He's in an old shed on the far side of town, directly below the cave."

"Is he hurt?" she asked cautiously but still with a sense of relief in her voice.

"Yes, Mother, he is hurt," Caleb replied. "That's why I'm here rummaging through some of the old ointments and salves we kept for the animals."

"How badly?" Miriam demanded with the anxious worry of a mother.

Caleb hesitated and once again debated how he would respond. He decided the honest truth would be best. “He’s very bad. He’s been shot with three arrows.” Miriam drew a breath as if to ask another question, but before she could, Caleb continued. “All the arrows have been removed, and I’ve been able to stop the bleeding, but he’s weak, very weak, and I’m worried about infection in his wounds.”

Miriam squared her shoulders and let out a sigh. Weakness and infection she could deal with; another death she could not. “That’s all right,” she said in a determined tone. And then as if imploring good news, she asked, “And what of Gili? Do you know where she is?”

The momentary small spark of hope they had felt about Uzzi was about to be hopelessly drenched, and Caleb dreaded the words he was about to utter. Bracing himself for the shrieks and tears he was sure would come, he calmly said, “She’s been taken as a slave.”

Rather than wailing and tears, there was only silence. There was no flinching or sagging shoulders, no grief-stricken expression on Miriam’s face. There was nothing. She sat there as if she hadn’t heard what had been said. Finally she looked at Caleb. “But she is alive; do you know if she’s alive?”

“I’m quite certain she’s alive. I watched soldiers carry her toward where other villagers were being gathered. She was kicking and screaming, but she was alive.”

Caleb watched as a strange sense of peace enveloped Miriam’s countenance. In a clear voice, she said, “As long as she is alive, I have hope.” She rose to her feet with an aura of resolution Caleb had never before seen in his mother. “Is it safe to go to Uzzi?”

Even though he didn’t mean to, Caleb chuckled and said, “Safe? With the exception of a few dogs, some chickens, and a couple stray sheep, there is nothing and no one left in Edrei. Yes, Mother, it is safe.”

“Good.” Dragging the stool back to the sheepskin pile, Miriam reached up on the shelf and took down two earthen pots with lids. “I’m not sure what ointments you took,” she said, holding out the pots. “But what Uzzi really needs is what’s in here.” Turning to Samara, Miriam said, “I will need some help tending to Uzzi. Will you come with us?”

Samara wiped back the tears that were still rolling down her cheeks since she’d heard the news of Hanan’s death. “Yes, I have no other place to go, no one else I can turn to.”

Walking over to Samara, Miriam put an arm around her shoulder and gave her a consoling hug. "I'm so sorry," she said. "I understand your pain." And then in complete confidence, she added, "We will get through this. Somehow, we will get through this."

Chapter Thirty-Two

"If you don't stop kicking and screaming, I'll kill you right here," the powerfully built soldier hissed angrily through gritted teeth.

"Go ahead," Gili said defiantly, calling the man's bluff. "I'm not afraid of you."

And she had no reason to be. Although screaming and crying when she was pulled from Uzzi's body, she'd heard Naaman's command to the soldier: "See that this child is taken to the village and put with the other captives. Be sure she is unharmed, or I'll have your life."

Now Gili was tucked under the man's left arm like a doll, arms and legs bouncing and her side being jabbed with the hilt of his sword with each hurried stride. "Your sword is hurting me," she complained. "Please put me down and let me walk."

"Humph," the man grunted. "If I let you down, you'll run away like a frightened rabbit."

"Please, your sword is hurting my side, and I promise I won't run away."

"Why should I trust you?" the man asked as he dodged his way around rocks toward the main road.

"Because I was taught never to lie," Gili replied, surprised that he would question her word.

Slowing but not stopping, the soldier lifted his arm and set Gili on the ground. "Walk ahead of me," he commanded.

Gili stumbled as he set her down but quickly recovered and settled into a pace that was half trot and half walk, just fast enough to keep from being stepped on by the man's large feet. Whenever she slowed to catch her breath, the soldier would push her in her back, and twice she fell to the ground. "Be kinder," Gili chided as she picked herself up and brushed dirt and twigs from her dark brown robe. "I'm going as fast as I can."

Turning from the rough path onto the main road, Gili stared in dismay at rubble from toppled houses that littered the road. She choked on the smoke spilling from those that still stood. Ahead of her, women with panic-stricken faces stood in huddled groups with crying children clinging to their legs, surrounded by soldiers yelling and screaming incessantly. Beyond them, the men, some bloodied, were seated on the ground with their hands on their heads as soldiers walked around them snapping whips in the air or lashing backs or legs. Half a dozen men were stretched out on the ground, writhing in pain, arrows sticking from their bodies.

As Gili approached the group of women and children, she was kicked so violently from behind that her head snapped back as she tumbled forward. She landed in an unmoving heap on the ground. It was the wrong thing to do at precisely the wrong moment. As the soldier turned around with a sneer on his lips, a gloved hand struck him across the face with such force that he reeled back and fell to the ground. "I ordered you to see that she arrived here unharmed," the man said calmly. Then taking a step toward Gili, he said, "Pray the girl isn't injured, or you will die."

The soldier sat splayed legged in the dirt, shaking his head. Adjusting his helmet he stammered, "I'm sorry, Captain Naaman."

Naaman walked to where Gili lay and carefully rolled her onto her back. Moving her dark brown hair from her face, he lightly tapped her cheek. "Are you all right?" he asked.

Slowly, Gili's world changed from black to gray and then to daylight as she opened her eyes and blinked several times. "I don't know what happened," she said quietly.

"You were knocked out for a moment," Naaman said. Then pointing to a thin, middle-aged woman who stood nearby, he said, "You there, see to this child."

The woman looked from the man to Gili and back, confused why this Syrian commander would care for an Israelite maiden. "Now!" the man said as he stood up. The woman instantly rushed to Gili's side, dropped to her knees, and scooped the girl into her arms.

Naaman walked back to his chariot, and as he passed the offending soldier, who was rubbing his stinging face, Naaman said, "You're lucky. She seems to be unhurt." Stepping into his chariot, he reined the team of horses and rode up the street.

Gili attempted to pull her legs under her but was stopped. "Don't try getting up just yet," the woman said as she held Gili's head and shoulders in her arms. "Rest for a moment." Gili's head hurt so much that she just smiled faintly and closed her eyes. "What's your name?" the woman asked above the din of confusion that surrounded them.

"Gili," she said with her eyes still closed.

"And mine is Keziah," she said. "Who are your parents?"

"Gideon and Miriam," Gili replied as she opened her eyes. "We live in the hills a few miles from town."

Keziah smiled at Gili's response. "I know them," she said, nodding her head. "But I know your brother even better."

Gili pushed herself to a sitting position, and with her brow wrinkled in thought, she said, "My brother?"

Nodding her head, the woman said, "Hanan. Don't you have a brother named Hanan?"

"Yes, I do."

"He and my Samara are very good friends," Keziah said warmly.

Chapter Thirty-Three

An overwhelming sense of sadness enveloped Caleb, Miriam, and Samara as they entered Edrei. The happy laughter of children and sound of shopkeepers haggling with customers over the price of cloth or fruit were gone, replaced with the mournful sound of silence. Where the fragrant smells of cooking meals once filled the air, now it reeked of the pungent stench of death and burnt homes. With the exception of a few smoldering roof timbers that sent almost invisible spires of smoke curling heavenward, all the fires had burned themselves out.

Cautiously, almost reverently, Miriam and Samara stepped over fallen block walls as they followed Caleb through the empty streets. A nondescript dog lay whining beside the bloating body of an old man, growling at them as they walked past.

Turning down the last street on the edge of the village, Caleb pointed to the burned hulk of a house. "Uzzi is in a shed behind that house."

Quickening their pace, the trio strode across what had been the pleasant outer yard of the home and pushed open the door of the shed. "He's over here, Mother," Caleb said as he moved a dilapidated feed trough and other things out of the way to reveal Uzzi lying on a bed of straw.

Miriam let out a slight gasp as Caleb carefully lifted a tattered blanket from an unconscious Uzzi. The injured boy was covered with dirt and dried blood, and his wounds were red, swollen, and inflamed.

"Hello, Uzzi," Miriam said quietly as she wiped away the tiny beads of perspiration dotting his forehead. "Everything is going to be fine, and before long you'll be running and laughing once again." After tenderly prodding and examining each wound, she turned to Caleb and said, "We need to bathe and clean these wounds. We'll need a fire to warm some water and some clean cloth to use as bandages."

Caleb smiled. "I've already been up to the cave and have a linen tunic we can cut up for cloth, and I can easily build a fire."

Samara pointed to a large metal pot on the ground just outside the door of the shed. "That will do for heating the water." Turning to Caleb she said, "I'll get water from the stream while you build a fire." Then she disappeared out the door.

* * *

An hour later Miriam began carefully washing each wound, and an hour after that, she was applying a combination of honey, herbs, and ointments she had concocted. The task completed, she brushed the hair from her face and looked at Caleb and Samara, who had been coming and going during the entire process.

"You look exhausted," Samara said as she watched Miriam slowly rise from kneeling beside Uzzi.

"I have one more thing I must do today before the sun sets," Miriam said looking at Caleb. "You told us you buried father and Hanan yesterday. Will you take me there?"

Caleb gave a weary smile and said, "Father is buried not far from here, but Hanan is buried up on the hillside, and you look very tired."

As if to add more strength to Miriam's request, Samara said, "I would like to go to Hanan's grave as well. We can help each other."

Caleb wasn't sure if her last comment meant they could physically help each other or if they could lend each other emotional support. Either way, he thought, they were determined to go. "Follow me," he said. "We'll go to Father's grave first."

Walking out of the shed, Caleb led the two women through some empty sheep pens to a trail that ran behind the last row of houses. There, in a lonely plot of earth surrounded by rocks and weeds, stood a lone cedar tree. Caleb walked toward the tree, following two small gouges in the dirt made by the heels of his father's sandals as Caleb had pulled him to the grave.

"He's buried here," Caleb said as he stopped and pointed to the ground.

"Where?" Miriam asked as she examined the dirt.

"Right here." Caleb used his finger to trace an imaginary outline of the grave in the air. "His head rests beneath that small pile of rocks."

Miriam shook her head in dismay. "But it doesn't appear to be a grave," she said, the disappointment evident in her voice.

"I made it to look as natural as possible. I was afraid soldiers or others might come back and disturb it. The only marker is that loose pile of rocks."

Miriam looked at Caleb with an expressionless face. "He deserves so much better than this." She sank to her knees, picked up a handful of sand, and let it trickle through her fingers.

"I know he does, Mother. I wanted to bury him at our home, but I couldn't carry him myself," Caleb said sadly.

Miriam looked up at Caleb through eyes wet with tears. "Thank you for what you did. Would you allow me to spend a few minutes here alone?"

"Take as long as you want."

"Perhaps you two would like to go to Hanan's grave. I will find you in a few minutes."

The two of them silently backed away from Miriam. Caleb said quietly to Samara, "Hanan's grave is up the hill. This way." He started weaving his way around the rocks and up the hill.

Hanan's burial spot was more of a monument than a grave. Caleb had managed to scrape away only a few inches of topsoil and weeds before hitting a solid layer of volcanic rock. Laying Hanan's body in the shallow hole, Caleb mounded dirt on it. Then, to keep animals from scavenging, he gathered every rock he could lift and piled them on top of the small mound. Caleb had made no attempt to disguise Hanan's grave, and the two-foot-tall tower of stones was so orderly no one could have mistaken it for anything other than what it was.

As Caleb and Samara stopped beside the pile of black rocks, Caleb said simply, "I'm very sorry for you. He was very concerned about you."

The corners of Samara's mouth lifted into a slight smile. "I'm sorry for you as well."

Sensing she might want to be alone, Caleb said, "I'm going to walk back to the cave to see what we can use. I'll wait there for you and Mother."

Caleb gathered a handful of dried grass and a few twigs as he walked. Using a small piece of flint and steel, he started a small fire at the mouth of the tunnel leading to the cave. Lighting an almost-full oil lamp he found sitting beside the entrance, he picked his way down the tunnel and into the cavern. Walking around the cave, he shook his head in amazement at the food, clothing, and supplies his father had secretly stored. The four of them, assuming Uzzi recovered, could easily live for two or three months.

As he began back up the tunnel, Caleb could see Miriam and Samara silhouetted in the entrance. As he approached, he asked Miriam, "Were you able to find Hanan's grave?"

"Yes. You did a very good job. Thank you," she said in a halting voice as she wiped a tear from her eye.

"I've been looking at the supplies in the cave. Father prepared very well for us. There's enough food to last for months and plenty of clothing."

Looking at Caleb and Samara, Miriam asked, "Do you think we should stay in the cave?"

The two looked at each other and then at Miriam and nodded. Caleb said, "I think we'll be much safer here, at least for a little while. The only problem is getting Uzzi here. He can't walk, so we'll have to carry him."

"Can we fashion a litter of some kind?" Samara asked.

Caleb nodded. "Easily."

Miriam looked down the hill to the dilapidated shed where Uzzi lay. "Let's move him now."

Chapter Thirty-Four

Naaman stood patiently outside the massive wooden door awaiting his summons. His feet hurt, his fingers ached, and the red blotches of skin on his face throbbed. He wished this meeting could have been delayed until he had bathed and soaked in the cool waters of the Albana River. The water always made him feel so much better.

A squeak of the hinges caused him to look up, and he watched the door swing open to reveal a smiling servant dressed in clean clothes—a luxury Naaman wished he enjoyed at the moment. "The king will receive you now, Commander. Please follow me."

Naaman returned the smile but said nothing as he gingerly followed, gritting his teeth against the discomfort in his toes as he walked. The servant strode across the floor of the spacious room to where Ben-Hadad was seated at a desk with his back to the approaching men. Clearing his throat, the servant said, "Commander Naaman is here as you requested."

Ben-Hadad whirled around on the elegant stool on which he was perched. "Ah, my very best commander. Welcome home!"

Naaman bowed his head slightly. "It's good to be back."

"I've received your dispatches, and the news is excellent. You've done an admirable job cleaning up Edrei."

"Thank you," Naaman replied in a solemn tone.

Rising to his feet, Ben-Hadad walked to a small table holding a tray and two brass goblets. Offering one of the goblets to Naaman, Ben-Hadad said, "Please, enjoy a drink of wine with me while you give me a few details of your adventure."

Naaman readily accepted the goblet and drank a mouthful, swishing it around to wash the dust from his teeth before he swallowed. Raising the goblet to his mouth again, he rapidly drank several swallows. He was thirsty, and the cool liquid was refreshing.

"It's too bad about Adad," Ben-Hadad said, clearly not troubled by the death of his distant relative. "I haven't told his father of his death, but I suspect I must. Did he die honorably?"

"An arrow in the back of his neck."

Ben-Hadad raised his eyebrow and gave a slight chuckle. "In the back of his neck? I hope he wasn't running away from the fight!"

"He was foolish," Naaman said with a bit of disgust. "He was more concerned about dragging a young Hebrew girl by the hair than paying attention to what was going on around him. The girl's brother was hiding, and when Adad and two archers passed by him, the boy rose from a hiding place and shot them."

"One against three?"

Naaman nodded then added, "And the Hebrew was already wounded."

A look of approval spread over Ben-Hadad's face as he slowly nodded his head and took a sip of wine. He respected bravery in anyone, enemy or otherwise. "Did you see it?"

"Yes, I was standing in my chariot not far away." Then after only a slight hesitation, he added, "I was more concerned for the Hebrew than I was for Adad. He was far braver."

"I would have been as well," Ben-Hadad said, and then with a wave of his hand to dismiss the topic, he said, "I never liked Adad." Naaman smiled slightly and was about to agree when Ben-Hadad added, "And what of the captives?"

"As you requested, the healthy men have been sent on to Emesa and Apamea to work on the projects there."

"Good. Even with added men, it will be years before we finish the fortresses and complete the canals. And what of the women and children?"

"They are being marched to Damascus as we speak. They should arrive within the next few hours."

Ben-Hadad placed his goblet on the tray and held his hand out to take Naaman's goblet. Naaman gratefully surrendered it because that meant the meeting was over and he could return to his home, his wife, and especially the river.

"You've done well, Naaman," Ben-Hadad said as he placed the goblet on the tray.

"Thank you."

Ben-Hadad put his arm around Naaman's shoulder and guided him toward the door. "You know you are my favorite commander, don't you?"

Naaman stifled a smile but said nothing.

Reaching for the door latch, Ben-Hadad said, "As an added token of my appreciation—and as a way of telling your good wife thank you—you may choose any two captives to become slaves in your household. Pick a young one—a girl who can serve for many years!"

Naaman stared at Ben-Hadad in surprise. This was an unexpected and expensive gift. "Thank you, your Excellency," Naaman said. "That is very generous of you."

"It's nothing. Besides, you deserve it," Ben-Hadad said. Then he ushered Naaman to the door. "Go now and choose your slaves. By tonight the best will be sold or given away."

* * *

Gili clutched Keziah's hand even more tightly than before as they looked down on Damascus from the crest of the hill. Day after day for a week, the column of soldiers had forced them to plod along the dusty road toward this city, and now that they had arrived, neither of them was sure if they were relieved or sad.

"It's the biggest city I've ever seen," Gili said in amazement.

"And me as well," Keziah said but with far less awe than Gili. Every night as the captives gathered around the campfires to cook, Keziah had listened to the disturbing tales of slavery. Many of them she dismissed as idle rumors, but one thing was certain: she would never see her husband or children again. Although she hadn't seen her husband since they had all been dragged from their home in Edrei, she had been told by others that all the men were gone, forced to march to some other city in Syria. Gili had told her about Samara, but as for the other children and grandchildren, no one had seen them. Every night Keziah prayed they had somehow escaped.

Looking up at Keziah with a furrowed brow, Gili asked, "What will happen to us when we get to Damascus?"

"I'm not sure, little one," Keziah replied as she gave Gili's hand a squeeze. "Whatever comes, we must be strong and have faith in Jehovah."

The soldier standing beside them jabbed his spear into the air and shouted, "March!" The weary captives began the descent into the pitiful world of slavery.

* * *

Two hours later, they were herded like sheep into a dusty, barren compound surrounded by block walls eight feet high. On top, the walls were embedded with sharply pointed steel spikes. Until then, Keziah had kept going by telling herself that, at some point, she would escape and once again be free, but at the sight of the thick walls and steel spikes, reality descended with a crashing blow. There was no hope of escape, and all she would ever know until the day she died was confinement, restriction, hatred, and abuse. Her shoulders sagged, and she let Gili's hand slip from her own.

"What's wrong?" Gili asked as she looked up into Keziah's distraught face.

Keziah looked down at Gili and was suddenly overwhelmed with pity. Keziah was middle-aged, and her life would end in not too many years. Gili was young and would be hopelessly trapped for many, many years. She would become intimate friends with hunger and thirst; she would feel the repeated sting of a whip's lash. She would come to know the evils of the world.

"What's wrong?" Gili repeated as she tugged on the sleeve of Keziah's dirty robe.

Keziah let out a deep sigh and choked back a tear, but all she could say was, "Nothing. I'm all right."

Gili frowned. "Keziah, you'll see. Everything is going to be fine."

"It will?" Keziah replied with a weak smile. It was a question not a statement.

"Yes. I know it will. You'll see. Prophet always told me I should have faith in Jehovah, even when things aren't going well."

"And you do have faith," Keziah replied genuinely. "It's—"

"You, the young one, come here this instant." The soldier's voice was harsh and vindictive. He was pointing at Gili.

Gili turned to face the massive soldier who had kicked her in the back and instantly slid behind Keziah.

"I said to come here," the man bellowed as he pushed Keziah roughly aside and grabbed Gili by the arm.

"Take your hands off the girl," Keziah demanded as she reached out and grasped the soldier's arm.

The soldier raised his free arm as if to strike Keziah but stopped and glanced quickly over his shoulder. In a markedly less hostile voice, he said,

"The commander wants this young maiden brought to him now!" He forcefully removed Keziah's hands from his arm and pulled on Gili.

Being careful not to touch the girl with any more strength than necessary, the gruff soldier guided Gili across the compound, weaving in and out of women and children, who stared at them through large, fright-filled eyes. When he was within a short distance of the gate, he removed his hand entirely and hung back while Gili approached Naaman.

"Do you understand why you are here?" Naaman asked in a weary voice.

"Because you attacked my village and your soldiers killed my father and brother," Gili replied without the slightest intimidation.

Naaman's eyes widened at the response, and he replied equally bluntly. "You will not be able to return to Edrei; Damascus is to be your new home, and you are to be a servant in my home—to my wife."

"What if I don't want to stay in Damascus?"

"You have no choice. You must stay in Damascus."

Gili paused for a minute before saying, "How long must I stay here before I can go back to my mother?"

Naaman shook his head and opened his mouth to reply, but Gili cut him off. "I won't go with you. You took me away from Uzzi."

"He was dead," Naaman replied.

"He was still alive when you made me leave."

"No, he was dead. His heart had stopped beating." To end the conversation, he pointed to the gate and said, "See that woman standing next to the soldier by the gate? Go and stand by her."

"I don't like Beulah. She's mean, her breath smells, and my mother says she is lazy."

Naaman stifled a chuckle. Then, looking pensively at Gili, he asked, "Do you know all these people?"

"Not all, but many," Gili replied.

Sweeping his hand over the pitiful-looking group he said, "If you don't like that woman, which of all these women do you like?"

"Keziah," Gili said instantly.

"Which one is she?" Naaman asked, surveying the hundred women scattered throughout the compound.

"The one I was standing next to; the one in the brown robe," Gili said pointing in Keziah's direction.

Turning to the soldier who had delivered Gili, Naaman pointed to Keziah and said, "Bring that woman here."

As Keziah joined Gili and Naaman, he said, "This girl is going to serve my wife. She has told me you would also be useful. You are both to come with me."

Keziah looked at Gili. Giving the young girl a reassuring smile, she looked back at Naaman. Very guardedly she said, "Yes, sir," and took Gili by the hand.

Turning back to the soldier, Naaman said, "Tell that other woman, the one by the gate, to go back in the compound." Then pointing to Gili and Keziah, he said, "Deliver these two to my home at once," and then he added with great emphasis, "Safely."

Chapter Thirty-Five

Uzzi sat up on the side of the sheepskin bed and grinned. "A week ago I wouldn't have been able to do that," he said to Samara, who was standing on the far edge of the fire's light.

"And three weeks before that you were more dead than alive," she replied lightly as she walked to the fire and bent over to stir the pot of chicken soup that was simmering.

"The food smells good," Uzzi said, realizing that for the first time in weeks he was genuinely hungry. "You're a good cook."

"It's your mother who's the good cook. She made this; I'm only stirring it," Samara replied as she brushed her dark bangs out of her eyes.

Struggling to his feet, Uzzi carefully walked to the fire and stood close, watching as she stirred the pot. Then placing a hand lightly on her shoulder, he said softly, "I've never thanked you for—"

Samara cut him off in midsentence. "There is no need to thank me," she said coolly as she swept his hand away and rose up to face him. "It's your mother you should thank. I've only changed your bandages once or twice. She has changed them many times—and sat up with you when you were burning up with fever."

Uzzi stepped back slightly and stammered, "I was only trying to say—"

"I know what you were trying to say." She pulled her lips into an artificial smile. "And . . . well . . . I really don't care to hear it." Then as if issuing a command to an underling, she said, "You should rest." Wiping her hands on her robe, she picked up a lamp and scurried to the tunnel.

Uzzi raised an eyebrow and tilted his head in confusion as he watched her walk away. He could understand why Hanan was attracted to her beauty, but he couldn't fathom how his brother could overlook the sharpness of her tongue. "I was just trying to be nice," he mumbled to himself.

Caleb walked into the cave carrying two freshly killed chukars from which he'd already plucked the feathers. "What's the matter with her?" he said, jerking his head in the direction of the retreating figure.

"Don't ask me."

"What did you say to her?" Caleb asked, laying the birds on a small table. "Something sure upset her."

"I told her thank you; that's all."

Caleb gave Uzzi an incredulous look. "You told her thanks, and she's upset?"

"Exactly, all I—"

Miriam entered the cave holding a small oil lamp. She reached out and extended it toward Caleb. "This is one of the lamps from the entrance tunnel. It's out of oil and needs to be refilled." Then looking at Uzzi, she said, "Why is Samara upset?"

"That's what I asked him," Caleb said as he took the lamp from Miriam's hand. "He says he told her thanks for taking care of him."

Caleb and Miriam both looked at Uzzi and waited. Uzzi looked back and forth between them and raised his hands in frustration. "I told her thank you; nothing more. I don't know why she's upset." Dropping his hands to his side, he turned and made his way back to his bed.

Miriam looked at Caleb, gave a slight smile, and winked, but Caleb simply shrugged his shoulders and shook his head, totally confused. Pointing to the table, he said, "I killed two chuckars with my sling while I was scavenging around the village."

"That's wonderful." Miriam eyed the birds. "We can save the soup for another day, and I'll roast these for dinner tonight."

As Miriam busied herself with the chuckars and Caleb poured oil into the lamp from a goat-skin bag, Uzzi slowly walked over and sat down gingerly on the wool sheepskins that made up his bed. He watched as the flames from the fire created dancing shadows on the walls and ceiling of the cave, and he absentmindedly began rubbing his hand lightly over the soft white wool. Looking at Miriam, he said softly, "What are we going to do, Mother?"

Miriam let the question hang heavy in the air as she sprinkled a mixture of salt and spices over the birds.

Caleb walked over to the fire. Squatting down he set the filled lamp on the ground. But rather than pick up a burning stick and light the oil, he looked up at Miriam and waited silently for her response to Uzzi's question.

Miriam turned one of the chuckars to its other side and reached into the dish for another pinch of salt and spices. Letting the mixture fall through the air and onto the meat, she finally said, "Do about what?"

"We can't stay here forever," Uzzi replied as he stopped rubbing his hand through the sheepskin. "We only have food for another few weeks or month, and there's no time to plant grain and nowhere else to get food." He paused briefly. "We must do something soon."

Miriam began massaging the spices into the second bird as if she hadn't heard anything Uzzi had said. Only after she had finished her task did she look over at him. "I understand we can't stay forever, but what you don't understand is why I can't leave." Pointing toward the cave's entrance, her voice trembled as she said, "My husband and son are buried out there." Choking back a tear, she stabbed her finger at the ground. "And this dark hole is the last place I saw my daughter."

The silence in the cave was as thick as the darkness. Uzzi and Caleb looked at their mother, but Miriam looked at neither of them. She leaned on the table with both hands, her head hanging, and made no effort to control her tears.

The crunching of footsteps in the tunnel caused all three of them to look at Samara as she entered the tunnel carrying another lamp whose oil had burned out. "Another lamp is out of oil," she said as she walked into the circle of light from the fire. But as soon as she said it, she realized she had inserted herself into a serious conversation. "I'm sorry. I didn't mean to interrupt."

"You're not interrupting," Uzzi said. "It's good you're here. This involves you. We were just about to discuss our future plans."

Miriam stood tall and brushed tears from her cheeks. Looking at Uzzi, Samara said, "Oh? And what have you decided?"

"Nothing," Uzzi quickly replied shaking his head. "We've decided nothing yet, but we need to make some decisions."

"Decisions about leaving here?" Samara asked.

Uzzi looked at Miriam and waited for her to respond. When she didn't, he said, "Leaving, yes, but more than that—where shall we go?"

Samara stood motionless, holding the small oil lamp in both hands.

Caleb suddenly stood, walked to Miriam's side, and asked, "Why can't we stay here? We can rebuild our house, plant grain, and do as we were doing before."

"And live every day in fear of the Syrians returning?" asked Samara.

"Why would they come back? They've destroyed this place," Caleb replied.

"But what if they do?" Samara fired back quickly. "I don't want to stay here."

"Jerusalem."

Uzzi, Caleb, and Samara all jerked their heads to look at Miriam. She returned their stares and repeated, "Jerusalem. We'll go to Jerusalem."

Chapter Thirty-Six

Two years later

It was the first time in two years of slavery that Gili smiled happily. She watched the little baby drool and blow tiny bubbles from his mouth. "He is so cute, Mistress Karinah," she said as she gently touched the downy black hair on the baby's head.

"I love it when he does that," Karinah responded, pointing with her fingertip to the tiny bubbles and gently stroking his cheeks.

Karinah and Gili both heard the door squeak, but neither of them looked up. "And how is my little nephew?" Naaman said as he walked into the room, his feet tucked inside sandals lined with soft sheepskin to cushion the jolt of his stride.

"He's adorable," Karinah beamed as she looked up at her husband.

Naaman smiled at the comment. "All babies look alike," he replied, only partly in jest. Then patting his wife on the arm, he said, "I must leave for a few hours. I will return before nightfall."

Gili lowered her eyes and backed away, discretely lifting a small pouch filled with crushed spices to her nose. It masked—but didn't eliminate—the stench that came from the man. She had overcome the awkwardness of seeing his disfigured face, feet, and hands, but her stomach rebelled at the smell of disintegrating flesh, and more than once she had wretched in his presence.

"Have the cook prepare you a small cloth like this," Karinah had instructed Gili after seeing her wretch the first time. Showing her a small white linen pouch filled with spices, Karinah explained, "It helps mask the odor."

Karinah smiled to acknowledge her husband's comment but turned her attention back to the baby and its mother before he was even out the door. "You're very lucky," Karinah said with more than a tinge of envy as she handed the baby back to her sister.

"I know it," the beaming woman replied as she cuddled the child against her.

Gili stood in the corner of the room and watched her childless mistress coo and fuss over the two-month-old baby. For reasons Gili didn't know, Karinah and Naaman didn't have any children. And seeing the baby made Gili temporarily forget her own situation. But as the woman and her baby began saying good-byes, the familiar loneliness and longing for her own family crept back, and Gili's mind raced back over the two years since she had been taken from those she loved and forced to serve as a slave.

Not a day passed that she didn't immediately drop beside her bed when she awoke and offer up her morning prayers. And every day they began with exactly the same plea: "Jehovah, Lord God. Thank you for allowing me to sleep safely last night and for another day to live. If you will, let today be the day I am freed from slavery and return to those I love and miss. But if not, give me the faith and courage to be strong until I see them again, and bless them to know that I am alive and well." Her petition continued with expressions of gratitude for her knowledge of a prophet as well as a plea for God's protection. And though she was a slave, she expressed heartfelt gratitude for being a slave to Naaman and Karinah. Every few weeks for almost two years, she had heard rumors of the brutal mistreatment or death of someone she had known in Edrei, someone else who had been forced into a life of slavery.

"Gili!" Karinah said forcefully.

Pulled from her mental ramblings, Gili said, "I'm sorry, mistress. I didn't hear you."

Pointing to her sister, Karinah said, "Will you please escort them out and then come back here and brush my hair."

"Yes, certainly." Gili walked from the room with the woman and her baby trailing behind. A few moments later, Gili returned, picked up a wooden comb, and began carefully combing Karinah's hair.

Looking in the thin sheet of polished copper, Karinah tipped it so she could see Gili's reflection. "You no longer find it so difficult to look at my husband's disfigured appearance, do you?"

"No, he no longer looks strange to me," Gili said as she gently glided the comb through the dark brown hair. "In truth, mistress, I never think about it."

"Neither do I," Karinah said. After a long pause, she added, "He's a very good man."

Gili nodded her head. "He is."

Karinah lowered the copper sheet to her lap and sat silently as Gili repeatedly pulled the comb through her hair.

"Mistress, may I speak?"

"Certainly, Gili," Karinah said.

"There is a prophet in Israel who can heal Master Naaman," Gili said as she quickly plucked a wild strand of gray hair from Karinah's head.

It wasn't the sudden pinprick of pain that made Karinah twist around to face Gili. "There's a what?"

"A prophet," Gili said.

"What is a prophet?" Karinah asked. She took Gili's arm and guided the girl around so she was standing in front of Karinah.

"A prophet is a man who speaks for God, a man who has wonderful power to heal people. He can cure your husband of his leprosy."

"Ah," Karinah said, nodding her head. "Like our priests of Baal and our sorcerers."

"No, mistress, not like those men. They do their work by evil power. A prophet works by the power of God."

"Baal is a god," Karinah insisted.

"But neither you nor Master Naaman believes in him."

Karinah smiled at the perceptive child. "No, we don't believe in him."

"I believe in Prophet," Gili said proudly. "He can heal people if they believe in God."

"Do you know this man?"

"Yes, mistress; others call him Elisha, but to me he is Prophet."

"How do you know him?" Karinah said with suspicion, not really believing this young maiden could possibly know a man who spoke for God and could miraculously heal people.

"He's been in my home many times," Gili said. Reaching inside the folds of her robe, she extracted the leather pouch holding a small but beautiful pale pink stone. Removing the stone from the bag and holding it in the palm of her hand, she said with reverence, "He gave this to me many years ago. It is my most valuable possession."

Karinah picked up the delicate stone and held it to the sunlight. Its crystal shape refracted the light and made the beautiful colors of the rainbow appear on the white wall beside them. "He gave you this?" Karinah asked.

Gili nodded her head and said, "It's the reason I'm here."

"This stone?" Karinah sked as she placed the stone back in Gili's palm.

"I was hiding from the soldiers with my mother, but I forgot the stone. When I went back to get it, the soldiers captured me."

Karinah looked at Gili's brown eyes and was suddenly assaulted by sadness and shame. In the two years the girl had been her slave, Karinah had never asked how Gili had come to be there. Not once had she asked about the child's father or mother or anything about her as a human being. And now this young maiden was standing before her and unselfishly offering a cure for her husband, expecting nothing in return. Shaking the thoughts from her mind, Karinah asked in a subdued voice, "How do you know this man can cure my husband?"

Gili looked at Karinah but said nothing. The pause was long enough that Karinah shifted in her seat and nodded at Gili to prod her response.

Still Gili hesitated. Her wrinkled brow, downturned mouth, and narrowed eyes all seemed to be evidence of an internal conflict. After a long moment, she said quietly, "Other than my family, I have never told anyone what I am about to tell you."

Karinah inclined her head slightly toward Gili. "Why is that?"

"Because it is a sacred experience, and we don't speak of it, especially to . . . a nonbeliever."

"I see," Karinah said. "Do you think I will ridicule your beliefs?"

Gili shook her head. "No, I don't think that; I just don't know if you will believe as I do."

Karinah studied Gili's expression. Placing the polished brass mirror in her hands onto a table, Karinah said, "Gili, if you know something, or someone, that can heal my husband, I ask you to tell me. I give you my word I will not ridicule you or your God. Do you understand?"

Gili nodded.

Karinah smiled slightly. "How do you know this man, your prophet, can cure my husband?"

"Because he brought my father back to life and healed him when he was gored by an angry cow."

The words had been spoken with such simple conviction. Pointing to a nearby chair, Karinah motioned for Gili to sit. "Please, will you tell me more of how this man healed your father?"

Gili examined the earnestness in Karinah's eyes then hesitated only slightly before saying, "Yes, Mistress." Drawing the chair so they sat almost knee-to-knee, Gili sat down and began.

The suspicious look on Karinah's face was replaced with curiosity as she listened to Gili's words. For twenty minutes Karinah sat transfixed, listening to Gili's subdued voice as she gave a vivid description of her father's terrible injuries and miraculous healing. When Gili finished, the two sat in silence for a moment. Then with earnest pleading in her voice, Karinah asked, "Do you honestly believe this man, this prophet of Israel, can heal my husband?"

"No, Mistress," Gili replied warmly. "I don't believe he can heal Master Naaman. I know he can do it if God wills it."

Karinah slid forward in her chair and lightly grasped Gili's arms in each of her hands. "Where can we find this prophet?"

Chapter Thirty-Seven

Naaman lay on his back on a wooden couch from which the cushions had been removed. Little streamlets of warm water ran down the sides of his temples, saturating his hair and then dripping onto the wooden plank, turning it dark.

"She says he can heal you," Karinah said softly as she dipped the coarse rag in a clay basin, wrung the cloth out, and began lightly scrubbing the flakey white skin on her husband's forehead.

Naaman blinked repeatedly as an errant drop of water slid into the corner of his eye. Whatever concoction the medical man had put in the water stung, and Naaman reached up with a stubby finger to wipe his eye. "And what do you think?" he asked sincerely. "Do you think a prophet of Israel can heal this hideous flesh?"

Karinah shifted in her chair, dropped the rag in the basin, and picked up a soft cotton cloth. Patting the water on each side of Naaman's face, she said, "You should listen to her. She speaks so reverently of how he healed her father. It brings tears to my eyes even now when I think of it. She has unending faith in this man, and although I don't know him, I believe in her and her faith."

Naaman turned his head and gazed at his wife tenderly. Her long hair fell in loose curls on her shoulders and was a stark contrast to the almost-white robe she wore. "I'm a lucky man," he said as he lightly stroked her cheek with the back of his painfully sore hand. "You deserve more than this grotesque appearance." Swinging his legs from the couch, he sat up and clasped both of her hands in his. "I'm meeting with Ben-Hadad this afternoon; I'll ask him to write a letter to the king of Israel so that I may meet with this prophet Elisha."

A delighted smile spread over Karinah's face as she gently squeezed her husband's hands. "Gili believes he will heal you, and I believe Gili."

Naaman returned the smile. "The little maiden has faith; that much is certain." Pushing himself up from the couch, he winced as the weight of his body settled on his damaged feet. Bending slightly he kissed Karinah on the top of her head. "Thank you for once again scrubbing my head," he said, and he shuffled uneasily from the room.

Naaman ate a lunch of dates drizzled with honey, almonds, and bread. Then he changed into a dark gray robe richly embroidered with white designs around the sleeves and collar. Stepping into the courtyard, he yelled to a servant trimming fronds from a miniature palm tree, "Obed, get my chariot. We're going to the palace."

Naaman looked up at the cobalt-blue sky and watched two Egyptian geese float to a graceful landing in the far corner of the courtyard. The massive birds honked noisily but didn't fly away when Obed drove the team of black horses pulling the gleaming, copper-covered chariot up to where Naaman stood.

Tying the rawhide lines around a small post protruding from the front of the chariot, the middle-aged Obed jumped from the chariot. "It's ready for you, Commander Naaman."

Holding up his gloved hands for Obed to see, Naaman said, "My hands ache too much to hold the lines; you take me."

"Certainly," Obed said obediently and reached out his arm. "Let me help you step up."

Pulling out of the gates, Obed slapped the lines on the horses' rumps, and the two animals stepped out in a lively trot. The chariot's steel-rimmed wheels rumbled against the hard-packed dirt road, churning up very little dust. Recent winter rain had left the ground damp but not muddy. As they approached groups of people, Obed's deep voice bellowed out, "Commander Naaman's chariot! Clear the way." As if by magic, the crowds parted. It wasn't out of respect that the people darted out of the way; it was out of fear. As much as Naaman had chastised him, Obed wasn't above running into or over someone if they failed to move.

Reining the horses to a stop in front of the massive palace, Obed helped Naaman down from the chariot. Looking up at the hundred steps leading to the multi-pillared building, Obed asked, "Would you like me to help you up the steps?"

"That won't be necessary," Naaman replied. "But please wait for me here. I won't be longer than one hour."

"Yes, Commander," Obed replied, as he walked in front of the horses to keep them calm.

Removing a black scarf from around his neck, Naaman carefully draped it over his head, letting it cover his ears and as much of his forehead as possible. As he ascended the stairs, he mused to himself that there was one positive thing about leprosy. Nobody wanted him around for any longer than was necessary. Slaves, servants, and all levels of assorted officials were eager to get Naaman out of the palace as quickly as possible, so when he arrived, they made certain he was ushered in ahead of anyone else who might be waiting. And that suited Naaman as well.

The meeting lasted much less than an hour. After quickly reviewing the strength of the Syrian army and the likelihood of war with the Phoenicians, Ben-Hadad changed the subject. "And what of your . . . condition?" Although less concerned about Naaman's leprosy than the others in his palace, Ben-Hadad was troubled by Naaman's unpleasant appearance and odor.

Naaman tugged uncomfortably at the scarf draped over his head and cleared his throat. "There is a little maiden, an Israelite captive from Edrei, who serves my wife," he began. "She has told Karinah of a man in Samaria, a prophet by the name of Elisha, whom she insists can cure me."

"Is there such a man?" Ben-Hadad asked skeptically.

Naaman nodded and continued. "She relates a story to my wife of his amazing power, of how her father was healed after he was gored by an angry cow."

Ben-Hadad cocked his head slightly to the side and peered questioningly at Naaman. "And you believe this captive slave?" he asked as if Naaman was a gullible child.

Naaman took a deep breath and slowly expelled it through his nose. "I have consulted and followed the requirements of Baal's priests, done as the best medical men of Syria have instructed, and even consulted sorcerers my wife has brought—all promised a cure if I gave them money and riches." Raising his gloved hands, Naaman removed the scarf from his head to reveal the white, flaking skin on his face, the lesions on his nose, and his missing ear. "Having done all they required, I stand before you looking like this—worse than ever before."

Ben-Hadad stole only the slightest glance before averting his eyes. Pausing only long enough to take another breath, Naaman replaced the scarf and continued, "Now comes a little Israelite maid, a slave, who has every right to wish I was dead for raiding her village and killing her family.

Asking nothing in return, she tells me of a man in whom she has complete faith, a man who speaks for the Israelite God, Jehovah. Do I believe her? Yes, I do." Naaman said with full conviction. "I believe her not only for the story she tells of the prophet healing her father but because of her example. There is no guile in the child. She's incapable of lying or misleading." Then after a short pause, he added, "Yes, Excellency, I believe her."

Ben-Hadad stood in complete silence, mesmerized not only by the words Naaman spoke but the strength with which he'd said them.

Rising from his chair, Ben-Hadad said, "You shall go to this prophet immediately." Turning to an aide who stood on the far side of the room, the king bellowed, "Call the scribe!" Then turning back to Naaman, he said, "Do you know where this prophet resides?"

Naaman shook his head. "Only somewhere in Samaria."

Ben-Hadad pursed his lips and thought for a moment. "I'll send a letter to the king of Israel. Certainly he will know where to find this prophet of their God Jehovah."

At that moment, a frail little man dressed in an ink-spotted tunic entered the room carrying a beautifully carved box in both arms. Ben-Hadad smiled and said, "Dagon, I wish you to write a letter to Jehoram, king of Israel."

The little man nodded and walked to a table, where he set his box down. Conscious that the king and Naaman were watching, he lifted the lid with an exaggerated movement and extracted a small piece of parchment—an extremely thin piece of sheepskin—and placed it on the table. Next, he removed a quill, a small pot of ink, and a bowl filled with white powder. Sliding a chair up to the table, he sat down and proclaimed, "I am ready."

"Most Excellent King Jehoram," Ben-Hadad began boldly as he strutted back and forth. But then there was a pause, a very long pause, as he continued to walk. Suddenly stopping, he turned to Naaman with a look of deep consternation on his face—he didn't know what to say next! The frown on his face deepened as he stared at Naaman for one minute and then two. And then as if he had just solved the greatest mystery of mankind, a big smile spread across his face. "With this letter I am sending Naaman, my chief captain and the commander of all my forces, to you to be cured of leprosy." He stopped and bobbed his head up and down in complete satisfaction.

Naaman looked at Ben-Hadad, waiting for him to say something more, to add a reference to the prophet, but Ben-Hadad simply looked at him with a smug smile and said conspiratorially, "That should make Jehoram uncomfortable and nervous enough to eagerly seek out this Israelite prophet." And then with a hearty laugh, he added, "He's going to think this is a trick and I'm trying to goad him into a war." And Ben-Hadad was right; that's exactly what the king of Israel would think.

Naaman raised his eyebrows and gave a weak smile. It wasn't how he would have phrased the letter, but he had to admit there was some logic to it. Certainly the Israelite king would know where such an important man was residing and would make an effort to pacify Ben-Hadad by locating him.

After the little man concluded making his marks on the parchment, he sprinkled a fine dusting of the white powder on the wet ink to keep it from smearing and rolled the parchment up tightly. Then he brought the roll along with a small candle to where Ben-Hadad stood. After he had dripped several drops of wax on the edge, Ben-Hadad removed a signet ring from his hand and pressed it into the hot wax. A moment later he removed the ring from the wax and slipped it back on his finger. Returning to his box, the man removed a small leather container, slipped the roll into it, laced a lid in place, and then handed it to the king.

Ben-Hadad took the container from the little man and handed it to Naaman. "Naaman," he began earnestly as he placed his hand on the commander's shoulder, "you are my most trusted leader, the one to whom I turn when I need military counsel, and more faithful than all my other soldiers combined. I know these Israelites; they will want payment for curing you, so I'm giving you 750 pounds of silver, 150 pounds of gold, and 10 changes of clothing to pay this prophet."

Naaman was taken aback and stared at Ben-Hadad in total surprise. He wasn't shocked that the king told him to expect to pay for the healing—that was common—but that the king was willing to pay it was beyond belief. Had Ben-Hadad looked carefully, he would have noticed a small tear forming in the corner of his battle-hardened commander's eye. Naaman cleared his throat and stammered out a simple, "Thank you."

Squeezing Naaman's shoulder tightly, Ben-Hadad said jovially, "Now go, and don't come back until your skin is clean!" Leaving Naaman holding the letter, the king walked briskly out the door with a huge smile on his face.

Chapter Thirty-Eight

The chariot was much longer and somewhat wider than the battle chariot in which Naaman normally rode. Standing in the middle was Obed, rawhide lines to the horses playing lightly in his hands. Naaman sat beside him on a comfortable cushioned seat that faced forward. Ahead of the chariot rode four soldiers, two abreast, on matching white horses.

Immediately behind Naaman's chariot followed another, this one somewhat smaller but no less lavish than the first. A massive man with arms the size of tree trunks stood at the lines, urging the horses forward. He was uncomfortable in his role. He was a soldier accustomed to riding horses, not driving them, and although they'd been traveling for several days, he was still not at ease. But driving the horses wasn't his prime role; he was here to protect the occupant in the chariot. If necessary he would die before he would allow any harm come to the little maid seated to his right.

In single file behind the second chariot followed ten camels. Four of the recalcitrant beasts plodded along with a combination of gold, silver, and costly apparel securely strapped down. The last six were laden with food, tents, and supplies for the people in the caravan.

Following behind the camels were six more soldiers. Like those at the head of the column, these soldiers were on stout horses, riding two abreast, and were outfitted in full battle armor. Should anyone be foolhardy enough to attack the little caravan, they would be met with full resistance.

The audience with the Israelite king had been uncomfortable at first. When the high-strung and almost irrational Jehoram had read Ben-Hadad's letter, he assumed the delegation was there as a trick, that Ben-Hadad was creating a scenario to begin a war. It was only after more rational people got involved that Jehoram understood the nature of their visit and eagerly directed them to where Elisha the prophet was residing.

"Amon, how much farther is it until we reach Prophet's house?" Gili asked with so much excitement she could hardly contain herself.

Amon clucked at the horses and lightly slapped them with the lines. "Not far, perhaps another two hours, maybe less."

"Do you think Master Naaman would allow us to race ahead?"

Amon shot an incredulous look at Gili but said nothing. He didn't need to; the expression on his face said it all.

His attention distracted by Gili's comment, Amon didn't see the four-foot-long Palestine viper until it was too late. The snake had been basking on a rock in the warm sunlight as Naaman's chariot rolled past. But as Amon approached, it uncoiled its scaly, tan body and slithered onto the road, its forked tongue constantly licking in and out. The black snake's rapid movement startled the flightier of the two horses pulling the chariot.

At the sight of the snake, terror struck the horse, which reared into the air, its front hooves thrashing wildly. As the horse rose, the tongue of the chariot to which the horse was yoked also went up, tilting the chariot just enough to knock Amon off balance and throw him backward onto the floor of the chariot. As Amon fell, he released the rawhide lines that ran to the horses. With the tension on the lines released, the spooked horse's powerful hind legs lunged forward as its front legs came down to the ground. In a panicked attempt to keep stride with its confused partner, the second horse lunged forward as well.

In only a few seconds, calm turned to chaos, and the wide-eyed horses bolted off the narrow roadway and onto a rut-riddled open plain. It was only her death grip on the top rail of the chariot that kept Gili from being tossed out of the chariot as the wheels slammed into the first rut. Amon had fought his way to his knees, but as the chariot bounced into the second rut, he sprawled on the floor.

Two things happened to keep the occupants from certain injury and probable death. On seeing the runaway chariot race off onto the plain, two alert horsemen at the rear of the column dropped their spears to the dirt and spurred their horses in pursuit at a full gallop. Racing up on each side of the chariot, the soldiers pulled alongside the out-of-control horses and leaned out to grab the rawhide lines attached to the bits.

As they fought to control their own horses as well as the runaways, the second thing happened. The bouncing and jostling had sheared the stout wooden dowel that held the right wheel on the axle of the chariot. As the chariot slammed into a third deep rut, the wheel flew from the axle, and one side of the chariot dropped to the ground, its wheel-less axle acting as a plow.

The combination of the axle plowing into the dirt and the quick action by the horseman slowed the chariot and eventually brought it to a halt. While the soldiers struggled to keep the panicked horses under control, Amon struggled to his feet and worked his way to a wide-eyed Gili. Amon chuckled as he looked into her ashen face and asked, “Are you all right?”

Gili stared blankly at him. Amon slipped a hand under each of Gili’s arms to lift her from the chariot, but she only moved a couple inches. “Gili, you must let go of the chariot,” he said with slight laugh. When she didn’t respond, he reached out and slowly pried each of her fingers from the rail of the chariot. Picking her up, he tucked her under one arm, inched his way to the back, and stepped from the chariot.

A moment later more horsemen rode up and began surveying the damage to the chariot. In the distance, the small caravan had come to a halt, and most of the people were looking to where the damaged chariot rested awkwardly in the middle of the plain. Soon a lone rider came galloping across the plain. He reined his horse up beside the chariot, sending dust and dirt flying. “What’s your status?” he called to Amon in true military fashion.

Amon was on his knees on the ground, examining the chariot’s axle. Looking up at the rider, he said, “We could be much worse. We’ve sheared the pins holding the wheel on. Other than that, I see no damage to the axle or the chariot.” Standing up he slapped the dirt from his hands and looked back over the furrow the axle had made in the soft dirt. “I don’t see the wheel, but if it isn’t damaged, this should be easy to repair.”

“I shall report back to the commander,” the horseman said, and he wheeled his horse about and dug his spurs into its ribs.

Pointing to two horsemen, Amon said, “Go find the wheel and bring it here.” Then to the other two horsemen, he said, “Unhitch the horses and cool them down.” He pointed down the slight incline to a big thicket of trees. “The Jordan River flows down there. When they’re cool, lead them to water. Then bring them back and let them eat some of this grass while we repair the chariot. We’ll hitch them again when we’re ready to go.”

The two soldiers dismounted their own horses, tied them to the remaining wheel of the chariot, and began their tasks.

Amon looked up to see the rider now coming back across the plain at an easy gallop. Reining his heavily breathing horse to a stop, the rider said,

"Commander Naaman says two horsemen are to remain with you to help fix the chariot. The rest of us will continue on to the Israelite prophet's residence. After you've made the repairs, all of you are to join us there."

Gili listened to the rider, obviously in dismay. "I should be there," she blurted. "Shouldn't I go with—"

"Gili," Amon bellowed as he shook his finger at her, "don't even ask. You heard the commander's orders."

Gili let out a deep sigh and fired a crestfallen glance at Amon. She turned and slowly walked to the shade of a scrubby cedar tree, where she sat down, watching the caravan until the last rider disappeared from sight.

Amon glanced at her a couple of times, and after a while, she stood up, dusted off the seat of her robe, and walked quickly to where Amon and a soldier were struggling to set the wheel-less axle on a tree stump they had scavenged. Putting her hands on her hips, she asked, "How much longer is this going to take you?"

Neither of the men answered; they were straining too hard under the weight of the ornate chariot.

"Let's try one more time," Amon huffed to the soldier. "On the count of three. One, two, three." In an explosive burst of strength, the two men let out fierce grunts, raising the chariot the final inch and unceremoniously dropping it on the stump.

"Please, Amon, can you tell me how much longer it's going to take you?"

Amon wiped sweat from his forehead with the back of hand. He sucked in a breath to yell angrily at Gili but stopped short when he saw her pleading eyes. "I know you want to be there, Gili, but you must be patient. We're working as fast as we can."

Gili pouted. "They'll meet with Prophet and be coming back before we ever get there."

When Amon only glared at her, she spun on her heels and walked back to the cedar tree.

Nearly three hours passed before the wheel was on and the horses were again hitched to the chariot. "Come," Amon said as he brushed dirt from his tunic and wiped away the rivers of sweat that had streamed down his face and soaked his beard. "We're ready to go."

A soldier stood in front of each of the chariot's horses, firmly gripping the bits in their hands. Gili jumped up from beneath the tree and ran to the chariot. Amon helped her step up, and then he climbed aboard and picked up the rawhide lines. Only after he had them firmly in hand did the soldiers let go and swing up into the saddles on their own horses.

Guiding the chariot around rocks, ruts, and clumps of grass, Amon eased the horses across the plain and back onto the road. With the horses in an easy trot, they began the bone-jarring journey toward the prophet Elisha.

Chapter Thirty-Nine

Gili rose to her feet as the chariot crested the hill so she could see what lay ahead of them. She surveyed the road, which wound down the grass-covered hillside to the valley below, disappeared momentarily in the slow-moving waters of the Jordan River, and reappeared on the opposite bank. A panicked screech erupted from her as she grabbed Amon's arm. "What are they doing?"

Amon pulled back on the lines, drawing the team to a standstill. "I don't know," he said as he gazed across the river to the hill on the other side.

"They should be going the same direction we are, not coming toward us," Gili said anxiously.

Amon and Gili watched in stunned silence as the small caravan of horsemen, camels, and a lone chariot descended the far hillside toward the dirty brown Jordan River.

"Something's wrong," Amon said ominously as he urged the horses to begin their own descent to the valley floor.

Gili's heart began racing but not nearly as fast as her mind. Something was indeed wrong, and she struggled to figure out what it could be. "Faster, Amon. We must go faster."

"If we go faster, we may lose a wheel. Be patient; we'll get there."

From her own slowly descending chariot, Gili watched carefully as the small caravan reached the bottom of the hill and entered a lush, grass-covered clearing and stopped.

"Now what are they doing?" she asked again.

"Probably stopping to water the horses and camels in the river," Amon said, concentrating on keeping the horses under control as they descended the hill.

Gili shook her head and watched in stunned disbelief as Naaman eased up from his seat in the chariot and gingerly stepped to the ground. Even from this distance, she could tell the curse of leprosy still had a firm grip on him. "Faster, Amon! Please drive faster!"

Amon held the horses in check and approached the Jordan. The horses stopped at the water's edge and dropped their heads to try and get a drink. Hauling back on the lines, Amon forced their heads back into the air and snapped the lines to encourage the team into the slow-moving chocolate-colored water.

Fording the shallow river, they came up on the opposite bank, and Amon eased the chariot into a space well short of where Naaman's chariot was standing. Gili pushed past Amon, jumped down from the chariot, and ran through the conglomeration of men and beasts toward the tree under which Naaman stood. When she was less than halfway there, an arm reached out of nowhere, grabbed her tightly about the waist, and lifted her off the ground. "I would not advise you to approach Master Naaman," a deep voice said seriously.

"What happened?" Gili said as she looked into the man's frowning face.

Obed set Gili on the ground but held onto her arm to prevent her from leaving. "He's in a foul mood; do not go near him."

"What happened?" Gili pleaded. "Did you not see Prophet?"

Obed shook his head slowly and said in hushed tones, "No, we didn't see him."

"But why? Did he refuse? Tell me."

Obed looked down into Gili's anxiety-laden face. "As we approached his house, Naaman commanded the lead riders to fall behind him so no one would be between him and the prophet. I drove the chariot near to the door of the house, and before Master Naaman could even step from the chariot, a servant came out."

"Gehazi?" Gili asked.

"Yes, that was his name," Obed replied as he nodded his head. "Jehoram, the king of Israel, had already sent word we were on our way, so we thought this servant was coming out to greet us and take us to see the prophet."

"He didn't?"

"No." Casting a furtive glance over his shoulder to make certain Naaman was still standing under the tree, Obed said, "This Gehazi looked directly at Master Naaman and said, 'Go wash yourself seven times in the Jordan, and your flesh will be restored and you will be cleansed.'"

Gili furrowed her brow at hearing the unusual instruction. "And did the master do it?"

"No," Obed said forcefully. "He was angry, very angry. He said he thought the prophet would surely come out and talk to him. He said he expected the prophet to call upon the name of your God and wave his hand over him and cure him."

Gili grabbed the sleeve of Obed's robe and asked, "And then what happened?"

"Master got very upset. He told Gehazi the rivers of Damascus—the Albana and the Pharpar—are far superior to the waters of Israel and asked why he couldn't just wash in them and be cleansed."

"And . . ."

"And then Master Naaman got back in the chariot in a rage and told us to turn around. Now here we are."

Gili's shoulders dropped. Confusion and uncertainty spread over her face. Releasing Obed's sleeve, she quietly thanked him. As she turned to walk away, she added, "You have been helpful."

"I wouldn't go near him," Obed warned again as he watched Gili slip around a camel and disappear from sight.

Gili wound her way through the noisy throng of men, horses, and camels to a thicket growing along the riverbank. Holding her hands in front of her, she parted the deep green ocean of grass as tall as she was. When she was far enough away that she could no longer hear the cacophony of men and animals, she carefully knelt down, folded her hands in her lap, and began to pour out her heart to the Great Jehovah.

As with all her prayers, this one was simple and spoken with reverence. But unlike the prayers of most other people, it was spoken as if Jehovah was her closest friend and sitting beside her, listening to every word. In the solitude of the deep grass, where the only sounds were the gentle gurgling of the river and the calm cooing of doves, she told Him of her troubles and then paused to hear His answers. They came in sudden bursts, like pure intelligence flowing into her. Closing her petition with a heartfelt expression of gratitude, she rose from her knees and took a deep breath of the refreshingly fragrant air. Then she hurried toward a lone figure standing with his back to everyone.

"Master Naaman," Gili said without the slightest hesitation as she came to a stop directly in front of him.

Naaman raised his eyes from the small anthill he had been observing and said, "What is it, Gili?" Whatever volcano of anger had been raging inside him had spent its fury, and his voice was soft and quiet, without emotion.

In a calm, confident voice spoken so softly that Naaman could hardly hear it, Gili said, "Master, if the prophet had told you to do some great thing, would you not have done it?"

Naaman looked down at Gili with a face that bordered on hideous but with warm brown eyes that radiated the soul of an honest and sincere man. "Whatever he asked of me, I would have gladly done," Naaman replied confidently. "Nothing would have been too great."

Gili smiled innocently but paused a long moment before she said, "Yet to be cleansed, all he asked of you was a simple thing."

Naaman looked at Gili but said nothing as he tried to sort through what she was saying.

"All he asked you to do," she said quietly, "was wash seven times in the Jordan River."

Naaman stood looking contemplatively at the unassuming young maid. "Pride," he said in self-indictment.

Except for drawing her lips back in a slight smile, Gili neither moved nor said anything.

Shaking his head, Naaman dropped to his knee and scooped her up in his arms. After a tight hug, he released her and extended his gloved hands. "Will you help me?" he asked.

Gili beamed. "Yes, master," she replied and carefully helped him remove his gloves and sandals, followed by his scarf.

Taking Gili's delicate hand carefully in his own, Naaman and Gili began walking. As if on some silent signal, the men and animals parted before the two of them as they made their way to the river. At the edge, Naaman dropped Gili's hand and, with his stubby fingers, removed his elegant robe so he stood in his white linen tunic and breeches, dressed like any common slave.

Men stopped tending to animals, and every eye in the caravan looked on as Naaman limped down into the Jordan River until he stood waist deep in the muddy water. With his back to the group, he bent his knees and submerged himself one, two, three, four, five, six times. Each time he emerged, water cascaded off the ugly lesions on his forehead, ear, nose, and lips.

Naaman paused before dipping the seventh time and turned around to face the shore. Raising both hands to his face, he used his white, scaly, leprosy-infected fingers to wipe water from his eyes so he could see clearly. There on the bank of the river stood a dozen people—soldiers, servants, and slaves—each waiting in eager anticipation for his final immersion. But he focused on only one person, the young maiden at the front of the group who stood with her head slightly bowed, eyes closed and both hands tucked tightly beneath her chin in an attitude of prayer. He watched until her lips stopped moving and she opened her eyes. Only then did Naaman take a deep breath, close his own eyes, and slowly slip beneath the water's surface for the seventh time.

Chapter Forty

The noise of the horses whinnying and the camels braying caused Elisha to look up from the parchment scroll that lay before him on the simple table. As he leaned back in his wobbly chair, a knowing smile creased his lips. He knew who it was before he rose on his unsteady legs. "Gehazi," the kindly prophet called to the man in the next room who stood grinding wheat, "our visitors have returned. We must greet them."

Walking slowly to a shelf on the far side of the small room, the prophet lifted the lid of a carved wooden box and carefully removed an elegant red scarf with gold threads—the mantle of the prophet of Jehovah—and reverently draped it around his shoulders. The contrast between the superior quality of the mantle and the simplicity of his robe was stark. Walking to a peg protruding from a wall near the door, he retrieved a gray-and-white scarf. Placing it over his head to protect him from the glaring rays of the sun, he opened the door and stepped out into the bright sunshine and hot afternoon air.

The horses ridden by the four soldiers pranced nervously as they approached the two-storied home they had left only a few hours before. Behind them rolled two chariots followed by camels and more horsemen.

The dust created by the convoy rose like a brown cloud and was instantly picked up by the wind and blown ahead of them, arriving at the humble house before they did. Elisha covered his mouth and nose with the corner of his headscarf and watched through squinting eyes as the procession lumbered forward.

As the first of the two chariots came to a stop in front of the house, Elisha's lips spread into a gentle smile, and he nodded his head ever so slightly. Driving the chariot was the Syrian nobleman; the grotesque lesions and ugly flesh that had disfigured his face were gone, replaced with skin as clean and healthy as a young boy's. But it was the small person seated next to the healed leper that caused him to stare. Blinking several times to remove the bits of dust that had settled in his eyes, he whispered to himself, "I know this face."

Before his mind could sort through the thousands of names and faces he had seen, the young girl jumped down from the chariot. With legs pumping as fast as they could and her long brown hair trailing behind her like the tail of a horse, the young maiden called, "Prophet, Prophet, Prophet," as she raced toward him with outstretched arms.

"Gili?" he called softly. He said it as a question, not a statement, his mind unwilling or unable to believe what his eyes were telling him. But with each stride she took, his doubt lessened until it vanished. "Gili!" he loudly exclaimed and began hurrying toward her.

A fraction of a second before the two bodies collided, Elisha dropped to a knee, and the force of the impact nearly knocked him over. "Prophet, Prophet, Prophet," Gili repeated, throwing her arms around the man's neck so tightly that he gasped for breath. Burying her face in his flowing white hair and beard, Gili sobbed uncontrollable tears of joy.

"Dear, dear, child," Elisha said softly as he hugged her tightly and patted her back. "I never thought I would see you again."

Naaman stepped down from his chariot and walked toward the man and young maiden, pausing a short distance away to watch the tender reunion.

Sensing the man's nearness, Elisha rose to his feet, keeping Gili close. A dozen questions about how Gili came to be in this Syrian's presence flooded his mind, but they would have to wait.

Standing before Elisha, Naaman raised his arms to reveal perfectly formed hands and rotated them so Elisha could see the healed flesh. Then he reached up and slowly removed the scarf that encircled his forehead. The deep furrows were gone, the skin smooth and perfect. He pulled back his long, dark, gray-streaked hair to expose two normal ears. Next, he reached down and slightly lifted his robe. Wiggling in his sandals were ten toes, all exactly as they should be. Lowering his robe, he bowed and said reverently, "Now I know that there is no God in all the world except in Israel."

Elisha nodded his head, but before he could speak, Naaman gestured toward the heavily laden camels and said, "Please, kind sir, will you now accept a gift from your servant."

Elisha separated himself slightly from Gili and in a firm voice declared, "As surely as the Lord God lives, I will not accept anything."

"I offer it as a gift—a token of my sincere gratitude for what you have done for me this day."

"I have done only that which the Lord God has allowed me to do."

"Even so, I have brought 750 pounds of silver, 150 pounds of gold, and 10 changes of costly apparel for you. Please, you must accept it."

Elisha shook his head, and although he knew Naaman would never understand, he asked, "Would you have me accept money for doing the works of God?" Before Naaman could reply, the prophet smiled and added with conviction, "I will not do it!"

Naaman drew in a deep breath and stood gazing at the dignified old man. "Then how can I repay you? Certainly there must be something I can do."

Elisha shook his head. Patting Gili lightly on the shoulder, he said, "You have been healed this day that the works of God might be manifest through you."

Naaman looked at Elisha's modest robes and surveyed his small house with its dilapidated outbuildings and shook his head at the refusal of the wordly wealth. Then he looked at Gili, who was still clinging to Elisha's side. "I am standing before you a different man than just a few hours ago," Naaman said humbly. "Not only am I healed on the outside," he said raising his hands, "but on the inside." Then as a small tear formed in the corner of each eye and with a voice choking with emotion, he pointed to Gili. "Had it not been for her, I would not be like I am."

Elisha smiled, not knowing exactly what role Gili had played in changing the man's appearance and heart but mindful that it had been something significant.

Naaman cleared his throat and began speaking slowly and deliberately. "She was taken as a slave during a raid on Edrei some two years ago," he began. "She had reason to hate me, but she didn't. Instead she has been faithful and even chose to help me."

Except for the slight movement of their heads as they exchanged glances, Gili, Naaman, and Elisha stood motionless and silent. After a long moment, Naaman smiled warmly and looked directly at Gili. "For all that you have so selflessly done, I now give you a choice. You may come back to Damascus with me, not as a slave but as my daughter. You shall have the finest clothes, the best food, and your own attendants. You shall be educated by scholars and have everything you desire." Then pausing to calm a quiver in his voice, he softly added, "Or you may remain here, in Israel, as a free person. The choice is yours."

Chapter Forty-One

Naaman shouted to be heard above the clatter of the chariot's iron wheels rolling over dirt and gravel. "Obed, stop at the front entrance!"

Obed shot him a quick sideways glance while abruptly steering the cantering horses around a young boy who darted into the street. "The front entrance, master?"

Naaman nodded, gripping the chariot's railing to keep from being tossed out.

Obed raised his eyebrows and shouted, "But you always go to the back entrance."

Naaman grinned. "Not today. Stop at the front entrance."

Obed shrugged, guided the horses around the final corner of the journey, and coaxed them into a loping run. Two minutes later, in a maelstrom of dust, he hauled back on the lines, stopping the chariot in front of the house's main entrance.

Waving his hands in a futile effort to clear the dust cloud, Naaman stepped down and watched as the second chariot approached. As it slowed, Naaman cupped his hands and shouted, "Amon, drive to the stable and wait for me there!"

Acknowledging the command with a flip of his head, Amon slapped the horses' rumps with the lines and continued onward.

"Go now, Obed. Take care of the horses."

Obed hesitated. "Master, I don't understand. Why are you going to the front entrance? And why are you wearing the robes of a Hebrew?"

Naaman smiled but said nothing.

Obed sighed, shrugged, and turned to the team. Clucking loudly, he drove off, shaking his head.

Naaman waited until both chariots were out of sight before he walked to the door. Brushing a thick layer of dust from the long shawl on his shoulders, he pulled it over his head so it draped his forehead and hung close to his cheeks; then he pounded loudly on the door. The heavy door creaked open, and Naaman tried to suppress a grin. A slave who was almost as wide as she was tall stood in the doorway, hands on her hips. "What do you want, Hebrew?" she said brusquely.

"I'm here to see Captain Naaman," he said in a barely discernible voice.

The woman shook her head and scowled. "The master isn't home."

"His wife, then, Mistress Karinah."

The woman eyed the unusual robe, the covered head, the partially concealed face. She must not have liked what she saw because she extended her arms to block the doorway. "Who are you?"

Naaman pulled the edges of the shawl closer to his face and answered, "A traveler—from Jerusalem—who comes bearing news."

The woman hesitated, staring intently. After a long moment, she tightened her glare and barked, "Wait here," then slammed the door closed.

Naaman chuckled as he heard the locking bolt slide into place. A moment later he heard the bolt slide again, and the door opened. The same rotund slave said gruffly, "You are to follow me." Then pointing down, she added, "Stomp the dirt from your feet before entering."

Naaman nodded, lifted his robe enough to expose his sandaled feet, and stomped forcefully on the mat.

"This way," she said.

Clenching his jaw to keep from smiling, Naaman obediently followed the woman through his comfortable house and out into the back garden. "Mistress Karinah is there," the woman said, pointing to the large arbor covered with grape vines.

Naaman smiled and nodded. "Thank you."

"Humph," the woman grunted as she waddled into the house.

Naaman closed his eyes, drew a deep breath and savored the scent of roses and lemon trees that filled the air. Letting the breath slowly escape, he swallowed hard and walked toward the arbor.

The crunch of his feet on the uneven pathway caused Karinah to lift her eyes from the baby blanket she was stitching and smile at him. It was a congenial smile, nothing more. The kind of smile Naaman had seen her give to people she passed on the street or a merchant who sold her honey or nuts. While still a dozen steps away, Naaman stopped and spoke a single word. "Karinah."

At the sound of her name, Karinah's face began changing. Her smile faded, slight wrinkles formed in her brow, and she tipped her head slightly. A fraction of a second later, her lower jaw dropped, and she raised both of her hands to her now-gaping mouth. "Naaman?" she stammered, barely louder than a whisper.

Naaman reached up and removed the shawl from his head.

"Naaman?" Karinah repeated. Then, "Naaman!" Her scream shattered the garden air. Tossing the baby blanket aside, she leapt to her feet and charged into Naaman at a full run. The force of the impact made Naaman stumble backwards. Only by wrapping his arms tightly around Karinah's waist did he keep from falling.

As the couple stood teetering, Karinah's hands shot to Naaman's face, her soft fingertips exploring his dirty but soft chin, cheeks, forehead, ears, nose, and lips. "You're . . . you're . . ."

"Healed," Naaman whispered.

Kaniah shook her head. ". . . perfect." Taking hold of Naaman's hands, she examined each of his fingers then suddenly dropped to her knees and lifted his robe a few inches. She carefully ran her fingers over each of his toes, sank back on her haunches, and gazed up into his face. Tears streamed from her eyes and splattered on her pink robe.

Naaman reached down and lifted Karinah to her feet. Wrapping her in a tight embrace, he kissed her softly on the lips.

Karinah's scream brought the rotund woman racing into the garden brandishing a steel sword that was nearly as tall she was. Seeing an unfamiliar man's arms wrapped around her mistress, the woman hurried forward in the closest thing to a run her stubby legs would allow. "Get away from her! Get away from her," she screamed.

"Butul! No!" Karinah shouted. "It is Master Naaman!"

If Butul heard Karinah, it didn't register because she didn't slow her charge. "Get away from her, or I'll cut you in half," she yelled, raising the sword high above her head.

Karinah broke Naaman's embrace and stepped between him and Butul. Extending both her arms in front of her, Karinah shouted even louder, "Butul! It is Master Naaman. Stop!"

With Karinah standing between her and her intended victim, Butul slowed her awkward run to a waddling gait. Two steps away, sword still extended high above her head, she stopped.

With her arms still extended toward Butul, Karinah slowly and emphatically repeated, "Butul, it's Master Naaman. He's been healed. Put down the sword."

Except for narrowing her eyes in a piercing gaze, Butul stood like a statue, staring at Naaman's perfect face.

Naaman stepped beside Karinah and said, "It is me, Butul."

Butul's jaw dropped, and she shook her head slowly. Then, without any warning, the sword slipped from her hands, and she crashed to the ground in a complete faint.

"I didn't think I looked that bad," Naaman joked as he knelt down beside the servant. Removing his shawl, he lightly fanned the unconscious woman's face. Looking at Karinah, he said, "Perhaps you should call other servants to come help. If I do it, I might get the same reaction."

"You've had quite an effect on us women, that's for sure." Karinah smiled as she walked toward the house.

* * *

The rays of the setting sun turned the sky a soft turquoise and made the few billowy clouds appear whiter than snow. The slightest whisper of a breeze kissed Karinah's cheek as she hugged Naaman's arm and leaned her head on his shoulder. "Again," she said. "Tell me one more time of your cure."

Naaman chuckled softly as he shifted on the bench and splashed his toes in the Albana River's cool water. "I've told you twice already."

"I know, but that was earlier. I want to hear it again."

Naaman kissed her lightly on her head. "What if we talk about us? Our future."

Karinah lifted her head from Naaman's shoulder and turned to face him. "What is our future?"

"Whatever we want it to be."

Karinah went silent. "Then I want to have children and grandchildren," she said softly. "I want us to grow old together. I want us to shuffle around this garden smelling the roses and listening to our grandchildren laughing as they splash in the river." Running her finger across Naaman's cheek, she said, “I want to touch your face when it’s old and wrinkled and hear you snore at night as you lay by my side.”

Naaman looked into Karinah’s eyes for a long moment and then at the river’s sparkling water. “When I meet with Ben-Hadad tomorrow, you want me to tell him I’m through soldiering. Is that what you’re saying?”

“I want to grow old together,” Karinah replied. “You have served him well. There are others who can take your place and fight his battles. You can be of service to him in some other capacity—something that will keep you nearer to home and to me.”

Naaman sat unmoving, watching the little ripples formed by the water as it splashed against his perfect toes. At length a slow smile spread across his mouth, and he reached out and squeezed Karinah’s hand. Then he simply said, “Old together.”

Chapter Forty-Two

Elisha reached out his hand and rapped his weathered knuckles three times on the splintered door. Lowering his hand, he placed it lightly around Gili's shoulders and drew her close in a gentle hug. When she looked up at him with anxious eyes, he drew his lips back in a reassuring smile. "These past two months must have seemed like two years to you. But we're close. Very close."

The worn leather hinges creaked as the door opened slightly, letting a sliver of pale yellow lantern light spill out into the black night. "We have come," Elisha said softly to the small man peering out from behind the door.

"Welcome," the man replied with a warm smile, backing away and opening the door only wide enough for Elisha and Gili to walk through one at a time.

Elisha placed his hand on Gili's back, giving her an encouraging nudge so she would walk ahead of him. "Jehovah with thee," he said quietly in greeting as he pushed past the man.

"And with thee," the man replied in a gravelly voice, closing the door and sliding the wooden peg into the hole that would hold it secure. Turning to a frail woman standing in an adjoining room, he called out, "Woman, the prophet has arrived."

"I can see that," the diminutive woman retorted as she shuffled into the room. Looking at Elisha she bowed ever so slightly and said, "We welcome you, master." Then shaking a bony finger at him, she scolded mildly, "But you shouldn't be out so late; the streets of Jerusalem are not safe at night, even for you."

"Especially for me," Elisha replied wearily.

"Humph," the woman grunted in disgust as she shook her head. "Israel will mourn the day it treated its prophets with such disregard." Then looking at Gili, she said, "And this is the little maiden you sent word to us about."

Elisha nodded.

The woman eyed Gili carefully for a full minute before she said, "You don't remember me, do you child?"

Gili narrowed her eyes and stared at the wrinkled face. The woman was old. Deep lines carved through her face like dried streambeds in the desert sand, and in the lantern light, her skin looked pale and sickly. Her fingers were long, the joints protruding in small bulges, and ended with cracked fingernails caked with soot. Her black robe was threadbare, and it dragged on the dirt floor, concealing her bent and frail body. The gray scarf covering her head was an almost-perfect match to the stringy gray hair that stuck out wildly in a hundred directions.

Shaking her head a single time, Gili replied timidly, "No, mistress, I do not."

"Of course she doesn't," the man snorted from beside the door. "She was a babe."

After a short pause, the woman said, "I am Abish. I helped your mother as she gave birth to you; I helped you enter this forsaken world, and may you forgive me for it."

Gili narrowed her eyes and looked at the woman as if trying desperately to bring back some recollection of the old woman.

Abish dismissed Gili's efforts with a wave of her bony hand. "It makes no difference. Welcome, child," she said warmly. Then looking at Elisha, she said, "We've already eaten, but I have hot mutton stew and warm bread. Are you hungry?"

"Of course they're hungry," the man answered before Elisha could reply. "They've been walking all day." Pointing to a rickety table, he said, "Please, master, sit. And you too, girl."

Elisha and Gili sat at opposite sides of the small table and slid their chairs forward until their knees unexpectedly touched. Still too far away to eat comfortably, Elisha twisted sideways, extending his legs into the cramped room and scooting his chair forward until he could rest his elbows on the edge of the table.

"I'm glad you're here," Abish called over her shoulder from the fire pit as she ladled the stew with its pungent odors into two clay bowls. Placing the bowls on the table, she picked up a loaf of dark, unleavened bread and broke it into several chunks, which she carefully arranged on a wooden plate. Setting the plate on the table, she smiled. "Please eat." Then looking over at her husband, Abish said, "Reuben, pull the other chairs over here so we can sit and talk while they eat."

Gili made no effort to reach for the wooden spoon that lay on the table beside her bowl. She had dutifully followed Prophet from village to village throughout Northern Israel, and she knew he would not eat so much as a crumb without first giving thanks to Jehovah. Lowering her head she listened as he sent a simple prayer of thanks heavenward.

The prayer finished, Gili picked up the crude wooden spoon and attacked the stew, shoveling in two mouthfuls with hardly a single chew. "Easy, child," Abish said with a smile. "No one will take it away from you. You needn't eat so fast."

Gili smiled and wiped a dribble of juice from the corner of her mouth. "I'm sorry," she replied, shifting a piece of the stringy meat to her cheek so she could talk. "We haven't had much to eat the past few days, and this is delicious."

Abish looked at Elisha and scowled slightly. Elisha only raised his shoulder in a shrug. Crunching down on a slightly undercooked carrot, he said, "She's right; we've been traveling for three days."

"We expected you last week." Abish pushed the plate of bread toward Elisha. "The word we received from your messenger was that you'd be here several days ago."

Elisha raised his eyebrows slightly and shook his head. "I meant you no anxiety. I—we," he said with a sideways glance toward Gili, "detoured to Bethel."

"Bethel?" Reuben questioned. "To warn them?"

Elisha nodded as he spooned a piece of mutton into his mouth.

"And did they listen?" Abish asked.

"A few did." Elisha dipped a crust of bread into the stew's dark brown juice. "Only a few."

"So, they didn't listen," Abish said with disgust. "They ignored you just like the people here in Jerusalem." She shook her head. "Will they ever heed the warnings of Jehovah's prophet to turn back to Him or be destroyed?"

"That's my prayer." Elisha dipped another crust of bread into the stew. "But now," he said, taking a deep breath and motioning toward Gili, "we must talk of Gili."

"Ah," Abish said, "little Gili, the joy of Miriam and Gideon."

With two mouthfuls of stew still in her bowl, Gili quietly placed her spoon on the table and looked back and forth between Elisha and Abish, listening to their words and carefully watching their expressions. After a brief moment, she turned to Abish and anxiously asked, "Have you seen my mother and brothers? Do you know where they are?"

Abish looked into Gili's anxious eyes and quickly shifted her gaze to Elisha before looking back at Gili. Tilting her head slightly and leaning forward, she placed her wrinkled hand on Gili's. Her cracked lips parted in a slight smile, and she said softly, "Yes, child, I have seen your mother."

Gili closed her eyes, breathed a sigh of relief, and then flashed them open. Her reserved, timid demeanor evaporated, and she excitedly grasped Abish's bony hand. "Where? Here? In Jerusalem?"

The corners of Abish's mouth that had been drawn back in a tight smile eased slightly as she slowly answered, "Yes, I saw her here in Jerusalem."

Gili jumped to her feet, sending her chair skidding across the dirt floor. "Please," she begged, her eyes dancing with excitement and swiveling her head rapidly back and forth between Abish and Elisha. "Will you take me to her now? Please!"

Abish looked over at Elisha. "Gili, we can't."

Gili recoiled slightly. "Why? I'm not afraid of the dark or of the thieves. Please, let's go now."

Elisha let a muffled sigh escape from his lungs and watched as Abish pushed herself from her chair and shuffled around the table. Resting a bony hand on Gili's arm, she said softly, "Child, they were here, but not now."

"But you know where they are, don't you?"

Abish looked deep into Gili's eyes and said, "Come sit back down, and I'll explain."

Gili shook her head and fired back, "I don't want to sit down; I want to find my family."

Silence filled the room. The three adults gazed solemnly at the young girl as small tears welled in the corners of her eyes.

Ever so slowly, Elisha extended his arm to Gili and softly said, "Please, Gili, sit and let Abish speak."

Gili looked back and forth at Elisha and Abish. Finally she pulled her chair back to the table and sat down, unconsciously smoothing the wrinkles in her robe as she placed her hands in her lap.

Abish smiled gently, sat down, and rearranged her own tattered robe. Looking at Gili but nodding her head toward Elisha, she began, "One month ago the prophet sent word of your freedom and asked me to make inquiries about your family. Since then, Reuben and I have spoken with many people."

"And do you know where they are?" Gili asked, wiping away a tear that had left a tiny streak through the dirt on her cheek.

"Yes and no," Reuben blurted out from the far side of the room. "We—"

Abish abruptly turned and scowled at him, cutting him off midsentence and making him cower in silence. After a long pause, she took a breath and faced Gili. "We know where they were."

"Were?" Gili asked.

Abish nodded her head. "As the Syrians began raiding villages, many of us moved to the safety and security of Jerusalem. Two years ago, your mother and brothers lived in a rundown house only a few hundred yards from where you now sit. They had no money, and when the owner demanded they pay or leave, they had no choice but to move." Expelling a heavy sigh, Abish said, "That was the last time I saw your mother."

Shifting noisily in his chair, Reuben said, "You're taking too long; tell the girl what we know."

Abish didn't bother to look at her husband. Instead, she smiled warmly at Gili and continued with her narrative. "We have learned that they moved to a small house on the outskirts of Bethany, a small village a mile or two from here."

"And that's where they live now?" Gili interrupted with a slight hint of excitement.

It was Reuben who answered. "No, Gili. They do not live there." Then looking at Abish, he said, "Woman, why do you take so long with your story?" Not giving Abish a chance to respond, he said, "They were forced to move back to Jerusalem. But we have no idea where or even if they still live here." Then with a determined nod, he said, "That's all we know."

Abish rose, took two steps to where her husband sat and, shaking a finger in his face, said, "Be quiet." Then walking to Gili, she bent her frail body over and gave the girl a gentle hug. "Jerusalem is a large city," she said. "We don't know where they are at this moment, but it's possible they're still here somewhere."

Seeing the disappointment in Gili's eyes, Elisha cleared his throat as if to speak but, instead, smiled warmly and extended his arms toward Gili. Without hesitation, Gili rose from her chair and stepped into the prophet's outstretched arms. After wrapping Gili in a comforting embrace, he lifted his wrinkled hand and wiped the stream of tears from her cheeks. Gently pushing a strand of hair from her eyes, he softly asked, "Do you still have the faith you once had as a small child?"

Gili swallowed hard and wiped her leaking nose with the sleeve of her robe. Looking into Elisha's warm brown eyes, she said nothing, only nodded.

"And do you believe what I say?"

Gili nodded again, again wiping her dripping nose on the sleeve of her robe.

Hugging her close once again, he said softly, "Then do not doubt. Only believe. I promise in the name of the great Jehovah, you will one day be reunited with your family."

Epilogue

The house was perched on a desolate hillside well beyond the protection of Jerusalem's walls. It was constructed of light gray blocks held together by mortar the color of a muddy stream. In its early days, brilliant snow-white stucco covered the blocks and gave it a clean, cheery appearance, but not now. Long years in the wind, rain, and searing sun had peeled away most of the stucco, and the small patches that still stubbornly clung to the blocks were the color of dirty eggshells.

A narrow path made a straight line from the back door of the undersized house to a wooden gate in a rock wall that surrounded the house. Through the gate, the thorny path meandered down a slight descent to a parched plot of ground that pretended to be a garden.

"She's changed," Uzzi said, walking up beside his younger brother and laying his bow and quiver on the rock wall beside where Caleb was pounding a loose rock back into place.

Caleb cast an incredulous sideways glance at his older brother as he hit the rock with a wooden mallet one final time, wedging it in tightly. "She was a slave for two years, Uzzi. Of course she's changed."

Uzzi shook his head as he leaned forward and rested his forearms on the wall. "No, no," he replied quickly, "I don't mean her attitude. I mean, she's no longer the little girl who giggles at my funny faces and laughs at my pranks. Look at her; she's grown up. She's becoming a young woman."

Caleb shifted his gaze down the gentle slope of the hill to where Gili was stooped over, carefully ladling cupfuls of water onto a young squash plant. "She was robbed of her childhood," he said, shaking his head. "At the age when you and I were running around playing war games, she was being abused as a slave in the house of some pagan Syrian."

Uzzi gave a single nod of his head to acknowledge the comment as he raised his arm and waved to Gili, who was walking to another plant.

"You know," Caleb said evenly as he too threw his arm into the air in a wave, "she harbors no ill will toward the Syrian man and his wife."

"How do you know? Has she told you so?" Uzzi asked somewhat surprised, turning his head to look at his younger brother.

Caleb shook his head. "Mother told me."

Uzzi stood straight and brushed tiny bits of sand from the underside of his forearms where they had been resting on the wall.

"Do you remember a couple weeks ago—the second or third night after the prophet brought her home to us? The night she woke up screaming?"

Uzzi nodded his head. "Of course I do. She was terrified. She said she had a dream that everyone left her, and she was alone again."

"Mother told me that after you and I returned to our mats, she stayed up rocking Gili to calm her down. As they talked, she asked Gili if she hated the Syrians. Gili told her no and that she had even come to love that man and his wife."

Uzzi shook his head in disbelief and sent a stream of spit flying through the air. "I spit on the Syrians for what they did," he said, suddenly angry.

The sound of sandals crunching on dirt and weeds made the brothers simultaneously turn and look down toward the garden. They watched silently as Gili strolled up the narrow path toward them, the empty water pail swinging in rhythm with her steps. "There," she said, placing the wooden pail on the wall beside Uzzi's bow. "I have given each of them a good drink of water." Looking at Uzzi she added, "If I tend them carefully, by the time you and Samara are married in two months, we'll have big, beautiful squash to eat at the wedding feast."

"You think?" Uzzi said, reaching out and playfully tousling Gili's hair.

Gili swatted at his hand, "I know," she replied. Taking a step backward so she was out of his reach, she rearranged her hair. "What I don't know is why Samara ever agreed to marry you," she teased.

Uzzi smiled and took a breath to reply, but Caleb beat him to it. "That, little sister, is the mystery Mother and I cannot solve. Why anyone would choose to marry a soldier—and this one especially," he said, lightly slapping Uzzi on the shoulder, "is beyond us."

Quick smiles spread across each of their lips, but Gili's evaporated almost as quickly as it appeared. Looking at Uzzi she said pensively, "In some ways, you and Samara remind me of Master Naaman and Mistress

Karinah. You are a warrior like he is, and Samara is a musician and very artistic, just like her."

Uzzi's smile faded completely, and his eyes darkened. "How can you be so charitable toward them?" he snarled. "He killed both Father and Hanan and then took you as a slave."

"He didn't kill either of them. It was others who did it," Gili corrected.

"But he gave the orders," Uzzi fired back.

Gili paused, inclined her head in the barest hint of a nod and then said calmly, "I despise what they did, but I don't hate them."

"Humph." Uzzi gritted his teeth and reached for his bow. "I don't make such fine distinctions; I hate them, and I hate what they did to our family."

Gili leaned forward and placed her hand on Uzzi's. "Good has come from it," she said.

"What good?" Uzzi retorted, withdrawing his hand from hers and slinging his bow over his shoulder.

Gili tucked some errant strands of hair behind her ear. "What good? Well, for one thing, you're marrying Samara. That's a good thing. If none of this had happened, she'd be marrying Hanan, not you." Then leaning slightly forward, she added, "Would you rather that Hanan was still alive or be marrying Samara?"

Uzzi rocked back as the force of the question slammed into him. He stared momentarily at Gili then shifted his gaze to Caleb as if seeking some help with a rebuttal, but Caleb simply raised his eyebrows and waited for an answer.

"Uzzi," Gili quickly said, "I don't expect you to answer that question. I was just trying to tell you that even with all the bad things, there is also some good."

No one moved, and except for the soft cooing of a dove perched in an old, twisted olive tree, there was no sound. After a long moment, Uzzi slowly removed the bow from his shoulder, placed it on the wall, and walked through the gate. Opening his arms toward Gili, he said, "This place isn't as splendid as where you lived in Syria, but it's our home, and I thank Jehovah that you are here with us."

"There's no place I'd rather be," Gili replied as she stepped into his outstretched arms.

Caleb watched as Uzzi hugged Gili tightly, lifting her off the ground. "Uzzi," Caleb said anxiously, "put her down; you'll crush her ribs." As Uzzi lowered Gili to the ground and released her, Caleb said, "Gili, whatever became of that stone the prophet gave you, the one that caused so much trouble?"

Free of Uzzi's crushing hug, Gili took a deep breath and smoothed her robe. Smiling, she reached inside the neck of her robe and pulled out an elaborate gold chain that was fastened around her neck. Suspended from the chain was the topaz stone, held in an intricate gold setting. "It's here."

Uzzi and Caleb both looked in awe at the necklace. It represented more wealth than they had seen in years. "It's beautiful," Caleb said.

"Gorgeous," Uzzi muttered. "But, where—? How—?"

Gili smiled, and a little beam of light danced in her eye. "It was a gift."

Uzzi and Caleb exchanged quick glances, and then Caleb asked, "From whom?"

"Master Naaman," Gili answered.

"But why?" Uzzi asked, perplexed.

Gili held the stone between her thumb and forefinger. "It was his way of saying thank you."

About the Author

E. James Harrison was born in Salt Lake City and developed an early love and fascination with the great men and women of the Bible while sitting on his parents' couch, flipping through the pages of *Bible Stories for Children.* Those early seeds have sprouted and grown into a more serious study of the scriptures to help him gain a clearer understanding of God and the Savior.

He holds degrees with emphasis in creative writing and public relations and has written countless magazine articles, newsletters, advertisements, and commercials. He has authored dozens of books in his mind but has only committed five to paper. His first novel, *The Tomb Builder*, was published in 2011. His next novel, *The Cross Bearer*, will be released in 2015.

When not putting words on paper for himself or others, he can be found boating and waterskiing with his family and friends or traveling to see new things and meet new people.

He and his wife Deborah have two daughters and four grandchildren.